'BEFORE WE START ON DETAIL, I DON'T WANT YOU TO THINK YOU'VE SEEN THROUGH IT. I'LL TELL YOU THE PUNCHLINE FIRST. THE MARK GIVES US A PILE OF LOOT, FOR ALL KINDS OF REASONS CONNECTED TO THE BULLSHIT WE THREW AT HIM FOR THE REST OF THE SCAM, AND WE DISAPPEAR. IT'S THAT SIMPLE.'

'They're all that simple,' Silvester said. 'That's how cons work. You get someone to give you their money, for a week, a day, sometimes even a fraction of a second in some of the financial market scams, and you fuck off. That's all there is. That's confidence in a nutshell. Convince someone to hand you a big pile of their money and steal it. I have no illusion and neither should you: confidence is theft. I steal money for a living. I just don't use a blackjack. The only thing separates a good con from a bad one is the subtlety of the scam. If they're too wrapped up in the detail to think about the basic issues of trust, then you're away. So there's no need to apologize because your scam looks like a flat-nosed, stocking-over-the-head blag. It is. Give me the de...'

Born in Oldham in 1960, Mark Crompton was educated by the De La Salle Brothers. Following this, he spent several frivolous years travelling in Europe and Asia.

He lives in east London and is married with two small children. Combining his writing with a day job, he has worked as a barman, a guinea pig, a wine waiter, a heavy lifter, a freelance writer and a journalist. He now works as a spokeman for a major US oil company.

Promise is the first of the Patrick Old books. Any similarity between Crompton and his fictional hero is merely wishful thinking on his part.

MARK CROMPTON

A SIGNET BOOK

SIGNET

Published by the Penguin Group
Penguin Books Ltd, 27 Wrights Lane, London w8 5tz, England
Penguin Books USA Inc., 375 Hudson Street, New York, New York 10014, USA
Penguin Books Australia Ltd, Ringwood, Victoria, Australia
Penguin Books Canada Ltd, 10 Alcorn Avenue, Toronto, Ontario, Canada m4v 3b2
Penguin Books (NZ) Ltd, 182-190 Wairau Road, Auckland 10, New Zealand

Penguin Books Ltd, Registered Offices: Harmondsworth, Middlesex, England

Published in Signet 1995
1 3 5 7 9 10 8 6 4 2

Copyright © Mark Crompton 1995
All rights reserved

The moral right of the author has been asserted

Filmset in 10/13pt Monophoto Plantin
Typeset by Datix International, Bungay, Suffolk
Printed in England by Clays Ltd, St Ives plc

To Sue, Thomas and Alicia
What more could a man want?

PROLOGUE

Old's bones were jarred as they bounced and slipped along the rutted, rotten-leaf-covered forest path. He looked at Ibn Fahad, his face a mask; they might as well have been cruising up the half-mile driveway of his desert palace for all the reaction he showed. Houssain Shawaz, the Sheik's factotum, was gritting his teeth and holding on tight to the hand grip of the bouncing Land Cruiser. The light increased as they neared the edge of the forest. The driver stopped and cut the engine. The five of them moved just inside the tree-line, as arranged, from where they could see the soldiers clearly. The wind had a biting edge and the Sheik drew his khefiye across his face. Old stepped from the cover of the trees and raised his right arm. There was one officer with the men and he turned and seemed to nod. They were far enough away that it was difficult to tell. At a signal from Old, Tandy, the driver, opened the back of the Land Cruiser and took out two folding chairs. Tandy returned to the driving seat.

'Less the help see the better,' Old said to his partner. The Sheik overheard this and gave a near-smile of recognition of a sound principle of affairs.

As the Sheik and Shawaz sat, the helicopter took off from among the soldiers. It was a clean take-off, and it rose to a height of around two thousand feet in a gentle sequence of spirals and loops. Slowly, it achieved its altitude and took a wide parabola across the valley. When it was around a mile away, there was a deep hiss and a bright orange flash as a missile flew from the launcher mounted on the shoulder of one of the soldiers. The moment the missile set off, the helicopter rose in a fast, angled climb, only to flick back into a vertiginous fall as the missile appeared. The missile adjusted its angle almost instantaneously but the helicopter continued to fall. It seemed as if it might almost hit the ground – it seemed to be trying to fool the missile and make it do the same. As it neared the ground, only fifty feet away, it shot behind a rock outcrop and emerged on the other side. The Sheik nodded sagely at the dexterity of the helicopter as the missile shot past, but after only a few seconds it became clear the joust was not over: with a wobble in its tail, slowly, carefully, the missile leant into a turn. The helicopter again climbed, clearly about to try the same trick, but before it had a chance to fall, and thus increase its speed, the missile seemed to have a rapid acceleration, pre-empting anything the helicopter might try. It seemed to have learned from its mistake. The helicopter made a shuddering right-hand climbing turn but the missile anticipated. There was a pure white flash, a small explosion, and, as suddenly, the helicopter and the missile were gone, the skies clear. The helicopter pilot put down his radio console and the officer slapped his back. He had done well to avoid the missile on its first pass. It was meant to react as its full-size parent would. It was designed by the same engineers, made by the same company, and cost over eighteen thousand pounds. A lot of money for an unrepeatable trick – unrepeatable by that model anyway.

The Sheik nodded to himself, looked at Old and his

companion, making eye contact with them both, as if he were trying to see into their souls, and then he uttered a quick, sharp, guttural sound directed at Shawaz. Shawaz nodded and smiled at Old.

'Seventy-five. Terms and conditions to stand as agreed.'

ONE

The foyer looked as if it had been designed by someone with a Gatsby fixation, time-locked in the early seventies. More likely it hadn't been designed at all: some furniture had been bought, some pictures hung. The three couches were mid-brown with vaguely grubby cream throw cushions. The pictures on the wall looked like cheesecake: pouting nearly-lovelies with vertiginous cleavages, dangerously strained blouse buttons and hip-high denim cut-offs. They were probably the most artful and restrained pictures ever taken by a photographer in Barry Mee's pay and each was without doubt the herald for the rest of its film roll which would show the blouse buttons giving way to the pressure, the cut-offs getting mysteriously lost, and the gynaecological tendency coming to the fore as the models licked their glossed lips and tucked their ankles neatly behind their ears, knees squashing pale white breasts.

Old felt queasy. Mee's money had the scent of damp bedside tissues and Old was not sure if he wanted to get near without forceps and rubber gloves. On the other hand, tacky as his money was, there was lots of it, and he was at least interested enough to be here. His last three jobs had been errant spouses who disappeared as if they were playing hide and seek, popping their heads up after a count of fifty and expecting the world to clap delightedly at their reappearance. He gave them a yelling at and each slunk back home, tail between legs, their adventure over. Barry Mee might think sleaze was something to aspire to, but he was not grey. It was worth a listen at least if it might lead to a job with a bit of spark.

Mee bowled through a swing door and halted less than a pace from Old, so he had to lean back to let Old stand. Old stepped to the side to increase the gap and give them room to shake hands.

'Barry Mee, call me Barry. Patrick Old I take it.' His tone was cheery, which was in itself a first. By the time anyone came to a missing-person specialist they were usually near desperation and he was usually briefed in a tone somewhere between the confessional and the skyscraper-ledge, pre-jump rationalization.

Mee retreated back through the door, signalling that Old should follow. When they were in the room, Old again found himself nose to nose with Mee, who stood by the door, half blocking entry.

'Drink? Coffee or something a bit stronger?'

Old squeezed past Mee and glanced at his watch. Just gone twelve.

'Coffee, as it comes, Scotch chaser, as it comes.'

Mee nodded his approval and stuck his head through the still open door.

'Pot of coffee, Debbie love, when you can.' He crossed to a drinks cabinet which seemed to reflect what he wanted to drink himself rather than to offer a comprehensive selection. It contained a variety of whiskies – Scotch, both blended and a selection of malts, Irish, bourbon, rye – and a bottle of gin for variety. Old asked for Grouse and was given an over-healthy measure in a heavy, ugly crystal tumbler. Old raised his glass to Mee and was about to make a start when they were interrupted by the receptionist who, when he saw her, convinced Old that she was either angling for a spot in one of his magazines or had already done a stint and was getting her wear out of the clothes. She had a skirt that covered absolutely nothing. From his seated position he didn't need to wait for her to bend to see her underwear – thankfully, she was wearing some. Old wondered if she changed to go home or wore a long coat or what. Mee smirked as he saw Old's fixated eyes. The smirk looked comfortable on his face, as if it were a much used setting for his facial muscles. They waited for her to leave and Old decided not to comment, the quicker for Mee's smirk to subside. Mee shoved a cigar-box towards Old. Old refused, wondering how many more functions and procedures of etiquette were due before they could talk about someone who was missing, how they were to find them, the business of the day.

'I expect you want to know . . .' Mee began.

'Someone's missing. Tell me who they are, why you want them, what you have for me to go on, I'll tell you how much it'll cost you.'

'Good, OK. I'll start at the beginning. It's a bit of a long story but, like I expect you'd tell me, who knows what might be important? I tell you the lot, it saves you going over the story ten times, filling in. The point is, I got stung by a conman. Not a simple bit of business where I lost out and feel bad about it, a genuine con. I can't wait to tell you, you know. Apart from the wife, the only people know about this got stung with me. It's a tale and a bloody half, made me sick to the gut, to think someone could just take me like that, but to get my mates at the same time, sticks.

Sticks in the throat. Plausible bastard he was 'n' all. You look back, you can see a million places you should have thought: "Hang on here a minute, what's all this about?" but you don't, do you?'

'You said you were going to start at the beginning.'

'Yeah, right. So what it was, the con, right, started in London. I met the guy in London, but that was arranged, 'cause I'd already met him on holiday. That was where it really started, that was where he really hooked me, did it proper. Back in London was where he pulled me in. I'm in Antigua, me and the wife, Lisa. So I'm sitting in this bar. You're less choosy on holiday, right, which is why he's out there fishing. You let the barriers down, let people in. You meet them back at home and they're already in. He tells me he's a specialist car importer, I tell him I'm a publisher. Doesn't talk about work much though, which makes a change from most guys, right, look forward to their holidays all year and then when they get there they do nothing but talk about work.

'So we're getting along all right, talking about this and that, exchanging a few drinks, the wives are talking, then Lisa gets the craps, it happens, right. I'm just telling you so you know I didn't ask for it, I was set up. So the day Lisa's in bed, your man, says his name's Phil Goodman, he says he's out of cash, doesn't like the rate at the hotel, he's off to Freeport, change some money, have a look around. So there's me and his woman, Davida, which turns me right on; I love these snotty women's names, and she's a real fucking looker, you feel great just walking down the street with her, the looks and all. I mean I can get good-looking women on my arm any day of the week, and they'll do

7

what I want, but it's the job, you know what I mean, they're tarts, the ones aren't already on the job, and they've got the bodies but the eyes, you know what I mean, hard, doggy eyes. This Davida, she's just a stunner, right, I mean those jealous eyes from other guys are such a turn-on and she's giving 'em whiplash, and she thinks I'm the best thing since flavoured KY. I'm Mr Witty, Mr fucking Sex and Charisma. Next thing, fish worm, worm fish, we're in bed, at it like good 'uns. We get to be alone, one excuse or another, four more times, and they weren't all exactly good excuses, I mean, Goodman must have been wetting himself, playing the fooled and innocent husband. One time, we were all swimming, except Lisa, who's still a bit delicate, and me and Davida swim into a cave off the beach, all "Oh I wonder what could be in here," when we both know a good porking is what she'll find in there.

'Trouble is, I feel bad about it. Goodman's a nice bloke, easy company, I like him and I feel bad about dicking his missus. Next thing, about three days before we're due back, the room's robbed. They take the traveller's cheques and the slips with the numbers on and the cash and most of Lisa's jewellery. Worst is, the cheques aren't Amex and we haven't got the numbers anyway. I've got copies at home but that's not a lot of use. So before I even go to Freeport, get told to go whistle, try to draw money on a credit card when the banks are closed, all that palaver, up pops Goodman, don't worry, I've brought plenty, lends me five hundred, cash, no problem he says, we always say we'll meet people after holidays, when do you ever? This way we'll be sure to – have a few bevvies, sort

8

things out. So now I feel like a bloody millionaire with his hand in the poor box. He's being the stand-up guy, acting like a real friend, and me, who wishes he was, and really likes him, I'm stabbing him in the back, I mean look at it, I'm shagging his missus. We're sitting at a table in the hotel bar, he's sorting out the cash, counting it out, I'm coming over all grateful, Lisa's sitting looking sickly and watching the fan, and Davida's stirring her drink, except her other hand's in my pants. Next thing she's got my dick out, in the middle of the bar, and I'm about to burst. I thought she must be the biggest bitch the world had seen. Sexy bitch though. Turns out she's just a pro. Like your man.'

Old topped up his Scotch, did the same for Mee, who paused for breath and took a large swallow.

'Back in London, we arrange to meet, just the two of us. I'd already been thinking about getting in touch with Davida but was just coming round to deciding it wasn't a good idea. We meet and I give him the dosh, many thanks and all that, so I'm in his debt, then he shows me the holiday pics – all these pics of the happy couple, stretched out, him smiling and innocent, her topless, a body you'd dream of and this cheeky, sexy, bitchy little smile on her face. So now I'm extra in debt. But the guy probably studies psychology or something. On the one hand he's got the upper hand because I'm in debt to him – on the surface because I owe him one, and another he doesn't know about. On the other hand though, if we do business, I'd never think I could lose out, because you dick a man's wife, you're the big cheese, right, the dick of preference; so you're looking down at him – he's less than you are.

So this superiority, it's going to override your natural scepticism about what's basically an iffy deal, because you've got the measure of the man, and you can handle him.'

'You've been thinking about this,' Old said.

'Fucking right. I've been at this con from every angle. I'm like most people, I think a con makes a good story – little twist in the tail and all that. If it wasn't me I'd probably admire the bloke's cheek, the preparation, the lot. But it *was* me.'

'So he's about to start turning the handles,' Old interrupted, anxious to get back on track.

'That's what he does. Away go the holiday pics, the money in the inside pocket. "That's that for a few months then I suppose," he says, letting me know he gets a few holidays a year. Then he says: "Remind me what it is you do," – like he hasn't checked out what his mark does by now – so I tell him, roughly, we talk about that for a while. I'll hand it to him, he does the job right – no pushing, he waited till I asked him what he did. Says he brokers deals, whatever comes up, but what he does most is import fancy cars. He says he has a sweetheart deal at BMW. He gets their test cars – huge amounts off the list. Some of them are tested hard he says, some only for town driving or parking or hand-brake tests. They get a full service and computer check after that – any worn parts replaced. He gets great prices, import/export brokers them – the left-handers to Switzerland, the right-handers to the UK. He says he can supply a thirty K BMW for about twenty-two, plus a load of unspecified extras. Course, you might guess, he never asks for the sale. I ask him if he can get one for me. He says sure, he has fourteen coming over in the next three months. He's going over next week, should be back two weeks later with one, the other thirteen a month later. Before I asked for the sale though, honest as the day's long, Honest Phil Goodman, he's telling me the ins and outs of the business – how the glory is that there's no overhead, no debt, how he has so many people want the cars, he insists on at least half the money up front, keep debt cost small and short, everything clean and simple. He said that a lot now I think back – clean and simple, like he said it enough that's how I'd think of it, which is about right.'

'So what was the actual con?'

'I'm getting there. Like I said, this way nothing gets left out.' He topped up the coffees and leaned back in his chair.

'I'd made the sale for him, right. He says he hasn't pre-sold this next lot, so if I want to do anyone I know a good favour, favour, hell, what a cheeky bastard, then put them in touch, but there's no rush because, like he said, he's going over next week for one and then he'll sort it out when he gets back. So I hand over a straight twelve. Ten on delivery if I'm happy. Never occurs to me he might not turn up until two weeks are up, I'm getting reassuring calls, he's not back though. He said he'd be a week to ten days, in the end he's seventeen days. I'm just getting a bit leery when he turns up. With all the extras the car's worth about thirty-four. It's a fucking beauty – I'm still driving it even though it reminds me how I was turned over; I suppose really *because* it reminds me.

'You look at how he turned me over though, the bastard didn't make a wrong move. Even being late –

he turns up late, it means the next time, when he's a no-show, I'm reassuring everyone, telling them what a diamond he is, how he was a bit late last time but there's the car, just look at it and pant, cool it and he'll be here pronto.'

Old raised a hand to halt the flow. 'Just a minute, am I missing something here? What's the scam?'

'I'm getting there. I told you, you'll get the whole story.'

'Didn't you forget "And in the beginning God created the heavens and the earth"?'

'I'm getting there. So I've got the new wheels, I'm praising him to the skies, chuffed with my new toy, feeling like I'm the smart one, the man with the inside track, like I've got this fantastic bargain because I'm such a smart bastard. He just says: "Don't mention it, that's business, I've got my slice, you've got what you want, everybody's happy, that's good business, right?" It's all so fucking plausible, there we are, two successful businessmen doing deals, making money, looking sharp, like in that book, fucking Masters of the Universe. So I'm on the blower, telling the lads, driving them round, look at my new wheels. He didn't need to lift a finger. I was his salesman – that's the beauty of this – he doesn't need to part a load of idiots from their hard-earned, just one, then leaves the donkey work to his pet idiot, and because the idiot is selling it to his mates, not cold, they believe him. I wasn't just telling people what a deal I had, I was really egging them on, saying get in there – even if you can't afford it, it's a once-only chance to make a bob. Get the money, beg steal or borrow, get the twenty-two, you can flog it for thirty, you're quids in. You only have to put twelve down, the rest on delivery. If you're selling the car, you only have to find for a few days – money in your pocket. I pulled nine of the poor bastards in and I took another two. Can you believe that? I'm the lucky sod who – apart from being the stooge who gets to pull his mates into a con – wins out, I actually get the cheap car, and what do I do, I stump up for another two, seeing a nice sixteen K profit, minimum, take it off the twenty-two I paid and I'm telling myself I've got a thirty-four K BMW for six and I'm a happy little sandboy. We're like a fucking syndicate. He invites us all round his house to give him the dosh, shows us a load of BMW brochures – all in German, says he got them from the factory – and there's mine sitting on the drive like a fucking advert. It all looks like domestic bliss, there's Davida swanning around, bringing in the cold beers, giving me the eye, gives me a grope when I go for a slash, so when I come back I'm laying it on with a trowel, what a star Goodman is. He wasn't worried what form the money was in – asking for cash we might have got suspicious. One guy, Kevvie, runs a minicabbing firm, he comes up with cash, that raises a laugh – "I'm in the wrong business," Goodman says. Ho di ho ho. The rest of us, it's cheques and banker's drafts, Goodman says, well, it's off to the land of the Rising Kraut, comes out with bit of Kraut.'

'He speaks fluent German?'

'Sounded like it to me. Mind you, the only German I know is Heil Hitler and Halt Englander – whatever you get in *The Great Escape*. Sounded like the business to me though. So we have a couple more beers, I get a stiffy watching Davida drift in and out, we all shake on it, everyone, we talk about it later, everyone at some stage gets the full eye contact with Goodman, we all fuck off, pleased as Punch, that's it. That's the last we hear from him.'

'I'm still missing something,' Old said, worried that he was being terribly slow.

'The first BMW,' he started.

'The only BMW,' Mee interrupted.

'Yeah, the car, did he actually have contacts or what – how did he get the first car cheap?'

Mee smiled. 'That's always the tricky bit when you don't know the scam. That's the bit that gets you hooked when you're the mark and it's as simple as simple can be. He buys a fully equipped Beamer for about thirty-four K – airbag, ABS, CD, airco, electric sun-roof, the whole Monty. He re-registers it in Germany, then re-imports it, so the thing comes over with oval German export plates and some Mickey Mouse German company as the previous owner on the new UK registration document. He gets your twenty-two and takes a bath for twelve K. If he only gets two people to go for the next consignment, including the cost of the holiday that traps the initial idiot,' – he jabbed his thumb at his chest, identifying the idiot – 'then he's ahead. I'd guess he doesn't do it for less than half a dozen, with us it was eleven, two of them mine, which, if you need to figure it out, is a hundred and thirty-two thousand – twenty-four of it mine. Except it's worse. Most of the guys it was a big blow, but they could take it. Two of them really had to scrape to get it together, couldn't afford a car like that but did it to make the eight K. I gave them their money back. I didn't have to, I know, but I just felt low. Just really, bloody low. So apart from the original bargain which, apart from being a brilliant car I only keep to remind me to keep my eyes open and to keep me fresh for revenge, apart from what I saved on the car, I personally went down for forty-eight. That's a fuck of a lot of money. I can't believe I'm ever going to see it again but somehow he's going to get his if you can find him.'

Revenge. It was the first time the word had been used but it had been the bedrock for the whole narrative. Mee had told the story in a breezy, anecdotal fashion, but there had been an undertone of furious obsession. He wanted revenge and Old, presuming he found his man, would have to be very careful with his next step. If he simply handed him over to Mee, he was sure a serious beating would follow, at least, and that kind of thing can go very badly wrong. While in Army Investigations, he had twice had to find soldiers who had gone AWOL from duty in Ulster after giving a beating to civilians they considered too mouthy and had suddenly found themselves kicking a corpse. If he found him, probably the best thing would be to hand him over to the police. That was the right way to do it: it would give him points with the police, and the two or three years the conman would be likely to get would hurt far more than any beating he survived. Once they knew where he was, safely inside, they could try suing him. But first, find your man.

Mee signed a contract for two-twenty a day plus expenses, which he was warned could not easily be predicted and could mount up.

'I told you,' he said, 'I want him, and one way or another I'll see the bastard done for this. What it costs, it's not the issue. I've come to you on strong word of mouth. I trust you, more or less, as far as you're likely to trust someone you don't know personally, and when you've just been ripped off by someone you let yourself think was a friend. I'm sure it'll cost and I'm sure the bill'll be legit.'

Old wondered if he had ever met someone keener to use a hundred and ten words where two would do. When he showed him the contract, he could have said OK, or Fine, or That'll do. Instead, Old had to sit and take a further speech on honesty and trust. Whether it was defensive or instinctive Old couldn't say, but he couldn't recall anyone make more reference in normal conversation to honesty and integrity. It sat ill with his position as a porn publisher.

Two

On the way back from Mee's offices, in the tatty end of Shoreditch, Old hit traffic. A few hundred yards down the road, on a bend, he could see the traffic painfully squeezing through an artificial chicane where two Transit vans had double-parked, one twenty or so yards forward of the other. The heavy mid-afternoon traffic was performing an elaborate dance as each stream alternately dashed through the gap or judged it better to wait and, in a poor pretence of politeness, allowed a van or skip-wagon to come through. Further back, the traffic practised the first-gear shuffle. Old looked at the photo. It was effectively all he had. A name, Phil Goodman, and a photo of the man, his wife, if she was his wife, standing alongside Mee and his wife by a long fishing boat on the beach. Old knew that as photographic evidence it was as bad as could be. Who looks like their holiday snaps once back in working clothes, overalls, suit, whatever? He decided he would get the photos cropped to a simple head and shoulders – some of Goodman, some of Davida. There was surely as much chance of tracing her as Goodman and each should or could lead to the other, though typically it was only Goodman who seemed to interest Mee. In his business it was probably second nature to regard women as props, though from the sound hers was an important part of the plan – the essential hook which gave Mee both confidence and guilt – and the business was, after all, a confidence trick.

Old's turn came at the front of the queue and he slipped effortlessly through. 'There's always room for a Mini,' he sang to himself tunelessly, as he did many times a day as his car eased him through one jam after another. Five more minutes saw him parked up the pavement outside the photo lab.

They asked no awkward questions inside the lab, not because they were especially discreet, but because they simply didn't care. Photos were what they made and this was a photo – you could tell; it was plain on one side with a picture on the other. Old left with a hundred each of Goodman and Davida, fifty of the two of them together and a dozen of the whole photo. He left the original at the lab in case he needed to order up more. He thought passing them around might be the best bet – throw a wide net.

Sam watched as Old chopped the anchovies and mixed them with the tuna.

'They're very salty, Daddy,' Sam observed.

'You like this, though. When it's all mixed up it's your favourite.'

'Pizza is my favourite favourite. And crumpets with houmous. And chocolate.'

'Chocolate isn't meal food,' Old started, and paused, realizing he was about to be forced to try and explain a concept he'd just invented and already wished he hadn't.

'What is it then?' Sam interrupted.

'Just chocolate. Sweets.'

'It's not sweets. Sweets are different.'

Old took a deep breath. 'I know sweets are different. If we're being like that, sweets and chocolate and crisps are all confectionery but different kinds of confectionery.'

'What's confectionery?'

'I just told you.'

'Tell me again.'

'Sweets.'

'And chocolate and crisps?' Sam asked.

'Are you doing this on purpose?'

'Doing what?'

'Nothing. Anyway, this is still one of your favourites. Tuna, anchovies, olives and pasta. You like it.'

'I know. I asked for it.'

'But you were complaining about the anchovies.'

'I wasn't, Daddy. I just said they were salty. You don't taste it when it's all mixed up though.'

When the meal was ready, Old served it and watched as Sam heaped spoon after spoon of parmesan over his plate. He mused that he had probably not eaten pasta or parmesan until he was fifteen or so, while Sam saw parmesan as a routine condiment, in the same mental cubbyhole as pepper, ketchup and, in his case, olive oil, which he poured over pasta with the enthusiasm Old had as a child for raspberry syrup on ice cream. After dinner, they watched an animated alphabet video, which had the great benefit that it was quiet. It was Sam's favourite. He could read now, passably well, but liked the clever ways the crocodiles changed to clocks, ducks to dragons, eggs to elephants to ears. By the time they had made their way to T, he was becoming restless. Old picked up Sam's bag, packed earlier, and his own packet of photos of Goodman and his wife and led Sam to the car. He had a regular Tuesday night date at the swimming pool with a school friend. It was surprising, Old found, how his circle of acquaintances grew once he started meeting his fellow parents while dropping Sam off at school. This had made an appreciable difference to the quality of his life. Even though it was a Catholic school, there was still a significant number of single mothers. As a single father – a fact which was widely known in the gossip-ridden community of the parents' schoolyard – and a fairly attractive and clearly solvent one at that, for the first time in his life he was a property to be desired and to be pursued with some competitive drive. They were fully aware of sin and how to go about it, they simply had a proper sense of guilt about their actions. The Pope notwithstanding, Catholic women have the same desires as any other women, and if there were a God, Old thought, there for sure would be something to thank him for.

Sam's Tuesday night swim with Jimmy was one offshoot of this popularity. He took Sam to Jimmy's house and arranged a pick-up time. Jimmy's mother, Hannah, was attractive and full-figured. She was also intelligent, and though she was still unsure what Old did for a living, she knew he was self-employed and home-based, which she felt gave her some understanding of his problems and of his life, as she was a proofreader for a technical publisher; they could complain together, she thought and intended, about the perils of self-employment, about the blight of the late-paid invoice.

So far Old had not bitten.

Still, because of Jimmy and Sam's friendship, she was in pole position. Last week she had had Old and Sam round for dinner; the two of them trying to carve a peaceful niche in the evening while surrounded by the chaos and din of two rising-five boys playing at full tilt. As Old rose from giving Sam a kiss on the cheek, telling him to be good and be careful at the pool, he was surprised to get a light affectionate peck on the cheek from Hannah. He felt a blush rise, then saw a corresponding blush, a very fetching russet pink, appear on Hannah's cheeks and neck. It was too late to return the kiss, he would have been too self-conscious, but he gave as friendly and casual a smile as he could manage. Inside he was shocked and delighted. He had been unsure who was making the running; he had just been told and he couldn't have been more pleased.

'Eightish then,' he said, and heard that the timbre of his voice had dropped so the words hardly crawled out. Hannah nodded and smiled and Sam waved.

'Go on then, Daddy, we want to get off.'

He left Hannah's and drove off. He drove a few streets away, in the opposite direction from the one they would be taking on the way to the swimming pool, and parked the car. He knew when he set off he had a minute at most before driving became dangerous, and he couldn't drive dangerously in the built-up streets, so stop it was. And here they came: the insistent, slow, steady drip of tears as they wet his cheeks, his neck, his collar.

The kiss was guilty, had set them going, had reminded him of Siobhan and all the memories that simple word, that name brought with it. It reminded him how much he hated that she had left him – deserted her husband and her son – but how still he couldn't hate her. He couldn't even manage indifference. He still loved her. He wanted her back. He knew

Sam did too and he wanted to share his love and his longing with Sam. But he knew it would let too much go and hurt them both. And she had hurt Sam enough already, bruised his tender soul.

What he could manage – when he wanted to reject Siobhan and get on with life – was a bitter resentment of the way she went. She hurt those she should have loved the most – spat in their faces and walked away. She should have left some dignity, done it with a straight face. But she had to do it with a joke. Nothing wrong with a joke, Old thought, in its place. But this was not the place. It was the place for the most pokerish, the most deadpan of straight faces.

There was the Post-It pad on the hall floor. No explanation, just: 'I've left. I'm not coming back, don't look for me. The dinner's in the oven.' It was the language she used that told him from the first that this was real. No 'sorry', nothing. He walked, half awake, part stunned, into the sitting-room and across to the drinks cupboard. He opened the cupboard and reached for the Grouse. His eye lit on the Post-It note: 'And the oven's in the kitchen.'

She just shouldn't have.

He rubbed his face briskly, wiped his eyes and readied himself to drive home.

Old sat in his tiny office and opened a file for the case. He was not naturally organized, preferring a more intuitive approach, but he knew the benefits of well laid-out and organized information, especially when it came to proving the value of the work done to reluctant payers. With that in mind, he first described the job required, dropped the description into a standard contract, signed it and sent it off to Mee for his signature. With a legal document behind him there was far less chance of him getting stiffed. A week after the second demand for payment of a late invoice, it was his practice to threaten to bring in lawyers. A week after that, he issued summonses. It tended to work wonders. Threats of lawyers are ten-a-penny. Summonses still provide a fright. His payment more secure, he got down to the job itself. He sketched out the outlines of the case and listed the avenues he intended, in the first instance, to follow. Until he had got down to work it was extremely thin-looking down on paper, or on the monitor. Once he started it would quickly fill out, if only with dead ends. It took less than fifteen minutes, and with at least a couple of hours before Sam was due to be delivered he took the opportunity to do something he managed increasingly rarely and which he secretly missed. He took a couple of beers from the fridge, and sat before the TV with his feet up and idly flicked through the channels until he found something soporifically and easily watchable. He was still there when Sam was returned, asleep in the back of Hannah's car, and after he had thanked Hannah, carried Sam upstairs, slipped his clothes off and pyjamas on, kissed him and tucked him in, he was glad to return and watch one programme after another, flicking around whenever his viewing was interrupted by advertisements, until the BBC packed up for the night and he decided that sitting through the commercial night-time output was taking things too far.

Lying in bed with a cup of tea, he started to plan the next day but had decided no more than to get Sam to school, which, being mandatory, was no decision at all, when he fell into a deep sleep, no decisions made, and immediately started to dream lewd, fascinating and shockingly detailed dreams about Hannah, which could well form a basis for numerous decisions and plans of action.

McCreery shook his head as he looked at the photos.

'Not familiar. I'll show them around, see if anyone's seen the slag, but he's new to me.'

'Do you know any working cons?' Old asked.

'Not that I can think of; not working on the job right now. It's a very specialized field, the line you're looking at. There's a lot of crime gets classed as confidence and broadly it's right, but that's partly because the villains like to put it that way – confidence being the glamour end of crime. The point is, legally speaking, cons fall into two completely separate areas of law.'

Old wanted some specific questions answering, but, like most detectives, McCreery didn't like to be led. He liked to take his own time, go his own way, and if it involved explaining some aspect of police work, there was no such thing as not enough time. There is always time for a career policeman to talk about the job. Or The Job, as they would have it. Old thought better of interrupting and decided to soak up the background.

'Your two nasty little villains say they're the Gas Board, Water, TV Licence or whatever this week's scheme is, get in some old dear's flat and have away with her savings. That's a con. Legally, there's no difference between that and some gigolo in Belgravia talks his way into fifty grand off some rich bint with a

soft brain and damp panties. It's theft. Same as burglary or shoplifting – '68 Theft Act. Obtaining pecuni-
ary advantage through deception. Same as doing a
runner from a restaurant come to that – same section
of the law: obtaining service through deception. Refuse
to pay your bill, face to face, and that's breach of
contract. They might call the uniforms up but if the
boys who get there have any sense they won't touch
it – breach of contract's civil and they could find
'emselves with a false arrest charge. I'm drifting.'
McCreery smiled as he saw Old listening quietly,
waiting for the point to arrive, the details to build up.

'Then there's your big financial scam. What we call
the long con. In the trade it used to be known as a
fuck, which is what happens to the firm gets done:
they get right royally fucked. I'm told these days
they're calling it a Maxwell. No explanation needed.'

They were meeting in the station canteen at Lime-
house station. It seemed the relief was changing, because there was a sudden influx of uniforms in
shirtsleeves.

A PC stood at the chair next to McCreery. He had a
cup of tea in each hand and a Cellophane-wrapped
Scotch egg clenched between his teeth. He nodded at
the chair and grunted, indicating he wanted McCreery
to move his jacket and let him sit.

'I'm talking. Sit somewhere else.' McCreery said,
irritably. The young PC looked around the room and
made another grunt to show there were no free chairs.

'So stand. And don't grunt at me, son. Just because
this is the canteen doesn't mean you're not a fucking
probationer and I'm not a DS. Rank, son. A bit of
respect'd be welcome.'

25

The PC put his cups down, turning to put off another PC coming to join him, put the Scotch egg in his shirt pocket, mumbled an apology and took the drinks across the room where he perched them on a window ledge. No wonder they're rude to the public, Old thought, when you see what they're like with each other.

'Sorry about that,' McCreery said, as if he expected Old to be as disturbed as he was by the cheek of a PC wanting to sit while he drank his tea, after a morning spent on his feet.

'Your typical long con is basically a piece of piss. You set up a company, legit company but with some stooge at the head – you're nowhere on paper. You open accounts with a load of legit companies. It takes quite a bit to bankroll one of these. You flog the stuff, you have to be able to run a company, because you don't want to lose too much, but a bit of a loss is OK, helps to build up a clientele if your prices are low – obviously. Then you run up a stack of debt, order shitloads of stuff, sell it off fast – any price'll do, doesn't matter, you're not going to pay for the stuff – then the company folds. The poor sod you got in to run the company, put on the letterhead, he might get in some bother, but you're home and dry. Done right a long con should clear a million minimum and the operation takes eighteen months bottom end, bit over two years ideally. The whole routine is about building up a reasonable credit rating – which is a matter of giving someone else confidence in your credentials – then making it blow up in their face. So it is a con but it gets different law, different treatment. In the end it comes down to a tenth of a penny on the price of a can of soup or a Mars bar; forty pee on the price of a kettle, whatever the slags have been having away with. Ask me, it's theft, same as any other, but it gets covered by the fraud boys, who barely ever get a conviction. The trial can cost a million, the guy's covered in lawyers from day one – like their guru Maxwell – and he walks. In fact, this is strictly a bail number. Your guy gets away with more than your average thief will ever see and the only bars he'll ever spend any time behind are on the windows of his country house. Slags!'

'Don't you get worn out hating villains as much as you do?' Old asked, always surprised by the degree of vehemence of McCreery's contempt for criminals.

'The day it becomes routine, just a nine to five, a slog, you've lost it. You want to do the job properly, do it like it needs to be done, you have to know what they are, your villains. They're a bunch of dirty, deceitful, thieving scum. Remember that and you're there. That's why Serious Crime is such good crack. Proper villains is what we deal with. Petty crime and you're up to your fucking eyeballs in probation officers, social workers, Community Liaison plods, all turning out excuses like they were fucking worth something. Get involved with murders and you've got some poor stupid sod to lock up, caught trying to order a pint in his local, still got the hammer in his hand, dripping blood, spattered on his face, hasn't got a clue what's happened, gets fifteen years in Gartree for being a stupid bastard with fists instead of brains. I don't need any of that. I wanted that, I could be a social worker and do a thirty-five hour week and take my holidays. I don't think so. I get to do villains.'

He poked a finger in his cup of tea and scowled when, as he expected, it was cold. He gulped it down and offered Old another. As he went up to the counter, Old saw a few curious glances from officers who would rather they knew who he was and what he was doing in their station. Most likely would be that he was from another station, but why did no one know his face? It would be the subject of much speculation later, unabetted by McCreery, who thought station-house gossip one of the avoidable perils of the job.

Old took the plunge when McCreery returned. 'Seeing you don't know him, the guy in the photo, what I need is, do you know any working cons and if you do, how can I go about meeting them? I mean, is there any way it could be arranged that I could get to see them? Problem is, I'm poking around on the out-side; chances of finding anyone by myself are pretty slim. If I can get across a drink from someone, villains being the unprincipled, money-grabbing folk you were just telling me they were, I should be able to get at least a pointer in the right direction. Especially if I can prove I'm not one of you boys.'

McCreery's eyes narrowed slightly, deepening the furrows in his anguished-looking brow. McCreery always tried to dress well and generally he succeeded: just the black linen jacket he was wearing must have cost the best part of two hundred pounds, his shirt and tie another seventy. This was partly because he liked to dress well for its own sake, partly to avoid looking too much like a policeman. To Old, though, he always looked like a policeman dressed up for an occasion. Something about his face, looking well worn for its age, but not as if he was actually older – barely anyone looks more than two or three years away from their real age, they simply look good for their years or they don't. McCreery didn't.

'What's in it for us? Looks a pretty good deal for you, get the Plod to do your job for you.'

'Same as ever. I find anything can't get back to me, or if it does but it doesn't matter, and telling you doesn't get in the way of whatever I'm up to, then I'll pass it on. It's worked before, hasn't it?'

'So long as you don't try and pull any flankers and you're not always on the blower wanting me to hit the computer, I suppose so.'

That was what Old had liked best about McCreery ever since they met at an advanced detectives course at Bramshill Police Officers College; his unreserved and unstinting enthusiasm for helping out. McCreery was there on a course readying him for promotion, and for his first experience of command. Old was seconded from Army Intelligence, being trained in detection techniques, the better to haul back the AWOLs. Normally the AWOLs were looked after by the MPs. But an awful lot of soldiers, for one reason or another, had security-sensitive information. And no matter that to a man they vanished for the same reasons as every other soldier: pissed off; homesick; drunk; horny. But when they had that special, secret information tucked away behind the hangover, the Army took special care to ensure it knew where they were and got them back, double quick. And that was Old's job: from a small unit in Intelligence, he was tasked to find them and put them back where they belonged. It was supposed to be a short-term thing. He took a commission, ending up heading up the unit, and was still making a crust, the Army years behind him, finding the missing. And a good part of what enabled him to do that job was the outside training – the detection, the advanced driving techniques, all that good professional stuff, but also the contacts he made. Some of them had turned into friends and even among those who had barely a civil word to say, most knew the value of a favour.

Old waited, expecting more from McCreery.

'So?'

'Yeah?'

'Do you have a name then or what?'

'I suppose. Frankie Silvester. Not the classiest article there is. Not my nick, just a name I know. I had him in for questioning a couple of times for cheque fraud. Didn't have much but I thought I could lean on him. He knew what I had and what I didn't and so did his solicitor. One thing you'll find in confidence, they're always ready to get the law on their side. Not afraid of a few lawyer's bills. Villain's best friend's a brief. That's always true – without exception. The cons are just the ones who understand that best.'

'After you missed out on him someone else managed it then?' Old asked mischievously. 'Not quite slippery enough?'

McCreery's eyes darkened at the slight, though he knew as well as Old it was a simple wind-up.

'Different crime, different occasion. I just noticed the name when he got nicked. He was the support on this. We didn't even get to see the principal. Silvester kept schtum, which is a surprise. These guys'll usually do anything to keep out of nick. Never know though; might be working with someone handy.'

'What did he do?'

'Not sure exactly. He's a bit of a smooth-looking bastard. If he was working to form it'd be something to do with some stupid woman.'

'Do you make a lot of friends like that, the positive approach you've got when it comes to women?' Old asked.

McCreery scowled again, the most natural resting position for his features, Old thought.

'Best DC in our squad is a woman. Next best too. Before you jump down my throat, what I'm saying is that's what he works on, right – women. They fall for him, that makes 'em stupid, right. Some stupid woman, fuck it, pardon me while I do you a favour.'

Old ignored the reply, not wanting to make a debate out of it.

'So where do I find him?'

'Leave it with me, I'll bell you.'

'You know what this reminds me of?' Kevin asked. 'It reminds me of all those times we sat planning how we was going to get loaded. We was going to rob banks, but we wasn't going to get caught like all the silly arses do it usually, we was going to get away with it because we was different, like we wasn't going to go bragging, we'd just keep schtum and 'cause we didn't know nobody, nobody'd be able to grass us up. Or we was going to do some big financial scam, 'cause we knew a few blokes worked in the City said there was all these billions flying about, all it took was somebody on the inside and you were away; few million here and there, it'd take 'em till the end of the month before they knew, time it right and you were on the beach in sunny Rio, lying on the beaches looking at the peaches.

Problem with all that was there was something missing; had to be or else I wouldn't be here doing cab control on a day no one wants cabs.

'Bottle or "get up and go" or both. Like most boxers; talked a good fight. Came to the day and where were we? Didn't even get that far – to the day – to actually doing anything. None of it got past "I wish, I bet we could, we should you know." '

'What are you on about?' Mel mumbled through the roll-up attached to his bottom lip. 'Time o' the month, is it?'

'All this about what we should do to Barry, what we should do to hurt the bastard. Flash twat drags us into this bloody silly scam. We walk in there like a bunch of sheep. Baa, here's me money, baa, money I had to borrow, baaaaa, and off he goes into the sunset, your man Goodman, and what does Barry do? He says sorry. Fucking sorry. So what are we supposed to do? Anything, nothing or what?'

The phone rang and Kevin snatched it before the first ring was half way over.

'Reddy Cabs, help you?' He scribbled the pick-up and destination on the log sheet.

''Bout six quid,' he said to the telephone. 'On his way.'

He yelled out into the drivers' waiting-room.

'Who's next?'

A glum face appeared at the window.

'Me.'

'Number!' Kevin barked.

'Twenty-two.'

'Mount Pleasant. Know it?'

'Sort of.'

'Which means "no", I take it. Just ask and I'll tell you. This is a minicab office, you're not expected to have the knowledge or nothing. Islington, N1. You know Islington well? Silly question. It's the Kings Cross end. Head for Old Street roundabout, up to Angel, left at the top, right past Sadler's Wells and another right. I expect she'll tell you what she wants then. Probably the Post Office depot – 'sall there is at Mount Pleasant. Picking up 246 Dacre.' The driver again looked blank.

'Jesus, the fuck do you find your way here of a morning? Runs between Plashet – Road not Grove – and Terrace. Parallel Selwyn. And move it, I said you were on the way. And your car's outside, pointing the wrong way. And I had a look at it this morning, it's a sty, for a pig that's got bad habits. After this run get it cleaned. And I told her sixish so don't try and rip her off, make it six flat, she's getting to be regular.'

The head withdrew through the window with all the enthusiasm it could muster, which was none.

'I know it's hard getting drivers,' Kevin said, 'but some of that lot are beyond a joke. I doubt if they could navigate a straight route from one end of the Romford Road to the other. No wonder people take black cabs. Sometimes wish I'd done the knowledge myself when the waiting list was shorter than the Nile. Not going to get rich driving a black cab, but it's reliable. Less agg than all this.'

He waved his hand around the untidy cab office. He watched Mel roll another cigarette, probably less tobacco inside than paper out – a sure sign of an ex-con.

'Business flat for you an' all, then?' he asked.

'Crap,' Mel mumbled. 'Holborn Station and Oxford

Street, the only places worth doing, extra uniforms out for some reason, so you're closing the stall before you've got it open, and there's more doing it. Fucking drugged-up kids. No fear in 'em. Try to scare 'em off they just blank you. Don't want to lean on 'em, they're fucking mad. Pull a knife, like as not.

'Got bound over a month ago. Six months. Get pulled in, I get to serve a month. No thanks, not again, not so soon and for something so crappy anyway. Starting Monday, I'm doing Charlie's window round for a month while he hops off to his time-share.'

'Charlie who?'

'You know, Charlie Graham.'

'Charlie Graham,' he paused to think. 'Doesn't ring any bells.'

'Not Charlie Graham, I meant like Charlie – Graham,' pausing between the two words. 'He's called Graham but everybody on his round calls him Charlie, 'cause that's what his old man was called and it was his old man gave him the round, so as far as everyone sees it, it's Charlie the window-cleaner.'

'Short guy, mostly bald, always falling off?'

'That's him. That's why he's got a month. Fell off a first-floor window ledge when it crumbled, done his back up. Doc says a month minimum. He's had a fortnight, now his month's come up at the timeshare and he says the people with the next month don't always use it so he's going to hang on as long as he can. He's charging me seventy-five quid a week for the round. Keep me going for a while. Makes me fucking angry, though.' He paused to re-light his cigarette. The problem with ultra thin roll-ups is they go out so frequently they seem to cost more in matches than tobacco.

'Getting a ticket for trading without a licence now and then, it's part of the game. Gives you a break. It's kind of understood you don't do it when you're under a ticket. So that's fine, it's a good paying game, you make a bob, when you're pushed off the street you lie low, sit out, your time's up, out comes the snide perfume, crap jewellery, dust it down, out with the display box and back to business. Life's sweet. So what happens? Tell me, Kev.'

Kev nodded, let him carry on with his gripe.

'You hear of a chance from a mate where you can make a piece in a hurry, you stump up twelve grand and wave it bye bye. And to add insult, the day you throw it away, you get smashed, celebrating what a clever lad you are, and wake up with a hangover you'd get nick for if you made anyone else feel that near death. So next time you get kicked off the street, you're borassic lint, after you've bought your invisible motor, and you end up cleaning windows. I mean do I look like George bleeding Formby?'

'What are we going to do then?'

'Fuck knows.'

THREE

Old and Ras perched on stools at the end of the bar. In the dim mid-afternoon light Ras's pure white turban seemed to shine, setting off his deep dark eyes and thick black beard. Old explained the job and listed his activities so far.

'Can't really see a place in this for me, not so far at least,' said Ras.

Old agreed. 'You could keep an ear out, raise the subject, which increases the chances of learning something. Most people have heard of a con; people like them, the way they work. They make a good story – trust and lies, deals and deceit and a nice little sting in the tail.'

'I heard of one,' Ras said.

'There you go. Everyone knows at least one. How's it go?'

'A guy who comes in here, he got his car nicked. Reports it to the police, claims on the insurance, the whole Monty. Police say it should turn up in a day or so, no radio, few dented panels; joyriders. No go. After a week it turns up outside. Perfect; just as he left it, tidier if anything. There's an envelope taped to the dash. The guy opens it, there's a letter. "Sorry about taking your car, I realize it was wrong but it was a genuine emergency and I needed a car urgently. Unfortunately, I cannot tell what it was. I realize I must have put you to some inconvenience and though this will by no means fully compensate, as a gesture, these tickets are attached." In the envelope there's two theatre tickets for a couple of nights' time. They're brassed off but kind of pleased. Human nature comes up trumps and all that. They report the return of the car but don't mention the tickets – doesn't seem necessary. They go to the theatre on the night, when they get home, the place is stripped. Burglars, real pro job. Cleaned it out.' Ras smiled. 'Neat huh?'

Old nodded.

'It's a good trick, but strictly speaking it's not a con. It's clever but it's just an elaborate way of making sure a house is empty. The essence of a con is confidence.'

'No kidding!'

'It is, though; it's easy to forget that's what it's all about. The con artist makes the mark confident that they can pull a stroke. The mark hands over the money, sure that they are the ones doing well. Some of them, they're handing it over to get a bargain that's just a bit too good – like Mee's one; sometimes, they're elaborate enough that the mark thinks they're the conman. They work best, because the greed helps them not to look too close, and they're set up so they only look at one angle – the angle that means they make the money.'

'I think I'm missing something there. I mean, you know if you're a conman or not, right?'

'The point is to make the mark into a conman – a bad one – one who doesn't figure out the angles. I'll tell you what I mean. There's one, some old dosser, keeps accosting smart, affluent-looking guys, guys who look like they think they're something special, pretty damn sharp. Eventually one will listen, because the dosser's waving a legal-looking envelope at them.

When they listen they're hooked. He's got spit on his chin and snot on his lapel and his breath smells like Lassie with halitosis, but he can tell the story.

'He can't read, but he found this document and he's sure it's important. Can you help? He might be a dosser but that doesn't mean he's not honest. Big, dopey, soft eyes. Whatever he says he is you instantly want to disassociate yourself from – you think, big, stupid, innocent dupe. There's a number on the document. It's a nearby exchange, which the mark might know or he might not – the whole thing goes on within a mile or so of the legal district, and the envelope's this thick off-white parchment affair, a phone number scribbled on the back. The guy calls the number, gets through to some name or other, explains, the guy at the other end nearly throws a fit – valuable document, all that, a reward waiting, two hundred and fifty pounds or so, please, please get it here, gives an address. So your man says to your dosser, don't worry, give it to me, I'll sort it. Your dosser, all innocent still, but now: "It's my responsibility. I have to do it." Then, for the first time, a wise look in the man's eyes – "It may be worth money, you might be going to rob me." Your man is sussed. Shamed, he starts to haggle – now they're on the same level. The dosser usually gets fifty to a hundred.'

'And when he goes to get his money, there's no such address.' Ras beamed as he saw the con.

'Sweet, isn't it?'

'As a nut. Is this just made up or are there supposed to be people actually doing this one and getting away with it?' Ras asked.

'I read about this one in the paper. It was supposed

to be doing the rounds in New York, Chicago. They got a few complaints to the police, but when the police wanted to go trawling the dossers, and when it was clear they'd have to stand up in court and say they were outwitted by this specimen, they mostly dropped the complaint. The police said they didn't know if it was someone pretending to be a dosser or just a team of ingenious dossers, though they thought it was unlikely to be the latter as they were probably clearing a thousand dollars a day. They said it was their policy to pass these kinds of scams on to the press as the papers usually gave them plenty of space – they made good stories, and once the scams were widely known, their ability to find a mark dropped through the floor.'

Ras's eyes lit up.

'If that's the case, then that's where you can get a few leads – a few names even – check out the papers. You could probably do it from your desk, couldn't you – one of these search whatsits?'

Old nodded.

'That's the next step. Down in the diary. First, see Ras, second, call Toby Norton.'

'The four-foot financial whizz?'

'Mm hm, that's the one. Then check the papers.'

'You think Norton'll know anything?'

'I wouldn't be surprised at anything Norton knew, especially where shady money's concerned. I mean that's basically his job, right, shuffling money around so no one knows what it is, whose it is and where it comes from. Playing Find the Lady with other people's money.'

Toby Norton, at four feet ten, thought himself the top-earning man in the country – within his peer group of men under five feet tall. An employee of a previous client of Old's, he was now in business on his own account and was doing very well. Unhindered by considerations of business ethics and legality, he managed to gain handsome returns for his clients, enough to keep them all from raising a word about the outrageous commissions he paid himself.

'I thought he was working legit as a trader,' said Ras.

'He is, but with all the connections he made through Darnell, before he was top dog, he knows how sweet the margins are in the funny-money business and I couldn't see him passing up on them, so there's a good chance he'll know some people.'

'He's not what you'd call a conman, though, is he? I mean he's a pretty straightforward trader, if a bit of an unusual one – working outside the big houses.'

'Sure,' Old said, 'I'll give you that, he doesn't rip off his clients, he helps make them richer, just like he promises, but he rips the tax off blind, shuffling money through offshore centres, and cleans up dodgy money, dragging it back onshore and putting it through legit deals. All that dirty money must touch a few dirty hands and I'd guess Toby has a good idea where it all comes from. Anyway, after seeing him, or phoning to try to squeeze a half hour into his day, it's up to the desk, try to get a few decent stories off the on-line news libraries.'

Ras raised a finger.

'You don't pay by the item for that stuff, do you?'

'Nah, you pay an annual subscription, then you use what you want, you just pay for the phone time you spend hooked up. The sucker's thing is not to hang up. You should get what you want and drop it down to a file and break the connection. If you want more, call up again. It's easy to get sucked in, sit staring at the thing, looking up this, that and the other; your bill comes through and you see the one call cost over a fiver. Stuff like that, ninety days to the quarter, it can add up.'

'Do me a favour, then. Check out recent reports – last couple of years, nationals mainly, on smart drugs. The local nick's been breathing down my neck again and I want to make sure there's no precedent for a successful nicking and maybe even find out the right law to quote at 'em to have 'em get off my back.'

Old nodded. Ras ran a very trendy bar that, among its many fashionable quirks, ran a sideline in cocktails containing smart drugs said to sharpen memory and acuity. He sourced them all through upright Swiss drug wholesalers and obtained very proper import licences but had still had his stock seized three times by the police. He had writs out for all three cases – which woke the police up – once for damages, when they destroyed the drugs, the other two to get the drugs back and to obtain punitive damages. Ras was winning all round. The publicity was packing the punters in his bar until the walls were sweating; and the police were going to lose their cases and knew it.

'Are we still on for dinner at yours tonight?'

'Far as I know, Satya didn't say any different.'

'I'll bring round the copy tonight then. There's bound to be a fair bit and most of it'll be repetitive as the papers nick each other's stories, but there should be something in there.'

'Until later, then.'

No one would accuse Norton of being difficult to get off the telephone. If Old had anticipated any problem it was that he would be difficult to get hold of. He answered the first call on the first ring. Old identified himself to Norton, who had done the same with his first, his only word. Old started to sketch out his needs but before he was half way through his first breath Norton interrupted.

'Not now, Pat. Phone's busy. Lunch?' Old grunted a kind of assent.

'Two, dim sum, New China? See you later.'

Assuming Old agreed, he hung up and Old supposed, to himself, that the date was OK and that given that it was he who was asking the favour, he had no right objecting. Besides, if he was to eat at Satya's later, dim sum was enough to keep him going without overfilling him, so long as he avoided the suet.

A couple of hours in front of his computer, checking through possible names thrown up in connection with a number of criteria connected to confidence trickery. Trying to cut corners, his first attempt was Frankie Silvester. Not a single reference to the name in any context. Next he hit the wide angle and asked simply for reference to the phrase 'confidence trick' in any of the nationals. He was rewarded with over eighty stories, most of them different though a few were, as he fully expected, rehashes of the same story. None of them gave any useful names and a good number were the simple identity-card flashers described by McCreery who wangled their way into some poor dupe's house under cover of false ID and robbed them of their savings and anything else of value. Still, they helped Old get a feel for the type of thing that went under the label 'confidence' and gave him an idea. A number of the articles were features and outlined a few neat cons. One was a belated review of the video release of the film *Dirty Rotten Scoundrels*, a fanciful view of the confidence trickster and for Steve Martin a stinker, Old thought. But one or two of the cons described by the features were simple and elegant enough to inspire Old to try out his idea. If he was to find his man, this research was not just a search for leads but an attempt to get inside the head of the conman. If he was to do that, then he must do what the con did. Do the job. Understand a con: do one; be one. Nothing too elaborate, and nothing from anyone who couldn't afford it, but a con. Use his wits to take money off someone. Definitely. Oh, definitely yes. He could feel it was right. A definite definite.

Old took a bite out of what looked like an eyeball wrapped in oily clingfilm and dropped the remainder back on his plate, closing his eyes to savour the texture and the strange undefinable taste.

'I always get the feeling this is food from another planet,' he said. 'Apart from the suet, there's rarely a taste you recognize, or even one that reminds you of anything.'

'That's because it is food from another planet: the planet China,' Norton said. 'China's another thing again. Everything I ever see or read about the place, it just seems so alien I can't understand it. I mean, look at the language. Is that something you could even see yourself understanding? Eat at Pizza Hut, you can imagine you can guess what the waiter's thinking.

You're almost certainly wrong but you can imagine it. The girl pushing the trolley,' Norton nodded towards one of the three waitresses slowly pushing the dim sum trolleys round the restaurant, slowing by each table to give the diners a chance to stop them and choose something new, 'could you make a guess there? I couldn't make a guess about a single thought she's ever had. Ever. We don't want to get into clichés about the inscrutable Orient, but Chinese is what inscrutable means. You ever played cards with Chinese? Don't.'

Old gestured towards the waitresses: 'Bet when she was a kid and she ate this,' he held up the half-eaten item, 'she thought, "This looks just like an eyeball," probably still does.'

They ate in silence for a while, concentrating on the weird and wondrous things left them in the wicker baskets, all fantastic to see, strange and wonderful to taste, all food and all new. When the food was finished and the tea refilled, Norton broke the silence.

'How can I help you then? I presume it's not about the work I'm finding to keep your money busy.'

Old shook his head.

'I know where that money came from, you know. Sure enough to put my own money on it,' said Norton.

'If anyone was arguing or offering to place a bet. It's money. No deeds, no conscience, it's just money. If money talked, that chunk would give name, rank and serial number.'

'Tim was a friend.'

'And now he's not. The money was there, in my hands. What was I going to do? Give it to his father?

44

Send an anonymous cheque to the donkey sanctuary? I don't think so. I've got Sam to look after and a chance like that doesn't come up every day, not every lifetime, and I lose no sleep over it. I gain sleep over it. You like money, Toby. You know how it helps you sleep and helps you breathe and you've only got forty kilos of you to look after. You should understand. We both know money's important. It can even be fun. Every time – not nine times out of ten – if there's some to be had and I can get it at a risk I can handle, I will.'

'I only said I knew,' Norton said, with the nearest to an apology in his voice Old thought he was likely to hear.

'And I suppose that means I was right – it's not about the money.'

'It's not. The money's doing great; what can I say, you're brilliant.'

'No need for sarcasm.'

'None there. Really, I didn't think returns like that were possible. Last year you made me as much from the money as I did from actually going out and working.'

'If there was ever a contest, you're doing better from working than I thought you could.'

'Now where's the sarcasm coming from?'

Norton nodded that he conceded the point.

'What it is, I want to pick your brains.'

He explained the job, including the BMW scam. Norton spotted the scam as soon as Goodman brought the car back and announced he could get another dozen.

'The first he bought. He collects for the rest and Bam! He's gone.'

'You're the first person's worked it out without it being explained. You heard it before?'

'No. But there's a lot of snide money out there, and a lot of snide deals. Spotting them is what makes the difference for a broker at the risky end of the market. You've got to look at them or you might as well be investing in gilts and blue chips – risk means pay-off. You've got to have a nose and that scam of your man's stinks.'

Old was impressed at Norton's perception, but pained that he had said what he thought and given Norton a chance to brag. There was no doubt that Norton was a good broker. Dishonest, sneaky and good. Old could handle that. But he had a chip on his shoulder as big as he was small, and, to compensate, bragged whenever the opportunity arose. It was made far worse that he was not stupid. He knew he did it and he knew why, but still he did it.

'Just because you know you're a little squirt doesn't stop it being the case,' he said. 'Same with the bragging. The chance comes up, I take it; can't help it. I hear myself, think "Oh no, here he goes, fucking superman," but do I stop? What do you think?'

Regardless of all that, however, Old found Norton's company congenial, his conversation sharp, and his professional services very worthwhile.

'I need to know if you know any working financial conmen. Any conmen, come to that – you might always have someone investing money with you gets it that way. If you know anyone does that kind of stuff, I'd be grateful for an introduction, find out what the crack is from the horse's mouth.'

'What is it you want to know?' Norton asked. 'Most

46

financial scams are fairly straightforward. I know the details, how they work – it's mostly just a matter of keeping the money moving.'

'I don't mean just laundry. I've got a fairly good idea how that works.'

'I'm sure you have.'

'I mean your actual taking money by deception. I mean, it must go on, I know it does, it's just a matter of knowing how, so I understand it. Then, when I get to speak to someone, I don't sound like a complete stiff.'

'You're going to run a scam, aren't you?' Norton said, grinning inanely. Old paused for a moment, taking a sip of tea while he decided what to say.

'Sort of. I just want to talk to someone in a big scam, and I want to find my man. But I was thinking of doing a little one – one of the silly little bar tricks maybe. Take money off someone right before their eyes. Make them look silly when they fall for it, then insist on the pay-up. Be an exercise in bottle if nothing else.'

'You fancy a go, you mean, for kicks.'

'Well there is that. What about it?'

'There is someone I can introduce you to. He's been at it for years. Done very well out of it. If I tell you he lives in Virginia Water, it should give you an idea. I'll try to fix up a meet and, if I can, I'll fill you in on how a few scams work then. Meantime, piss off. I've got to get back; money to make, hustlers to hustle. You interested in forty grand's worth of papaya futures contracts by the way?'

'Don't you make those decisions for me? Papaya? Is this a wind-up?'

'Naturally.'

FOUR

The tyres crunched on the gravel as they pulled up on the small oval drive in front of Mee's neo-Georgian house in Chigwell.

'Size of this place,' Mel grunted. 'What's it called, Essex? Twelve grand bound to have hurt him as much as it did us. He must be worth a mint. Two.'

'You not been here before, then?' Kevin asked.

'Not been invited. Known the bloke long enough but never really seen much of him outside the pub, Friday night Indian, few trips to the races. You don't tend to go back for a few cans and a take-away to a bloke's house, he lives a ten-quid cab ride away. Got to say I always thought of him as a mate, though. Praised him to the skies when he came up with this car thing – bringing his mates in on a piece of action he could have kept for himself. Fucking star, I thought. Made a mistake, didn't I?'

Kevin stepped out of the car and Mel followed, scrambling across the seats as the passenger door wouldn't open.

'You don't still take this thing cabbing, do you?'

'Just take it out if we're pushed, and if there's only one or two to pick up, put 'em in the back.'

'It's a fucking wreck.' Mel glanced up and down the length of the big Ford Granada: nearly three litres of metallic gold tank.

'It's a lovely motor. Moves nice, well comfortable, it's just got a dodgy door. I'm waiting for someone to find me a new one. We've been here nearly five minutes, are we going to do something or what?'

'We should have planned what we was going to do, you know.'

'We just say what we want. Tell him it's his fault. Tell him we want our fucking money: if it wasn't for him we wouldn't have lost it. What else is there?'

'We could give him a smack.'

'You think that'd help?' Kevin asked.

'It'd help me. It'd take that fat grin off his fat, ugly face.'

They stood together and rapped loudly on the door. The Filipino housekeeper told them Mee was out. When Mel tried to push past, she stood firm.

Kevin gunned the accelerator and dug deep furrows into the gravel as he spun the car out of the drive.

'Should have rung first,' Mel muttered.

'She said.'

'She was right.' They sat in the car and seethed, thwarted by an elementary detail. They cursed Mee all the way back to Forest Gate, and all the way through four rounds in the Princess Alice. When they came back and found the car boxed in, they cursed him some more, and if they had been able to get the car out and drive, they would have blamed him if they were booked for drink driving. By the time they separated, promising to get together again, possibly next time involving more of the swindled friends of Barry Mee, the air was blue with insult and threat.

Satya cooked so frequently for Old, she had heard plenty of compliments for her cooking, and she knew it was a bit of a clichéd thing they did – the regular

49

Wednesday dinner date, the wife busy in the kitchen while the men opened a few cans, in this case also in the kitchen – but she still enjoyed the praise for the food. She liked to cook a traditional roast, and she knew that, with Old and Sam alone, there was little call for it round their place, little opportunity, so today that was what they would have. For her, apart from fry-ups and omelettes, it was the only bit of authentically English cuisine she knew how to cook. As the after-dinner conversation got down to business, she frowned. Her work, as a secretary in Ras's father's accountancy practice – a job she had before they met – was dull. Too dull to bring into the forum of after-dinner conversation, and the office politics was mostly family politics. Ras's business was the bar and restaurant, and Ras's musings were about the possibility of opening another. But much as he loved the bar, George's, Ras knew it held less interest to anyone else. He would admit no such thing about Old's business and tried to involve himself whenever and wherever he could, eating up the details and trying hard, if no practical help was possible, to offer some insight or some new angle of attack. It was undoubtedly work which, from a certain angle, could be seen as glamorous, but it was also true that it had its dangerous side. Knowing the simple way men's minds worked, Satya thought this was probably the root of the glamour. And it could be seedy. Like this new job. Conmen were simple thieves and if one could be caught, all well and good. But to work for this man Mee? Pornography was horrible. She had a friend whose father ran a newsagent with a full and ripe top shelf. She had spent some time in the shop and had always been curious about the top shelf. Occasionally she had been there while someone bought a magazine and had been quietly repelled by their manner – a strange mix of furtive shame and brave swagger. It also made her think her friend's father was not quite the respectable business-man he seemed, though she later realized, through the number of newsagents they had as clients at the accountancy, that in that business it was absolutely essential. Sell them or go under. People wanted them and there were sufficient newsagents that the custom of the wankers was as necessary as everyone else's.

For Pat, though, it was different. He didn't really need the money so badly he couldn't do without any case in particular – these days he could afford to be choosy. He was doing it out of interest, the challenge, all that testosterone-driven stuff. She didn't like the sound of what he was doing and she didn't like the thought of him touching that horrible man's money, still less Ras getting involved. Before she bothered to get involved in an argument she knew what their response would be – that what they were doing had nothing to do with porn – but they were wrong. It wasn't just money. She knew, or thought she could imagine, how most of those women would have felt as they were posing for the photo sessions. Whatever they said about it being their choice, how many of them would have said, five years earlier, that they wanted to feature in porn magazines, to be the subject of who knew how much damp and lonely thrashing of sweaty men and pimply boys. The thought was enough to make your flesh creep. She knew they would look at it differently – all boys had a few of those magazines as teenagers, and at least they had the decency to look ashamed as they bought them – but that exposure coloured their view of pornography for ever. It would always be a bit of a laugh and a hard on. It would never be looked at from the point of view of the women – couldn't be. It was too resolutely male. Besides, by the way they were talking, they were already well into the chase. They were getting into the nitty-gritty, enjoying their tales of clever deceit. They wanted to find their conman but she could hear in their voices, in their enthusiasm, how they admired his guile and his nerve.

'I was thinking about it,' Ras said, 'about as far as a physical ID goes, all you've got is the one crappy photo and a description from Mee, and it's wrong. There's more out there you can get your hands on. There was the other nine of them. They all saw him, they might all remember some detail or other that Mee missed. If you had a word with all of them, you might learn something. Probably take a while but it's got to be worth it.'

'That's a good point. In fact it's the best lead I've had yet, until McCreery turns something up, and it's been staring me in the face. Nine people who knew him, saw him, did business and gave him money and have had good reason to go over the whole thing a thousand times and fix every detail they can. I'll get the names off Mee in the morning. He should have no objection – when I turn up, asking questions, shows he's doing his best to get the money back. Two of them he paid back, said they were too skint, felt he'd pressured them, felt bad they were losing money they couldn't afford to lose. Pretty decent gesture really, from a low-life like Mee. Thanks for the thought.'

'Kind of help you get when you apply a real mind to the job,' Ras said.

'Although this time it was you thought of it.'

At six-thirty, the Star Inn was busier than usual, but only because it had a table of eight, already pouring the drinks down. The Star had a large car park and was a little out of the way. Many of the customers ate with their drinks – good high-margin stuff – but few drank to excess, as so many of them were driving, which all kept down the trouble. This lot, though, all arrived more or less together in a collection of beat-up minicabs. The barman knew this, because they were the first in and he saw them arrive while he caught a pre-session fag outside. They went straight on to pints with shorts chasers, half were on bitter, half lager, all the shorts were Scotch. They all sat together, pulled a couple of tables together to make one long table – more work for later – and they had not stopped talking. It seemed to be some kind of formal meeting, but the types who usually met in pubs for meetings – lefties and quiz and darts organizers – looked a different sort entirely. These were all East End and Essex boys, had it written all over them, often literally, on their arms, surrounded by garlands, roses and 'Cheryl'. They seemed to be trying to take it in order to speak, holding off and subsiding into a general chat whenever two of them had to leave the table to get a new round.

It wasn't working, they weren't committee types. Voices were occasionally raised, a few bangs on the table. Although the barman couldn't hear what the debate was about, it was obviously no issue of academic interest. This was best judged by the few words he did manage to pick up, very many of which were along the lines of 'bastard, fucking bastard and fat little cunt'. As the bar began to fill up towards eight, the ten downed their drinks, there was a deal of collective head-nodding, as if some decision had been taken, a plan of action settled, and they trooped out. If the barman could, he would have put the night's wages on the proposition that the bunch on the way out were planning something highly illegal. No takers.

Sam and Jimmy scaled the rope pyramid, howling with laughter as the rope wobbled, diving back into some surreal fantasy the rest of the time, with cartoon baddies, real-life friends, and sundry objects and strangers interweaving with no apparent distinction made between the real and the fictional. Old stood with Hannah, trying to make casual conversation and finding it easier than he had expected when Hannah invited him along. It was easier mostly because Hannah was good at it, leading the conversation, pausing just when he had something worth saying. The first few times they had met, conversation was restricted to kids. It was the one thing they knew held an interest for the other. They had moved on to new pastures and things were progressing well. Old knew that his hesitance would soon be gone. It only happened with women, and with women in whom he had an interest – it was fortunate Hannah didn't know that – but his small talk function froze completely. Soon they would know enough about each other that they would be able to talk as friends, conversation developing organically, developing offshoots by itself and sustaining itself, feeding upon whatever circumstance offered it. It was starting this process already, they were talking about the technical publishing business and where Hannah's skills could be of use to Old. This was not where they had started, but Old was sure this was more down to the skill of Hannah in keeping the conversation moving than to any effort on his part.

They sauntered across the playground, not intruding on the kids but staying near enough to save them from the occasional panics to which kids are prone when they momentarily believe themselves forgotten, abandoned in the park. They both spent a silent moment watching as Sam and Jimmy clambered up a steep-sided log rampart on a climbing frame apparently meant for eights and up.

'I've a big pan of risotto at home, if you'd like to join us,' Old blurted out, unsure where the words came from. 'Well, at least, I've made the stock, I've cleaned and prepared the fish, I've just to put it all together. Take about half an hour, forty minutes.'

'You make stock? A methodical man.'

'No choice is there, really? Stock cubes aren't worth the name, and if you make risotto without stock, you're just making chicken and rice, fish and rice, whatever. Stock's what makes it what it is.'

'Still,' Hannah insisted, 'most men wouldn't bother, especially not mid-week. They'd do it of a weekend and make an almighty fuss about it. On Wednesday it's impressive.'

'Risotto's what Sam and I fancied. Today just happens to be a Wednesday. What some other man, or some other woman come to that, what they'd do, it doesn't come into it. I'm cooking for Sam and me.' He stopped and realized he had flushed. Was he ranting?

Had he spoiled the moment? He was sure he had, but if so, Hannah brought it back from the dead. They had avoided mentioning their partners specifically, other men and women with regard to relationships in general, but she covered things up and broke that barrier too, before it had chance to develop into a taboo.

'I suppose I know about the wrong kind of man, and you've learned life without a woman.'

For a moment, Old resented the implied criticism of Siobhan, but after all, didn't she deserve her share of criticism? Where was she to say Hannah was wrong? Stand up and defend yourself or keep quiet. He didn't answer, his mind rushing too much to formulate a coherent reply, so full of defence and rejection for the absent Siobhan. Hannah seemed to pick up on this.

'Tell me if I step on any toes. Unasked-for honesty. I only thought I understood, that we were somehow in the same boat.'

'We are,' he said thickly. 'We are.' He put the first two fingertips of his right hand to his lips, kissed them lightly and touched them to Hannah's lips.

'No toes stepped on, I promise. You still didn't tell me if you were eating with us. Ask Sam. It'll be a good risotto.'

Now it was Hannah who was silenced by unexpected emotion. She nodded and smiled, then waved at Jimmy who had seen the smile and waved at her.

Later, as Old dropped Sam off at the childminder, he realized he had been smiling since he arose that morning. Dinner with Hannah had been great. She was appreciative, which was a pleasant change from Sam, who always said he liked food unless he was unhappy about something, and it bore little relation to how he actually felt about the food itself. By the time she left to get Jimmy to bed, they had been chatting like old friends. A couple of glasses of wine had given a glow to her complexion, which was anyway looking well in the sinking light as they finished the dinner they had eaten in the garden. He liked her, and he was pretty sure she liked him back. Potentially a very happy situation. Not wanting to push things, they had finished the evening with another quick exchange of affectionate pecks on the cheek, but this time they managed to avoid the embarrassment that went with their last goodbye kisses. It had been the best evening he could remember for some time.

He had also found himself thinking about her physically again. She was his type, there was no doubt. Women seem to dislike the idea of men having a physical template they aim for. But many do, even though for a million reasons they may end up happily attached to an entirely different shape, the preferences are still there. Hannah was a little above average height for a woman, she wasn't plump, but had the kind of body, the kind of face that suggested she could easily become so. She had a distinct waist, though no wasp-waist, and shapely hips, and breasts no one would describe as bee-stings. They were what Old thought of, castigating himself for his Neanderthal attitudes as he did so, as a perfect handful. She dressed in a way that showed off her figure, wearing conservative print dresses, with gathered waists and necklines just low enough to point out what it was they wouldn't let you see. They managed to be sensible, modest and at the same time to drive Old wild as he thought about her.

Now it was back into the mire with Barry Mee.

First was to get a list of his friends who had been done along with him in the con. Somebody, one of them at least, should be able to remember something of some use. The receptionist sounded as if she would have liked to stall but had been given instructions to put him straight through. She wasn't happy about it – obstruction was the one power she had, taking it away was too cruel. Like asking a sergeant-major to whisper.

Mee was as effusive and ebullient as ever.

'Good to hear you're still on the job, my man.'

Right away Mee, quite innocently, had hit a sore point. It was a well-paid job and the whole area of cons was of interest to Old, but the contact with Mee, the fact of working for his tainted money, was something Old was trying to keep from the forefront of his mind. The last thing he wanted was to be thought of as Mee's man.

'A lead I need to follow up – or at least, a lead I think might be there for the following. The guys you sold the idea to, your mates who were stung with you, can you give me their names and addresses, phone numbers, where I can contact them, and, if possible, a bit of background – like which were the ones could least afford to lose it? Just send me a fax with as much as you can get down, if you could. Better, fax me details on the first couple and I can be getting on while you get the rest of the information together.'

His suggestion was met with silence.

'When do you think you could get that to me then?'

'I don't think it's such a good idea. Get on with

58

doing whatever else you were doing, I'll have a word with the lads, see if they remember anything.'

'I'd prefer to do it myself. I hear what they say, I can judge it, see if I think it's anything new, put it in context. Send me the stuff, I'll get on to it, leave you to get on with business.'

'Just don't do it that way. It caused a lot of bad feeling I don't want stirred up. Find out but forget that angle.'

'I think that's a promising angle,' Old insisted.

'Find another one. I'm paying the bills, find the bastard some other way. That's the last I want to hear about it. Was there anything else?'

'It's the bills bother me. If I don't find him, you'll not be wanting to pay any more than the deposit you've already paid, and if you've the cheek, you'll be asking for that back too. So you tell me who you want me to find, I'm the one decides how I go about it. You don't give me the information, I'll find it anyway. What's the problem?'

'I said drop it.'

'I heard. Pardon me if I don't take any notice, won't you? Look, nine guys, all mates, lost twelve grand each and they can put it all down to you. Goodman isn't here to blame, you are. When I speak to them, I don't expect to hear them telling me you're the salt of the earth, I don't care what they think about you, I don't care if you are the salt of the earth or not. I care about finding your man because that's what I was hired to do. I'm the one with the know-how, I do know how, and for the moment, that's how. At least, they get me asking questions, they know you're doing something to get the dosh back. Stiffing up the money for two of 'em as well, you're trying, right. I mean, what do they want? Is it that the rest are pissed off because you put the money up for two of them but not for the others?' Old heard an almost indiscernible groan come down the telephone.

'It's right what you say,' Mee sighed. 'I ask you to do the job I should let you do it. I'll send you the names. Problem is I've got to change my story. I didn't think you wanted to do this so I painted myself a bit whiter than grey. I thought about giving the lads the money, all of them, then I realized how much it was. They went into it with their eyes open, let 'em bite it. Like I said, though, two of them hurt. Really couldn't afford it, and I'd really egged them on. So I thought I'd pay just them off. It would have been a nice gesture – expensive, but a really good thing to do. Make me a real *mensch*, right? 'Cept when it came to it, I liked the idea of the glory, but it was still too much money, however you looked at it. Know how many wank mags you have to sell to make twenty-four grand? Plenty, plenty. I might be loaded but I didn't get loaded by giving away money every time someone fell flat on their face.'

Smirking is nothing to be proud of but it was hard to resist.

'So you told me you were a hero when really you were just a plain old guy with his hands in his pockets and a smile on his face. So what? I never thought you were a hero in the first case, so just fax me the bumf and I'll get on with it and I won't mention your little story. I'm sure you feel better just getting it off your chest. Just like the letters page in the mags, eh?'

'You don't need to be so superior about the mags. Somebody's going to make the money, why not me?'

'Couldn't agree more, wouldn't want it to be me. Just make sure all the girls are old enough and you won't get me knocking on your door. Now send the fax and stop worrying about what I think or don't think. I'm not going to blackball you from the Garrick or anything.'

'I already was,' Mee muttered with the beginning of a laugh in his throat.

Old checked his messages and found that McCreery, good as his word, had fixed him up with an interview with Frankie Silvester, two days time, Ford Open Prison. The biggest and best known of the low-security, high-privilege prisons, it was usually criticized in the press when some white-collar criminal was sent there to live a life of deprivation, the simple thought of which would bring on tears in a journalist, but which failed to satisfy the bloodlust of the public, who seemed almost to relish the insanitary, violent, backward reputation of the older prisons. There was that to wait for. In the meantime, he had the fax on the contact numbers for Mee's fellow dupes. Most of them had home and work addresses or mobile phones supplied so he could contact them daytime and avoid letting the job spill over into his valuable personal time, but though he knew he should crack on, he felt like a break. He was enjoying day-dreaming about Hannah, and that brought on an easy-going mood that would be ill-served by badgering his way though Mee's list of misanthropes and ne'er-do-wells. If there was to be a right time to try out a proper scam, or at least a bit of crude trickery, this was it. He'd tried a trick in a couple of pubs, see how it went, but to do it well he'd up the stakes a little, be a bit more blatant about it and distance it from a bar trick. He showered and shaved, splashed himself with a handful of Eau Sauvage and hopped into the Mini. He was just hitting the Mile End Road when he had a thought. Not easy to get back in the opposite direction from here, but who said things had to be easy. He pulled into a petrol station and put the car next to the forecourt shop. He made a telephone signal to the attendant, who pointed at a booth in the corner of the shop. Old pulled out a handful of change and dialled Hannah's number. It surprised him that he could bring it up from memory, when he had expected to have to call Directory.

'Busy?' he asked.

'So so. Is that you, Pat?'

'It is. Why be self-employed if you can't take the odd affie for yourself? Can you spare the afternoon? Give yourself a break?'

'What did you have in mind?' she asked with, Old thought, a suspicious edge to her voice, as if Old was trying to nudge the relationship along the tracks a little prematurely to the bed they both thought it would eventually reach.

'Get your glad rags on and I'll pick you up in half an hour.'

By the time Old had stopped the car outside Hannah's house, he had decided they might as well make the most of the occasion. He had been intending to have a couple of drinks; if they were to make an afternoon of it, he would probably have more, so long as he remembered not to hit it until he had his work done. Hannah opened the door and Old was lost for words.

She was dressed simply but looked beautiful. She had on a pale print dress, with no jewellery on the neck, no jacket – the September sun was holding up well – and had her hair up, revealing a perfect elegant neck with tiny wisps of hair touching it as they escaped from the mass of hair above. Normally her hair was more than half way down her back, so there was plenty of hair to put up. She had a slight heel on her pumps, which gave her calves a lift, giving her legs a long sleek look that made Old imagine them going all the way up, past the knee-length hem-line. One thing looked strange. As he looked her over, she was not wearing a scrap of jewellery. Almost in the same moment that he noticed, he realized why. She had hinted in passing that her parting from her husband was not happy. They still fought when they met, they still had to meet because of Jimmy, but not too often, as he seemed to want to see Jimmy more for the pain and inconvenience he could offer to Hannah than from any genuine need or wish to see the boy. Few women, as far as Old knew, bought themselves jewellery, apart from worka-day junk – might seem too much like setting a bad precedent. And given feelings with her ex, she would be unlikely to want to wear anything he bought. Hence the bare arms, ears, fingers and wrists. He thought the look made her appear vulnerable and attractive. It was not a radical feminist statement, as when some women consciously shunned jewellery, seeing it as a descend-ant of slave bonds. This was clear, as she did wear make-up, but subtly and well. He promised himself that if they did become an item – as the terminology went when he was last dating women, in the days before Siobhan – he would buy her a nice piece of jewellery. His mind threw up the image of a diamond, but he told himself not to jump too far too fast. Diamonds are symbolic, and what they symbolize very quickly turns to reality. After diamonds, plain gold bands soon followed. He'd only had dinner twice and three pecks on the cheek and he was coming on like Satya's mother, planning the wedding. On the other hand, he knew he was very, very keen. And he knew what that entailed when you were dealing with a good Catholic girl. Life is so complicated.

Hannah was ready to go but they had to wait a quarter of an hour for a minicab from a decent firm who could be guaranteed not to send a '79 Datsun Cherry. To be sure, he specified a large car in good condition. They were going to Jack Spratts bar on the roof of the Consul Hotel. It was expensive and flash and he didn't want some liveried flunkey opening the door and prising him, creased and sweaty, from the back of some old heap.

There was an intangible but definite air to the bar which spelled money. It had neither the halogen up-lit, chrome and leather Bauhaus look, nor the other classic 'look money!' approach of dim table lamps, faded prints and overstuffed English country house furniture. Old realized that the reason he liked this place was that it simply didn't feel like a bar. Rather, he thought, with its pale unglossed wood, semi-translucent ceiling, large clear windows – especially novel to someone used to the hemmed-in gloom of pub-life – and its glass brick dividers and pale cotton-covered sofas, it looked like the home of a rich Swede, greedy for whatever light he could get after the starvation of the long winter. It was the nearest Old had seen to anything he could describe as an ideal look, a look he could copy if he ever had the money to own a room as big as the look demanded.

His first idea was that he would do his little con as a lone wolf – a romantic idea which showed how much he had fallen under the spell of the glamour of the conman. Now he had Hannah with him, he had decided that this was the better way; after all, didn't Goodman have a female accomplice or partner, a hench-woman? Alone, he could look like a real con, things could turn nasty. With Hannah, they would be a couple having a drink, making conversation, and look, a little trick I know. The stooge would willingly play along, fingers crossed, and then, especially if there were witnesses, as ideally there would be, he would pay up. Not a lot, and not anything he couldn't afford – sitting in Jack Spratts mid-afternoon, as like as not staying at the Consul. Chances were the whole thing would go down on expenses anyway – 'Lunch – con-tact'. Old knew he was dissembling and justifying himself. He was nervous. With the original plan if things went wrong he had only himself to blame, only the bet to pay, only a privately bruised ego. With Hannah here he could look a public fool.

He had tried a practice run in an anonymous pub just off the Romford Road the night before. The con was sweet as a nut but he needed all his diplomacy to quiet the growls of dissatisfaction from the aggrieved punter who disliked losing, disliked being held to his promise to pay and disliked the whole thing happening in front of his friends. What saved Old was that his mark would have looked such a terrible loser for starting a fight with someone who had beat him so fair and square, even if the loser's prize was to lose a few bob and look an idiot. He would have looked far less of an idiot if he had taken his loss with better grace, but good grace was not in his vocabulary and it was Old's bad luck that he had chosen as his trial stooge someone for whom that was the case.

He had explained the situation to Hannah on the way over. That was more of a challenge than the con itself. He half started over their last dinner to explain his job. But he had stopped well before telling her about specific cases, stopped before porn pedlars and conmen. Stopped well before becoming an amateur con. And he hadn't underestimated her shock, or even her distaste.

She seemed so unable to get over her shock that he was essentially a private detective, being paid to root about and find out people's business – a *real* private detective, she repeated several times – that he wondered if he had even started to get through to her before. Apparently not. She had taken it that he was some kind of business researcher. The next step, the current case, and the next, that he was on the way to a con, were too much. For about five minutes. Old could see that she was deeply shocked, genuinely outraged. For the first of those five minutes, she sat, open-mouthed and agog at the terrible thing they were about to do: find an innocent victim and take good money off them for sport. Old tried to pass it off as good-natured fun but she would have none of it. It was theft, she said. Plain and simple.

Since this was the basis of the law on cons and the

basis of his investigation – that the whole thing was simply theft by front – it was a hard proposition to counter. Still, he felt that it was necessary for him to work through the con, to get inside the head of the con, feel the pressures and the buzz. He was beginning to feel it was a bad idea to have invited Hannah. Soon, though, that idea evaporated.

As quickly as she became outraged, she lost the outrage and the reality of the exercise started to sink in. She realized this was no theoretical exercise but they were, as they sat in the cruising minicab, on their way to pull a con. She took on the look. That crazed madwoman look. Not bag-lady crazy, but crazy anyway. It could easily be mistaken for an old-fashioned smoulder. But it was out of context. In this setting, the Catholic Women's Apprentice Confidence Tricksters Guild, it was a madwoman's glint.

Old had taken Siobhan a couple of times to the casino. She took to it like a lawyer to misery, and across the floor he could see the slightly damp-eyed excitement of other women hopelessly gripped by the casino. And in Siobhan's case, the excitement lasted past the casino and brought out an animal side he had never seen before.

It was that same feral glint he saw now in Hannah.

Her final moral qualms were stilled when he agreed to prove it was good-natured fun by, after taking the winnings, insisting on sharing a round, dragging in the victim and have them share the laugh.

To Old it sounded like worse torture than his plan, but Hannah insisted it was the only fair way to do it. Women's idea of justice, Old mused, could be pretty arbitrary and unpredictable. Who was it said women weren't allowed into wars because the violence would get out of hand? Pretty glib, but you could see what they meant. And what man understood women's motivation anyway?

Once inside the bar, people being the self-deceiving creatures they are, Hannah, now convinced that the way they were going about things was perfectly fine and moral, was getting more and more excited about the prospect. A pretty curious bit of logic, Old thought, that led her to justify their trick and then carry on getting excited about it because of the danger. Still, he thought, the excitement of all this, followed by a good meal, should burn itself pretty strongly onto a few neurons – create a positive memory associated with him that she wouldn't forget in a hurry. That is, if she didn't decide first that his work wasn't just a bit too tacky to make involvement with him a viable prospect.

Hannah asked for a glass of white wine. Old nodded and asked the barman for a bottle of Laurent Perrier rosé.

'Pink do?' he asked, as the barman pulled the cork with a soft imploding pop which barely crept out from under his cloth.

'Wonderfully,' she said, eyes alight. 'I had a pretty mundane day lined up today. I was going to try and get through fifty pages or three hours, whichever was the longer, of proofing a manual on the development of a wide-area network for telecommunication managers.'

'Sounds like a bit of a giggle,' commented Old.

'The technical stuff is for someone else. If they get something wrong it's basically down to them. My job is to make sure the whole thing takes place in English, which, for these techies, is not a simple matter as most of them have English as a second language – second to incomprehensible jargon.'

'So part of your job is to translate their gibberish to English.'

'To clear and simple English. That's it.' She nodded at a man just seated further down the bar. 'Doesn't he look like what we're after?'

'We're,' thought Old. It's suddenly a co-operative effort. But still, when he looked, the man did look a perfect mark. His suit smart and well tailored, his demeanour on the brash side of confident, Old guessed he would be unwilling to think he made mistakes easily, happy to think others foolish. Old and Hannah had deliberately remained standing at the bar to make any moves less obtrusive. They had also placed themselves dead centre to close the possible distance to a potential mark. The mark was around ten feet to their left. Over the space of ten minutes, they manoeuvred themselves to within conversing distance. The person furthest from the mark would stand away from the bar and face the person still at the bar, then they would retake a position at the bar but on the other side. Eighteen inches gained. Then they would remain where they were for two or three minutes, letting the scenery settle down, and start again. Once they were within hearing distance of their mark they staged a small tiff then fell into silence. Old was nearest to the mark and, looking around, bored, commented on the splendid design of the bar to the mark. Bingo. The mark wanted conversation and leapt into a discussion on hotel architecture.

Once he was hooked, reservations or no, Hannah

joined in the fun with a vengeance, gliding into the conversation and almost flirting in a quiet way that seemed to Old far more alluring than a more obvious coquettish flirt could ever have been, though he knew that he was far from the best judge, since he was already thoroughly hooked and gasping for air.

On his trial run, Old had been unable to engineer a conversational link to his sting and hoped he would have better luck on the real thing. Why he thought of this as the real thing and the other a practice he wasn't sure – the scam was the same. Perhaps he was being a snob and this seemed like a better number, so he downgraded the night before. Lacking the link, he had simply forged ahead. Today he seemed no nearer to a feasible link – normal conversation seems to be lacking in run-ins to 'Pardon me while I rip you off and make you look a fool.' He turned to Hannah and raised his eyebrows, warning her to be ready; not that she had anything to do in particular, but he had told her it was important not to interrupt, though he had suggested she did interrupt once, early on, so he could warn her not to do it again, also suggesting that she was not familiar with the trick, as indeed she was not – he hadn't explained it, the better to add to the surprise. He thought it was the best time to go ahead with the trick, as the bar had filled up. There were a good half dozen people within hearing distance and if he said loudly enough what he planned to do, he would probably get a small audience, the better to ensure the mark paid up. Not that it was important in itself – he wasn't doing this for a living – but it made it a better way of getting inside the head of the con if he had a win.

'Listen,' he said, 'someone showed me a great bar trick. You like bar tricks?'

'Not if you mean all those ludicrous things like flicking beer mats with the back of your hand and drinking pints of bitter while you stand on your head.'

'Nothing like that,' Old said, smiling. He pulled a handful of change from his pocket and picked out three pound coins. He put the change back then put the hand with the three coins back in his pocket and brought it out again. Obviously he could have picked up or dropped any of the coins, but it was impossible to know what, if anything, he had done. His mark, who had introduced himself as Leonard, which, judging by his age, was probably a surname, already looked interested. He placed both hands palm down on the bar, held them for a longish moment, asking Leonard, 'You can count I suppose, big numbers – all the way up to ten?'

Leonard smiled and nodded.

'You should be on top of this then.' He moved his hands. Two one-pound coins lay on the bar.

'How many coins?' Old asked.

'Two.'

Old put his hands over the coins and shuffled them around in a hammy pastiche of the fairground huckster. Again he took his hands away to reveal the two coins and pulled his cuffs up.

'How many now?'

'I've not said I'm playing,' Leonard said, cautiously but still, for now, smiling.

'So don't answer. How many?' Old cajoled.

'OK, two.'

'You're sure it's not one or three?'

Leonard nodded.

'How many?'

'Two.'

'You're sure?'

'Yes.'

'Two?'

'Yes.'

'You want to bet?'

This slowed up proceedings while Leonard pon-
dered. He looked at Old, looked at the coins, evaluated
Old's sleight of hand.

'Yes. No.'

Old scooped the two coins back up.

'Never mind then, some other time.'

'Come on then, show me.'

'You didn't want to play. It's all part of it. The
price of admission. What've you got to lose? You not
sure you can count from none to two and back? Use
your fingers.'

'OK, I'll bet. There's two.'

'Now just to prove I'm not a shyster, and because
we haven't set the level of the bet yet,' Old glanced
round at Hannah and saw she was grinning like a
Cheshire Cat on Ecstasy. There was quiet interest
from five more casual drinkers. 'Just so as you know
I'll not deliberately make you look silly, I'll give you a
free go. You lose. There's none there.' A ripple of
gentle laughter, saying 'Glad that wasn't me,' went
through the audience. Leonard smirked bashfully.
Caught, and it had already dawned on him that he had
to lose – indeed had already lost and been let off. He
knew he wouldn't be let off next time. Caught, and
about to pay the price.

'Ready?' Old asked.

'Let's go.'

'For real this time?'

'Sure.'

Old put his hands back on the table and moved them around, again revealing the coins.

'A quick check then.'

'Two!' Leonard interrupted.

'I'd say it's pretty sure.' Hannah said.

'One at a time. One person only, sorry.'

Hannah flashed a delighted smile, her eyes wickedly alive and glad she was helping ensnare Leonard, their poor dupe.

'How many then?'

'There's two.'

'Bet?'

'Sure, how much?'

'Whoever's right buys the next round.'

Leonard glanced at the empty, upturned bottle of Laurent Perrier in the ice bucket and then at the two coins, still and certainly two. He nodded. He was grinning widely now. He knew the blade was about to fall. He still couldn't see it but he could almost hear its whistle. He was sure of two things: that there were two coins and that he was going to lose. The two seemed incompatible, but somehow he knew he was going to find out, both dreading it and, like the small crowd, wanting to see how the sucker punch worked.

'Whoever's right buys the next round?' Old repeated.

'Sure.'

'One more time to be sure; how many coins?'

'Two.'

'Say again.'

'Two, bloody two.'

'OK, you're right. Your round. Mine's the pink. Leave your drink out, share the bottle.'

Leonard was still waiting for the penny to drop; the audience was muttering – a couple seemed to have seen it, the rest were still behind.

'Sorry, what happened?'

'You lost the bet is what happened. Whoever's right buys the next round. You were right. There are the two coins. Always right. You're a good counter. Your round.'

Leonard nodded slowly as the simplicity of the bet sunk in. Suckered.

'You make a habit of this kind of thing?' Leonard asked.

'First time I've actually done it since I was caught out myself the other week. Might start though!'

'Guess I can think of a few people I could take for a ride, guys I'd like to see squirm a bit. What'll I get you?'

Old nodded at his bottle, still upturned in the bucket.

'You really expect me to stiff up for a bottle of pink fizz?'

'It's usual, you offer to buy a round, you buy what people want, what they were already drinking, not what you think might be a cheap round. You thought we might have half a shandy and two straws? Like I said, get the bottle and three glasses and we can drink to your future success as an amateur lounge-bar con.'

Leonard nodded at the waiter, who had been listening to the whole exchange, and as he did, Old saw

Hannah flush. She grinned. They had done it and he was half right. He felt as he had expected to feel. A giant adrenalin rush. He had walked into a bar, talked a little and now a complete stranger was buying him a bottle of pink champagne. But he had missed out a significant detail. A testosterone rush. He felt like he could service a stud farm for a month. Sod aesthetics, he needed sex. He had an erection that felt like it could be used as a scaffolding pole. And he felt like this, why? Because he had robbed someone and they'd handed over the loot with a smile. That was a rush. More!

FIVE

When Old returned home he checked his machines. Fax first, one only, junk. A four-page catalogue for an auction of used office furniture, computers, photocopiers and stuff. Going in the fax directory had been, on reflection, a bad move. The telephone answering machine held eight messages. Old wondered who was the pain. It was his experience that if there were more than four messages on the machine, without exception it meant that someone didn't believe the message saying he'd get back and was on there a number of times. He was right. In spades. One message was from an editor commissioning a short piece on combat simulation and could he call back. Ho hum, the drawback of keeping spare irons in the fire was that they all needed stoking and blowing to keep them hot.

The other seven were all the same person, calls left at thirty-minute intervals.

Dougie Owen.

Dougie's wife had left him.

If he was always this irritating, Old couldn't blame her, but missing spouses were bread and butter. Interesting stuff like this Goodman/Mee thing were great fun, but spouses on the lam were what filled the days. And ultimately they gave him the motivation to keep going – Siobhan's departure still hurt, and no matter who came into his life, he was sure it always would. People didn't have the right simply to vanish, not in Old's eyes, and he tried to find them if only to get the reasons. Sometimes he found them and he had them send a letter: 'This is why; I left because . . .'

As a solution for his clients, it didn't help when it came to getting bills settled. Clients wanted their missing ones bundled up and delivered, C.O.D., but it helped him sleep nights. He wasn't a kidnapper, he was a detective. He couldn't fix lives or make people live where they didn't want to but he could encourage them to explain themselves at least.

He called Dougie and fixed a meet for the morning. Dougie protested, squeaked, whined and moaned that this evening was half a day too late and no later than immediately would do. Old gave him a time, a place and a dialling tone.

The two men sat in the gloomy foyer. There almost five minutes, they had told themselves they were ready to wait all day if necessary and could get more angry with every passing minute. But all day was already looking like a long, long time. Mel deftly rolled a cigarette and popped it between his lips. The cigarette flared slightly as his match touched the end, a sign of the high ratio of paper to tobacco, itself a sign of someone who knew all there was to know about killing empty time and knew it well enough to hate it. He pointed at one of the framed photos on the wall, a big-breasted woman dressed as a pornographer's fantasy policewoman, with short skirt, no blouse, and the half-undone, too-tight tunic stretched by her giant breasts, squashed in and apparently plotting their imminent escape.

'Jugs on that one,' he leered.

Kevin nodded.

'Buckets and rope,' he commented.

'You reckon Barry gets to dip his wick?' Mel asked.

'Wouldn't surprise me, lucky bastard.' As he spoke, Mee rolled out of his office, all bonhomie and bounce.

'Been here long? Got stuck on the phone. Come on in, see the place. We'll pick up a drink in my office and I'll show you round.'

Before they had chance to do more than mumble greetings, he had them sucking on Havana cigars and holding Scotches that between the three of them polished off half a bottle of Macallan. He called the receptionist in to ask if there was a shoot in progress in the studio. Again she was wearing a skirt that barely qualified for the name and a sheer blouse over a similarly sheer bra that hid nothing, only pushed up her breasts for closer attention. Kevin and Mel stared, transfixed. Behind the reception, seated, and wearing headphones and a cardigan, they had hardly given her a second glance. Now their eyes were drying out for want of blinking.

As she leant over Mee's desk looking for his shooting schedule, he patted her bottom.

'Gorgeous arse, Debbie,' he said. She stood and pushed it towards him, hitching her skirt up as she did.

'You going to look, you might as well look proper,' she said. 'I seem to remember you didn't miss much last time I done a shoot. Was as much as Richard could do to keep you out of shot.'

Kevin and Mel gazed at her. Little was concealed by her underwear, which resembled three strands of silk held together by willpower.

'Your mouths are open,' she said to the two men,

and 'Richard's doing "Are You Finnish?" with the blonde from Leicester for November's *Stretch*,' to Mee. As she left the room she patted Mel's bulge. 'Calm down, son, you'll never last through a shoot without shooting at that rate.'

As she closed the door behind her, the silence hung heavily. Mee sat grinning, pleased as Punch at the reaction. All Mel could manage was a breathless "kin' 'ell', while Kevin could only shake his head in wonder that a scene, which could have come straight out of a dirty magazine, had happened before his eyes. Everyone he knew, while enjoying a good wank mag, among which Mee's were highly rated, still assumed that, good as they were, the stories were simple flights of the imagination. It was different again if they were simple reports from the world in which they were made, a world of total sexual hospitality in which he was a popular stud and all women his flirtatious admirers ready to interpret his every whim. When Mee opened the door to take them on a tour he had to pat him on the shoulder. He was lost in a world of the imagination and it was only the notion that he might see it for real that persuaded him to leave it behind.

Mee took them up to the next floor and opened a door where half a dozen people worked in a mundane office of unbelievable untidiness, the contents of one cubby-hole office spilling out to meet the mess emerging from the next.

'Subscriptions, advertising and mail order processing,' he said. 'Can't get the bastards to work tidy, but at least they work cheap,' he added under his breath in a conspiratorial whisper.

The next floor was one room, the windows blanked

79

out. Kevin and Mel knew where they were immediately. On one side of the room was a mock-up executive office suite, complete with leather-top desk and chaise longue. In the middle was a four-poster, with theatrical set flats on two sides, one showing a country-cottage-style picture, the other an expensive hotel room. Piled in a further corner of the room was a selection of S & M equipment: cages, chains, masks, a set of stocks and a dungeon wall flat. In the one remaining corner, bathed in light, was a collection of suburban semi furniture, with a curtained window, light behind it, signifying daytime sex, and on the couch, between takes, a pure blonde woman sat draped in a tatty dressing gown, taking deep tokes from a joint, while a nondescript man tried to tease a little erection into his nipples.

The photographer saw Mee standing in the shadows and snapped his fingers.

'Back in positions, I want another pop at the finger.'

The blonde casually slipped off the gown and draped it over a chair with no more self-consciousness than if she had been taking off a scarf. She waited while the male model lay back on the couch. His penis was twitching into life.

'Didn't I tell you to get rid of that?' the photographer muttered. 'This is a limp dick spread, newsagent stuff.' He checked with one of his sets of cameras, which was on a low tripod pointing down the length of the sofa, while the model tried hard to think his near-erection away. The blonde, meanwhile, stood behind the photographer, striking exaggerated poses of easy sexuality, obviously enjoying the difficulty this gave the struggling model.

Mel took a deep pull on his Scotch and Kevin followed suit. A few seconds later, they finished the drinks off, both flushing red as the alcohol quickly hit their bloodstreams.

'Positions,' the photographer barked. The male model lay on his back on the couch, one leg thrown over the side, the other leg firmly planted on the floor. The blonde knelt between his legs and bent over to take a nipple between her teeth.

'Lovely, hold that, lovely, now lick it, and the other.'

The male model's limp penis again began to twitch.

'Think of verrucas,' the photographer ordered, 'and don't smile. That thing gets any bigger I'm going to stick it to your leg with gaffer tape. Now, bring your left hand round, grab her arse.'

He pulled the tripod back, giving himself a wider angle, taking in the whole picture. Before he took up his position behind the camera, he took out a tube of KY jelly from his case, removed the lid and squirted a little onto the blonde's puckered red anus. She jumped as the jelly touched and turned as he spread it around.

'You ever think to ask before you go handling a girl's arse? It's freezing. You fucking enjoy that don't you?'

'What do you think?'

'And what are fucking Curly, Larry and Moe doing in the shadows? You selling fucking tickets now?'

'That's Mr Mee and a couple of business associates. Keep it down or he might invite them in on the shoot, and then it might end up on a different shelf – out of the newsagent.'

'That's no different to selling tricks,' she murmured.

She obviously believed she was talking privately now, but in the big empty room sound travelled and the three men could hear every word. Mee grinned at Kevin and Mel and shook his head.

'He's just winding her up,' he said. But Kevin and Mel were so engrossed by now they were willing to believe anything. They both had painful bulges; Kevin was holding his as if there was no one else in the room.

'Beneath turning tricks then are we, love?' the photographer teased.

'Just take your fucking snaps.'

They resumed positions and started again, the male's fingers playing idly around the blonde's anus, occasionally tugging at her pubic hair, but no more. There were complex rules on what was and wasn't allowed. She could penetrate herself, he couldn't, and neither could he have an erection, though she could be positively saturated and penetrated by any number of digits or inert objects. She held his hand on her buttocks with one of her hands and with the other she slipped a finger into her anus while the camera whirred and clicked. A half-choked moan came from the back of the room and Mel and Barry looked at Kevin, who blushed as his bulge subsided.

'Let's get on,' Mee said. 'That's the tour. I've had Debbie book us lunch. We'll get over there and then we can discuss business. I suppose you want to know what I'm doing about Goodman. I've got a man on the job, first-class private eye.'

They were walking back down the staircase and Kevin shook his head. Private eye. Too much. Take a trip to Genre County. Pornography over, now crime. He would be hardly surprised if he returned to the car park to find his car had been blown up by a robot warrior from his future.

They had been in the restaurant for less than half an hour. It was expensive and both Kevin and Mel felt uncomfortable – they were the only men not wearing jackets and ties and their clothes were not in the Soho tieless but fashionable mode, they were in the Ilford pub git mode. Mee had blitzed them with his ire at Goodman, pointing out, quite accurately, that he was the only one of them to lose on two cars, and that, above all, he was made to look the biggest fool, as he was the one sold the idea on.

Kevin and Mel ate solidly.

The food was modern English and they both felt comfortable with its simple sauces and generous portions. Mee ordered pints of porter to go with it and it was a solid beer, quickly re-ordered. The service was polite but brisk, most of the customers wanting to be in and out within an hour. Mee was half way through his main course when he was called to the telephone. He came back and apologized, saying he had forgotten he had a meet with his bankers, sorry, have what they wanted, no rush, the bill was covered.

'Good to talk to you,' he said in his parting line. 'Good to know we're all thinking on the same lines about pal Goodman.'

Kevin looked over at the disappearing back of Mee, down at his fillet in beer and barley, and across the table at Mel.

'Well that told him, didn't it? Put him right in his fucking place.' He grinned. 'Cracking day though. Can't remember a day like it. Jesus, couldn't you have just strolled over and popped one in that model?'

'Not many. Barry though, he done us up proper, ain't he?'

'I suppose so, but if this is being done up proper, I'll have a bit more, thanks, and I'll start with the Swedish bird.'

'Finnish.'

'Yeah, whatever, the blonde muff with the slippery arse.'

'But what we going to tell the lads?'

'Fuck the lads, we had a good day, and what Barry says, most of it's right. Sure he's a cunt but at least he held his hand up. Put yourself in his shoes. If you'd dragged us all in, you'd have been getting your back slapped: "Mel, what a fucking diamond, prince among men." Then next minute you're Mel the rancid dog-shit, and you've done nothing different. And he lost twice. And he's got this guy on the job, supposed to know what he's doing. What I say is, no way, even if this guy finds Goodman, no way he's going to come up with the money I can see. I say we get Barry to agree we all get a pop at him. Try to get back what money we can but we all get a pop. Feel the guy's guts heave a bit, feel his face split under your fist, give us a bit of respect back, eh?'

Old stood in the centre of the room. He declined to sit and was unsure what to do with his hands. He certainly didn't want to touch anything. The flat was a parody of the married man with absent wife, failing to cope. Old was sure it was not this way when the man's wife was around; the shelves were full of containers for this and that, expensive pans hung from the walls, sharp steel knives stuck out of the sink and good crockery tried miserably to show its quality from beneath layers of dried take-away and half-empty foil containers and pizza boxes.

Dougie Owen was a large man, big-shouldered, with a beer gut that without the rest of him to keep it in proportion would have seemed huge. He was pacing around the house, declaiming upon his wife's wickedness for abandoning him, kidnapping his child, his precious son for whom he would do anything, though by the state of the house and Owen's apparent abilities as a housekeeper he guessed he actually did little for his son beyond the occasional tousle of the hair.

'So, besides being a selfish bitch, why do you think she's gone and where do you think she might be?'

'Who the fuck knows? Like I said, she only thinks of herself.'

'But I presume that's nothing new. Why did she choose this moment to go? I suppose it's been a few days now.' Old glanced around the room as he spoke. Owen was not the least apologetic.

'That's her job, slovenly cow. Thinks I'm doing her work for her, she can think again. I go and earn the money keeps this family together. She has a bit more housework to do when she crawls back, tail between her legs, might make her think twice about it next time.'

'If you think she'll come back of her own accord, why did you call me in? Has she done this before?'

'A few times. Usually stays at her mother's two or three days. Four at most. Her mother died this year. What a loss to humanity. I suppose Jan was pretty upset.' It was the first time he had referred to his wife by name, previously using the generic terms, 'her', 'the wife' and 'the bitch'.

'We had a row, which has been known. It got out of hand and she flounced out like the fucking Queen of Tonga and I've not heard a damn thing. It's a week now. Eight days today. I want her back and I don't care what it costs.'

'While we're on that, it costs two hundred a day plus expenses, which can add up.' Owen's face dropped.

'Two hundred a day?'

'Plus expenses.'

'That's going it, isn't it? How long should it take?'

'It could take ten minutes, in which case you'll get charged for half a day. If she's shacked up with Lord Lucan it could take a while.'

'I'll pay for a week. See what you can do.'

Old mused on how long 'I don't care what it costs' had lasted when it became clear what it did cost.

And now the killer:

'In advance.'

'On your bike. Payment by results, old son, same as anyone else.'

Old particularly hated being called old son. He headed for the door.

'Nice meeting you, Dougie. Call me if you're ever serious about getting anyone found.'

'Hang on a minute. How about three days in advance? I'll write you a cheque now. Just find me the bitch.'

Old nodded his OK. He always insisted on payment in advance for missing spouses. It solved the biggest problems when he found his clients' loved ones and they insisted on staying missing. He never offered to return anyone, but his clients never seemed to see it that way. They seemed to think they had hired themselves a bounty hunter. He was keen to disabuse them of the notion, but he didn't want to talk himself out of work. So he would find his target, then spill the beans. The fact was, very few of the missing returned, though often those left behind felt much better when they had at least been given an explanation, even when it led to a blinding row.

He had only once returned anyone, bundling an errant fourteen-year-old from Covent Garden into the back of his car and taking her home to her father. Their gratitude lasted precisely seven hours and ended as the bread knife cut three tendons in the girl's father's hand. Since then, he had been rigid about that: no returns. And after a few initial calls, if they turned nothing up, he would wait for the cheque to clear before he put in any hours, though he had two days to wait before his interview with Frankie Silvester at Ford Open Prison, and little to do until then. He could always get Sam out of the childminder's early. Maybe take him and his father-in-law Barney to the zoo. Or maybe forget Barney, take Hannah and Jimmy.

Old had a bad feeling about Dougie Owen. He had paid the cheque in on the way back home, paying the surcharge for express clearance, which meant it would be through in two working days. But after a little thought about Owen he was reluctant to wait. He looked like a man with a temper, a man who would take no answer but the one he wanted. Old thought at first he wanted his maid-cum-whore back to pander to his wishes, but he couldn't get rid of the nagging thought that Owen was a bad 'un. It had never happened to him but it was not unknown with the police that someone would report missing the person they had just killed. They seemed innocently to believe that reporting a crime was as good as an alibi, that it somehow kept them out of the frame. Wrong. Old felt this could be the case. Maybe Dougie wanted him to find out she was dead, or missing, whatever, and if he had spent good money trying to get her back it would weaken the case for him as her killer. There was no real justification for the belief beyond the instant dislike he had felt for Owen. He would get on the phone, do what he could. The phone was the most important tool for this kind of job and if an hour on the telephone did no good, that was the time to hit the knockers, by which time the chances of anything turning up were much reduced in any case. It was a hard irony of this kind of case that it was by far the easiest work that turned up the most results and the most tiresome the least.

Because of the number of these missing spouse cases, and because the large part of these were women, he had a passable relationship with all the women's refuges in the area. Though some were more prickly than others, and some more helpful, they had come at least to accept that he could be trusted, to believe that anything they told him that they wanted to stop there would stop there. And it would. Still, he couldn't help thinking that his relationship with the refuges would be mortally wounded if they knew who he was working for on his other case, and who could blame them for feeling that way? He felt that way a little himself – the more he thought about taking Mee's shilling the more tarnished he felt, and that was as good a guide as any to what kind of work he should take. He knew why he was tempted; it wasn't the money. It was a principle of his – if principle was the word – that as he was hired to find missing people, any money that came into the story wasn't really the point. So if he could coax some of it his way, then he would. He had done enough jobs with the opportunity to get close to money that he was largely insulated from immediate money worries. That wasn't the problem with this job. Regardless of the money – which was good – it was the job. Conmen: they were fascinating. It was a real job. Ultimately it had less real importance than any one of these missing wives and daughters, fathers and sons – what was the damage but the wallets and egos of a few Essex wide-boys? But it was fun. A professional conman was a real target – stretching his abilities, he was already suspecting, at least as far as they would go. Goodman wasn't going to be hiding like an ostrich just waiting for Old to say 'Boo.' He would have a different name, different address, different hair colour possibly, certainly a different style, and quite possibly a completely different scam. A different continent even. Back to Janet Owen.

Someone answered his first call to Durning Hall Sanctuary then hung up as soon as he spoke. This tended to happen. It usually meant that someone answered the phone who was not supposed to. The people who ran the refuge had become used to the idea that, although many men, more than a lot of people supposed, beat up women, not all did, most never would and besides the world is full of men and if any kind of a life is to be lived, men have to be dealt with. They were running a refuge from which at some stage women would rejoin the world. The last thing they wanted was to run a Carmelite convent. The second time he tried he was answered.

'Durning.'

'Is that Kim?'

'Who's asking?'

'Patrick Old.'

'Kim speaking. Someone lost a woman then? Careless of them, isn't it?'

'She's a Jan Owen. There's no danger I'm going to tell her ex. I wouldn't trust him an inch. I'm a bit dubious about him, to be honest. If I don't find her soon, I might have to have a word with the uniforms, see if anyone's been in touch.'

'If I thought I couldn't trust you, we wouldn't be talking already. But she's not here. We've been busy and I've not spoken to any of the local places for a couple of days, so she could well be elsewhere. We're not exactly a network but we keep in touch about new admissions just so's we can be ready for raving men on the loose.'

'Thanks anyway, I'll stick a tenner in the post.'

It wasn't exactly part of the deal – if they didn't want to speak then they wouldn't. They were women who had enough of doing as they were told. What they gained from Old was the men off their back and the women with a little more peace of mind with the first contact with their ex-partner behind them – things said that needed saying. The tenner had developed as a custom. He slipped a few pounds in the box when he made visits, it was well received, so now he always paid a tenner for information, even when it was a no go. They didn't take advantage, having him calling round if they could save him a few calls, and he always paid, unprompted, and sent a cheque for Christmas. At least they knew his heart was in the right place. As important as anything, they also, most of them, said they would keep an eye and an ear for Siobhan, though he thought it unlikely they would hear anything, and even if they did, their loyalties were very clear and there was no doubt they would ask permission before they gave even a whisper.

He called the second, the only other in Newham. No luck. Owen said his wife came originally from Hackney. He knew a couple of the refuges in Hackney; he knew most in the surrounding boroughs as far as Islington and Tottenham. When it started to get into NW postcodes then he was lost and his contacts ran dry. He hoped it wouldn't go that far. If he didn't turn her up or at least get a pointer from his session on the phone, he decided, he would call the police, get the local nick to check if there had been any mysterious accidents; worse, any unidentified bodies, though he had seen nothing on the news. He hated thinking like this, but his bad feeling wouldn't go away.

'Erewhon Refuge.'

Old explained himself to the person on the line. He knew one person at this refuge, Katey Walgrave, and she was out, apparently acting as a witness in a court case. Old thought it remarkably forthcoming of them to tell him so much, but they would give him no more. He assured them he knew and was trusted by Katey, but no one there knew of him and that was that. He asked them to tell Katey he had called and hung up.

That was his only blank. He rang nine more refuges in five boroughs and was given a clear no at each. He was starting to frame his enquiry to the police when the phone went. Katey Walgrave.

'They said you rang. Who's missing?'

'Thanks for calling, Katey. I'm looking for a Jan Owen. It's for her husband, but I don't trust him.' Old repeated his misgivings and Katey pressed him for more details: was he aggressive towards Old, how did he seem to regard his wife, was he insulting?

'I take it this means she's with you?' Old asked.

'She is now. They discharged her from Homerton Hospital this morning.'

Old remained silent, the quiet pressing Katey for details.

'He broke her cheekbone, left wrist, two ribs and gave her internal bleeding, black eyes and a bruised nose. She looks a mess, Pat. I'd suggest you came over for a chat but she wouldn't go near anyone with a connection with her old man. He's a bastard though. She'll not be going back, you can take that from me.'

'I'd like to, Katey, and I believe you, but if I heard it from her, then I could tell him that, and it'd help put a stop to the whole thing. Then they both know they know.'

'She doesn't want to talk to anyone today.'

'Could you just ask? Please, Katey?'

Katey made a small humming noise which Old took for assent as she put the phone down, making loud steps as she walked the length of the uncarpeted hall, which Old could picture as he heard the hollow echoes reverberating down the line. He hung on and hung on and was wishing he was free to hang up without damaging an uneasy relationship when Katey returned.

'She'll speak to you. I'll put you through, she's in the lounge, trying to get a bit of peace. I'll be honest with you, she wanted to talk and I advised that she shouldn't. Don't pressure her. She's very fragile. I don't want her hurt. Just say what you have to and give the woman a break. She's not had an easy time, it just got much harder, and she might be about to start a life of her own.'

'I understand that,' Old interrupted. 'I want to help her put it, him, behind her.'

'But it's the husband who's paying you. Divided loyalties?'

'No, just a mistake on his part. Maybe he'll feel better about the break when it's clear in his mind she's gone. I just hope she doesn't go back like so many do.'

'I don't think she will. She seems fairly strong to me. He's been giving her a slap now and then for years, she says, but this was a first and she says it's the last. She knows she was wrong to let him get away with it before, but now she's gone. She won't go to the police, she's just closed the door. Don't make her open it again.'

'I promise I won't. I'll try and make him see it's closed too. Now can I speak to her?'

The phone was hung up and he was left in telephone limbo for another thirty seconds until another woman answered.

'Jan Conway. You want to speak to me.'

It was phrased not as a question but a statement and the voice was surprisingly firm and clear. Old supposed

93

he was expecting something trembly, weak and ready to break. But the women who came to the refuges, by the time they had made the move, for whatever reason, had usually found some strength inside and were just getting used to how it felt to have a little self-confidence. He was so surprised it was a moment before he realized she had changed her name – he somehow knew he was talking to the right person and didn't need to check.

'How much did Katey tell you?'

'Your name, that Dougie hired you, and that she trusts you and so can I, but that I should leave it anyway, talk to no one.'

'You believe her about me but you don't take her advice?'

'Everyone's getting over something here. I spent a week here once before. I didn't like it. The people are good but the atmosphere is bad. No one means badly, but the psyches are more battered than the faces. There are more good-hearted people here than you often find, but those damaged insides, damaged hearts, they affect the feel of a place, sour it. All the good feeling does no more than ease that, like honeyed vinegar. But the place is no less needed for that, by me too. Everyone here tells you all the time how men see you differently, not as real, separate people, you know the stuff – maid, therapist, nanny and whore. They tell you how you have to learn to see yourself as a real woman. And they mean it, but they don't do it. Katey is a darling. She visited me in hospital every day, she looked after my Jeffrey as well as anyone could while I was in hospital and kept him from seeing me, which was harder than bringing him in, but which I needed.

I look frightening now but seeing me a week ago would have given him nightmares.

'I was talking about Katey. She treats the women here like her children. That's why I don't take her advice, though I trust her without reservation. She's as quick to put us in a box as everyone else. The soft-headed battered wife. A few words with the husband and she'll be back on the doorstep and a week later it'll be the old routine: flattered, fucked and battered without rhyme or reason.'

'And you're not like that?'

'Don't patronize me.'

'I wasn't, I don't know you. It was just a question.'

'Good. Don't. No, I'm not like that. I can see why women go back – I stayed and once I left and went back. But it still wasn't the same. I trusted him once. Don't they say you should give anyone a second chance? Well that's what I did. And he spent it. So now it's over. He did this and he'll not do it again. And if he can do it to me he can do it to Jeffrey, and he'll never be allowed to do that. He's lost his son and I hope that hurts. It'll hurt Jeffrey for a while but it would hurt him more to be used as a weapon. I shouldn't have said that about losing Jeffrey hurting him. That's not why I'm taking him away. It's true though. Reason or not, I can't but see the pain as a bonus.'

'Can I see you? I'd really like to see you, and if you're as assured as you sound, it shouldn't be a problem, should it?' Old was getting as good answers as he could expect over the telephone. He felt sure she wouldn't return to Owen, but he didn't like the telephone. Though he did much of his work on the line, he never felt the same reality was attached to a telephone answer. He needed to see someone speak.

'No you can't.'

Old objected, tried to persuade her, but though the words came out, as soon as she had spoken he knew there was no point. There had been a simple and utterly lucid finality in the short phrase.

'You sound like a decent man. I'm not hurt enough by experience with one man to paint you all with the same brush and Katey vouches for you. Is there a woman you love?'

Old was taken aback by the course the conversation was taking. He was no longer guiding it and immediately Siobhan entered the scene he felt vulnerable.

'Yes there is.'

'Have you ever laid a finger on her?'

Old didn't like being questioned, just like most of those he questioned for a living. Like them, he felt threatened by it; like them he questioned the right of the other to ask him questions; and like most people, he kept his fears and his doubts to himself and answered anyway.

'Never. I love her too much, I always will. That's not why she left.'

'Sorry, I didn't know she'd left you. But it's still as I thought. You haven't and you don't expect to. I have no idea if you've ever seen a woman who's been beaten, but if you haven't, you don't want to, and if you have, there's no saying it was this bad. I wouldn't want anyone to see me if it wasn't absolutely essential. I look a bloody mess and that's about the size of it.'

'I'm sure it's a short-lived thing,' Old muttered, sympathetically.

'Oh, most of it is,' Jan said. 'It isn't one of these self-esteem problems I'm having. I wasn't Aphrodite before and I won't be later. I wasn't bad looking, and apart from a nose maybe a touch off-centre, the rest of it'll be gone in a month, the facial stuff at least. The arm and the ribs'll take a little longer. But listen. One eye is puffed and red with a hint of purple. The other is closed and blue, again with a hint of purple. My nose is in a splint. My lips are both split where they burst against my teeth, some of which he knocked out – I already have an appointment with the dentist and the crowns should be straighter than the old ones so there's a silver lining. Aside from all that, my face as a whole is swollen, discoloured. Do I have to go on?

'Go and tell Dougie if he ever sees me again, it'll be by accident. Tell him not to try to disappear with the bank accounts or sell the house because I got myself a lawyer, saw him in the hospital, and there's a freeze on everything. Tell him we'll be divorced within six months, and tell him to write by the end of the week agreeing not to contest it or I'll have the police on him for all this. I don't want to get the police in but if he thinks he could get himself in trouble, he'll be a lamb. The man's a physical and moral coward.'

She gave him the name of the solicitor. Old was stilled. She spoke with passion and nothing Old could think of seemed worth saying. He was about to hang up when he thought of one final point.

'You seem so sure of where you're going, so sure it's a closed episode, can you close it while you still hate him? Do you hate him or wish him ill or have you stopped caring?'

'I'll never stop having a part of my mind and my

heart for him, I don't think I will, but it'll be a different part than it used to be. I used to love him and now I have a living, throbbing hate. Sure I wish him ill, all the ill the world has to offer. I hope he turns alkie and loses his job. I hope his liver turns grey and his balls drop off. I hope he starts a drunken fight – which the coward never would – and gets his due. I wish him dead, but a difficult death. Now, thanks for listening, thanks for passing on the message, get off and leave me to my aches.'

SIX

Old was ushered into a small interview-room. It surprised him how little security he had to meet; no searches, no questions, simply check his ID and he was in. The room was like the interview-room in a thousand police stations. No windows, plain wooden table, three chairs, peephole in the door. The only thing missing was the tape machine now always present for police interviews. There was a small closed-circuit TV in the corner of the room, though it seemed not to have a mike. The room was probably used for interviews with solicitors and this allowed some degree of privacy.

Francis Silvester slouched elegantly in his chair. In his standard prison denims and freshly shaven, he looked as if he had been dressed in a country style by Ralph Lauren and looked more assured then Old could ever manage. Worse, he looked as if it was achieved without the least effort.

'I don't know why I'm seeing you,' he drawled.

'Mightn't it be because McCreery said I wanted to see you and you remembered what a pain he can be?'

Silvester smiled.

'You know, I think you might have it. Get on with it then.'

'Money come in handy in here? I understand McCreery got the money back from your last scheme, in exchange for a lesser charge and not being too unpleasant about you in court.'

'Money's always handy, no matter what's gone on before.'

'You got eighteen months, so you'll serve a year. You've done three months and it's starting to look like a long time.' Old knew from talking to lags in military prison that they hated to hear talk about length of sentence, especially from people outside. From screws it didn't count – they'd still be inside when you were long gone – but from anyone else it hurt. The advice was to do it one day at a time, don't look at the long stretch. Not easy when people rub your nose in it.

'Year from now,' he went on, 'you'll be out and you'll be skint. No one'll want to work with you – bad luck – and you'll need a bit of start-up.'

'Who's saying I won't be getting a job, going straight?'

'If you're going to mess about, I'll be off.'

'And I'll be so sorry to see you go, I'll be put off my mid-afternoon wank. For about five minutes.'

'Let's dance later,' Old interrupted, irritably. 'I want information. I won't hand anyone on to McCreery, he just owed me a favour. I need to find someone was on a scam. Doesn't matter why. Nothing to do with McCreery. He knows people on both sides of the fence, comes with the job. If we have a good chat, you co-operate, I'll see you two-fifty. I can drop a cheque in an account, post cash, whatever. If you give me a name and it turns out good, I'll give you a further grand.'

'Says who?'

'I do. What's the matter, you can't rely on a simple promise, you want a contract or something?'

Silvester nodded. 'A contract would be nice.' He

knocked on the door. After an interval a guard appeared. Silvester gave him a smile which seemed perfectly to balance liking and respect. Old thought it was a smile that would stand him in good stead with the guards who, as a group, were more demanding of respect than most; probably more needful.

'Would it be OK if we were to take a walk in the grounds, sir?' he asked. The guard shrugged.

'Suppose that should be possible, no harm done, eh, Frankie.'

'Thank you, sir.'

The two men sat under the cover of an old cedar tree on a solidly made bench which, according to Silvester, had been made in the prison workshops.

'They say these open joints are like holiday camps. Sure they are. People who say prison's a doddle, any kind of prison, they need to do a bit. Some bloke, on the dole a couple of years, doesn't get out much, starts saying how his gaff's a prison, he's missed the point. Your own gaff, you've got the keys. This place, might be the best prison in the system, but someone else's got the keys, locks you in at night, even here. And no women. You ever watch *Cheers*?'

Old nodded.

'Sam Malone: babehound. First time I heard that expression on *Cheers* I got a grin it took me a week to get rid of. The thing is . . .' and Old believed him as an enormous shit-eating grin cracked Silvester's face. 'The thing is, that's me. Frankie Silvester: Babehound with a capital B. I chase women. That's my life. I chase women and they let me catch them. I mean face it, I'm a good-looking guy, I can be charming, so I'm good at it. Doesn't leave much time for work – all those women out there and so little time, and they like having me around, so I let them buy me stuff, give me pocket money. Shit, got to be better than working. OK, so sometimes I go for the crinkly stuff, tarts with a few years on 'em, starting to go to pieces a bit, and that's not so hot on the ego, so I get tempted, tell a few fibs here and there, take more than I really need, but they wouldn't pay if they didn't want to. I don't tie 'em up or anything. Well that's a lie, but only when they ask me to, which is more often than you might expect. These old 'uns, they've done it straight often enough, and they've done it not at all for long enough, you find their imaginations tend to go off the beaten track a bit, their tastes get a bit fruity. Am I giving you what you want or I am going on a bit? Should we sort the contract out?'

'You were serious about the contract?'

'Contracts are serious things. A good contract is the basis of a sound business relationship.'

Silvester pulled an envelope from his jacket pocket. It contained a number of sheets of paper folded too many times and for too long. He flicked through them until he found one with one side empty. He scribbled on it in a neat and characterless hand the details of the deal they had made in the interview-room. They both signed it and Old hoped they could get back to business, but Silvester was gazing distractedly around the park.

'Shall we talk?' Old asked.

'A minute. There's someone.' He stood and waved at a young man walking across their line of vision a couple of hundred yards away. A few people returned the wave and started towards Silvester but he shook his head and pointed at his target. Eventually he put two fingers inside his mouth and let out an ear-splitting but surprisingly even-toned whistle. Old had not heard such a good whistle since he left the Army, where everyone seemed to be able to whistle that way. The figure turned along with the rest of the prison inmates within view and probably, thought Old, most of the dogs in East Sussex. He ambled across in an exaggeratedly casual manner, as if, not really wrongly, thought Old, he had all the time in the world and more.

When eventually he reached them it seemed as if the walk had used his supply of expendable energy and he had lost the ability even to speak. He slowly rolled his eyes across them and a decorous and plummy 'Help, Frankie?' trickled from his mouth like honey from an apostle spoon. Silvester passed him the contract.

'Have a dekko and, if it's OK, sign it and witness it, all right Jessa?'

The man looked down at them, again taking enough time to note details of the two men's appearance even they wouldn't have had the time to notice.

'First,' he drawled, 'I can hardly witness a signature that's already down.'

'Ask us if they're our signatures, and if there was any duress on either party. They are and there wasn't.'

'Hmm. I suppose. The contract is fine, then.' He pulled a slim black Cross pen from his jacket and crooked his finger at Silvester, who stood and turned his back so it could be used as a writing surface. A quick flourish and he handed the contract back.

'The fee.' He drawled, with what may have been the shadow of a smile, though on anyone else it would have been an echo of an involuntary twitch.

'Wind-up!'

'The fee?'

'Jessa, leave it out, I've business to do. I owe you one.'

'A professional witnessing is not professional unless it is accompanied by a professional fee. I will take services in kind. Please remember my name is Jeremy. Please forget your horrible diminutives and ask your few acquaintances to do the same.'

'Done. Jeremy. The business doing pleasure with you.' Jeremy was already strolling off but at Silvester's weak old joke he half turned, though without stopping.

'Now if you want to talk about doing pleasure, I've more time. You know my room.' And with a wicked grin, which shocked Old with the transformation it brought on his face, he left.

'Fucking trollop,' said Silvester, smiling conspiratorially. 'Don't know how he's got the bottle. Still, another few months in here and I'll probably be knocking on his door. The two of us are the only bastards in here with any kind of style. If I'm going to turn into a lock-up queen, I may as well get it right.'

Old took a look at the contract.

'I suppose that's a legally binding document now then. What's his story?'

'He's the same as everyone else in here. He's a greedy, lazy bastard. He was a solicitor with one of these flash City firms. A couple of their biggest personal clients had funny money he had to lose for them. He lost it right over to the Isle of Man. It was enough for it not to matter about the damage to his shiny little career but he made a big miscalculation. He thought the money was funny enough that they wouldn't prosecute. But they were madder than it was funny. Still, he got two and a half years, he'll be out in eighteen months, and the chancer is representing himself to stop the Law Society chucking him out. It won't work, they'll have him out, but they like to keep their bent solicitors quiet and they hate it when they fight back. Naturally, being lawyers, they've got a constitution with more loopholes than a trawling net, to let them off the hook when they're in deep, but Jessa . . .'

'Jeremy, remember.'

'Yeah, Jeremy. He's giving them a little lesson in why everyone loves lawyers. He's dug in there and it's going to take industrial plant to get him out.'

'Now earn some money.'

'What exactly do you want?'

'I'm not going to tell you why I want it but there's a scam on the go. I want to know where I can find somebody who uses it.'

He described the Goodman scam, changing only the car, making the upgrade to Mercedes 500S. Silvester's face told him nothing; no flicker of familiarity showed, but by the end of the story, though Old had told it relatively quickly, he was sure Silvester was more than aware of the scam. As soon as the first mention of a good deal on imported cars was made, the shine went out of his eyes. Conmen are always on the look out for a new con. As soon as a con hits the news it is dead, while a good but unknown con is money in the bank. Silvester's eyes went dead when it was clear he wasn't about to learn anything.

For Old that was already a result. Although Mc-Creery had told him they had no known associates for

Silvester, he had probably been involved in the con or at least knew someone who had done it.

'So what can you tell me about that?'

'What about it?' Be nice to know from the start, thought Old, if he intends to lie to me.

'Well, for a start, if you've heard of it, if you know anyone who works it, and if you do, who are they, what can you tell me about them?'

'And the name goes straight to McCreery, what is it, I look stupid?'

'The name'll go nowhere. You contracted to talk. I want some hard information and I guarantee it's for my use, my profit.'

'Are you trying to break into the business? You've got some front if you are and you're making your meets in here.'

Let him think what he wants to think, Old thought. As he fancied the idea anyway.

'Front's necessary though, wouldn't you say?'

Silvester nodded, slowly, looking Old over anew, appraising him, Old thought, and trying to judge how much to trust him or believe him. Old didn't really care what he believed; so long as there was a choice of possibles, Silvester couldn't be sure what the situation was and that was the way Old wanted it.

'I'm still waiting to hear what you know. If you don't give me anything, that's what I pay for. You know anyone working the con or you don't? Come on.'

'I do.'

'What do I have to do, buy it by the fucking word. Tell me who they are will you before my hair falls out and I get Alzheimer's, can't remember it when you do tell me.'

'I know one guy, works that exact scam. You find him I want the grand.'

This is like pulling teeth, Old thought, noticing he was beginning, gently, to grind his own teeth.

'I know three names he uses. Most people use more than one name, but for some reason they think it's funny to tell people about them. The ones I know, Angelo Tapley, God knows why – people like to get something positive in the name, all part of the psyche build-up. If you could be called Honest Jack, you would. I heard most of the Latin American cons are called Jesus. Clever huh?'

'Angelo Tapley . . .'

'Yeah, Tapley. Angelo. Guess he was going for the angel angle. Bit contrived really, though. James Good-enough. That was another and that's a cracker. It's a real name, I know. I looked it up in the phone book when he told me and there's quite a few of them – not him obviously. The other one is Bob Gold. No idea which is real, if any, though the Tapley one's got to be favourite, no idea where he lives. He drinks a bit in Tokyo Joe's when he's looking for stiffs, I think, or he used to. Best I know, he's based in North London. North North – the Herts end, posh end. Better than that I couldn't say.'

'That's supposed to help?' Old asked, pushing for more. As he was only fishing, damn-all was about as much as he allowed himself to hope for. Things were looking up. Press on. Assuming – which he wasn't – that one of the names was right, there were many ways to trace someone once there was a name, false or otherwise. Even a false name left tracks and smells if it was used enough.

'He's about forty, above average height, looks after himself, good figure, very dark eyes, bit hypnotic – very deep – greying dark brown hair. That might be a prop though. Lot of cons grey their hair, especially the younger ones. Bit of age is a big asset for a con.'

The description fit Goodman, though that was not one of the names he had been given. It was a fairly vague description, though the eyes seemed significant. Mee had mentioned repeatedly how Goodman made a point of establishing eye contact, though Old suspected that was probably standard practice for a con: Teach Yourself Hucksterism. Chapter One: The Basics. Look the suckers in the eye until they start to blink and blush.

'So what else should I know about this charming friend of yours?'

Silvester grinned.

'He is that thing. He's a very charming man. Charm the wallet off a Fraud Squad plod and the panties off his mother.'

'I should tell him you sent me?'

'Don't be silly. Say you found him through your natural ingenuity. Tell him you're psychic. Tell him what the hell you want but leave me out of it. People get narky about stuff like that. Unless you and Tapley do get a bit of business together, it works out sweet and you both make a bob. That way you can let it out I gave you the nod. Otherwise, keep schtum. And about that – pissing him off – he's even-tempered. Patience is a bit handy on this lark – it can take a long long time setting a job up, but he is a bit handy. Only once I heard of someone doing him a bad 'un and he was quick to get in there, show he was no mug. Threw him out of a second-floor window. Nothing broken, which was luckier than anyone has a right to expect, but last I heard the guy was out of business, delivering pies to chip shops. Straight and skint.'

After he exchanged pleasantries and signed out, Old left as fast as he could. He had a much better result than he expected and he felt like he could start to wrap this up. Those names – with Goodman there were four – would lead to something, and that something would be his man and a payday. He still had to talk to Mee's fellow dupes and that might turn up something, but he felt like he was already hot.

SEVEN

When Dougie Owen opened the door to Old he didn't look pleased. He didn't look as if he especially didn't want to see him, just that nothing in particular would have pleased him and hadn't for a long time.

'I left a message on your machine,' he said, belligerently. 'If I call I expect a reply, not to spend all day talking to a machine.'

'All day isn't really necessary. About thirty seconds usually does it.'

'You're a lippy sod. You should remember who's paying the wages round here.'

'Not wages, a fee. I work for myself, at the moment you're my client. In about two minutes you won't be.'

As he spoke, Old looked around the street. There were a number of people taking advantage of the late autumn sun. It was early evening and most people were home from work. There were no little kids around but a few teenagers. Nothing to cause a problem. He didn't want to upset any little ones. Neither did he want any witness problems, but as he wasn't expecting any complaints, it was unlikely there would be any. Not from Dougie and not from anyone else.

'You've found her then?' Owen asked, a sly grin creeping onto his face.

Old nodded.

'So where is the bitch?'

Old slowly shook his head.

'What's that supposed to mean?'

'It means I found her but she doesn't want you to know where she is.' Old handed Owen a sheet of paper with Jan Owen's solicitor's details.

'There's a message. Here's her solicitor's details. Be in touch with yours, give him this and agree to an uncontested divorce, your blame, mental and physical cruelty, by Friday, or she calls the police and gets you in. GBH at least.'

Owen had gone slack-jawed. He stared at the blank front of the folded sheet of paper in his hand and then at Old.

'*I* paid you. Not that bitch. I want her back here. I want my son. Where is she? Tell me where she is or give me my money back.'

Always an eye on the pennies, thought Old.

'You hired me to find her, which I did. I promised no more. Your wife said not to tell you, so I won't. I could give you the money back but I don't like you, so I won't. I've something from your wife in the car, c'm'ere.'

Old strolled down the path, crooking his finger at Owen. He peered down through the window of his car and smiled. Owen followed, still looking puzzled. Old wanted this to take place in full view of the street. They might pretend they didn't know he was a wife-beater, or they might not know at all. Either way they could behave normally. But if they all knew that they all knew, it would be easier to treat him like the piece of shit he was. Owen ambled over to the car and leaned towards it. He saw an empty back seat and looked up at Old.

'Eh?'

'Sucker!' Old spat, under his breath. Then he yelled

out. 'Message from your wife!' and his fist shot out and hit Owen in the stomach. Owen buckled. Old put his hand on Owen's chin and lifted it. He punched him full in the left eye. Owen toppled back against the car but there was not enough room to fall. As he moved back, Old hit his other eye.

'Your neighbour here beats his wife!' A quick pop on the nose; the first blood.

'In hospital for nearly a week!' he shouted. The neighbours were all watching, without exception, but no one moved.

'Black eyes, split lips, broken teeth!' he shouted, as he drove a jab across Owen's mouth, sending blood spurting as both lips burst against a simultaneously broken tooth.

'Did I forget anything, Dougie? Call the solicitor and do as I said. Don't call the police or I'll press charges myself and I'll visit again too. Ah, there was one thing. Ribs.' He let loose a barrage of powerful blows at the same point on the bottom left side of Owen's ribcage, finally smashing his elbow in, hard.

'For the next few weeks, when you breathe, when you feel your ribs ache, when you wake up with the pain of them, think of Jan and think what a piece of shit you are.'

Owen sank to the pavement and started to crawl, at first on all fours and then rising to a hunched and limping walk, not looking at Old or any of his neighbours and as quickly as he could getting inside his lair, the door protecting him from a suddenly hostile world.

Old rubbed his hands and tried to shake some of the soreness from them. A middle-aged man shouted from across the street.

'Well done, mate. He's deserved that for years.'

'Didn't get it though, did he?' said Old and shook his head in contempt at the people already gathering in bunches to discuss the spectacle, new ones already coming out, alerted by the buzz. He drove off, glad to get the episode behind him and hoping his hands wouldn't swell too badly.

Satya daubed the pungent, lime-green, muddy poultice over Old's hands, layering it thickly across his knuckles.

'I don't know why I'm doing this,' she complained. 'It's your Uncle's mud and your idiot friend's mess.'

'Thanks Satch,' said Old.

'Don't call me Satch. Satya or nothing.'

'Not Mrs Virdi, then.'

'Look, *I'm* doing this, not Ras, but I don't have to. I'm not happy with you, and I'm especially not happy about you getting Ras involved, which means I can do very well without your half-wit wit.'

'Didn't I get myself involved?' Ras put in when he saw that Satya's barb had quieted Old. 'No one held a gun to my head.'

'You got another chance to be the mysterious macho seeker after truth, husbandji, darling. It would have needed a gun to the head to keep you away.'

'Such sarcasm,' said Ras.

'Such truth,' Satya added. 'Deny it if you dare. You'd get involved in anything this idiot asked you to.'

'Thanks Satya,' Old repeated.

'And you'd do yourself a favour with me if you kept your head down and your mouth shut.'

'This is nothing to do with the pornographer, you know. This is another thing altogether,' he said, twitching his hands at her.

'You said. Keep your hands still.'

'So why the tongue lashing?'

'Because you're still involved in the other thing and I thought better of you. Helping drug dealers, now this. I'm disappointed. The stuff's finished. Now leave it for an hour, I'll take Sam to the park. Wash it off after the hour and give your hands a good wash and they'll stink for a day instead of a week. And if you expect it to help then you're as gullible as Ras, who still tries not to step on cracks.'

The two men sat in silence for a while, feeling chastened and suspicious that it was deserved. Neither felt comfortable helping Mee, though so far Ras had been involved only in advising and discussing the case: the bar kept him tied down most of the time and there was nothing special that merited his help. They both gazed at Old's mud-caked hands, watching as the shine went off the slimy poultice as it dried.

'She's got a point you know,' Ras said eventually. 'He's a pretty disgusting character.'

'Course she's right. That's the problem. She wouldn't have a go unless she'd had a good think about it. She's got bloody impeccable judgement and if she says she's disappointed then you can bet she is and that means we're a pretty sorry pair.'

'She does have good judgement, doesn't she?' Ras said, with a mixture of sorrow – that she had judged him to be doing wrong – and pride that she was so wise.

'Bit late to do anything about it, isn't it, though?' he asked. 'Now you think you're half way there?'

'Looks it; I mean what are we supposed to do – am I supposed to do?' he corrected himself. 'Just get the thing over with and see if there isn't maybe something helpful I couldn't do with the money. Or some of it.'

'You don't think he's involved with any dodgy stuff, do you?' Ras asked. 'With the porn I mean.'

Old shook his head.

'Hope not. I'd have to drop it if there was. Probably grass him up to McCreery as well, as if the Vice Squad boys don't already keep a close eye on the sleaze.'

'What do you think Mee and his lot will do if they get their hands on him – on Goodman? I would have thought they'd fucking kill him.'

'And that's another problem. Because I don't think they'd be too pleased with me if they knew I'd found him and was keeping it to myself. It's a problem.'

By lunchtime, Old had managed to see four of the dupes pulled into Goodman's scheme by Mee. He had no great insights but had a better picture of Mee. His friends were a bunch of deadbeats, some with money, some without; Mee was a deadbeat with a great deal of money. They were men with no aims and principles unattached to money and its acquisition, even though most of them hadn't even managed to make any. They were, in Old's eyes, simply low. With less culture between them than a small portion of butterscotch-flavoured frozen yogurt, the nearest they got to a read was the captions in Mee's magazines. It made Old remember the statistic he had read, that the average household had only seven books. When he thought of his own house, and Ras and Satya's and Barney's all with hundreds, he realized that that statistic was a few people like him and loads of Barry Mees with no books at all. He hated to think of himself as a snob – what right did he have, he had the same background as they did. But they brought it out in him. Rub two neurons together, he thought, and the shock of the thought might kill them. Showing the loyalty of best friends who had lost money, none so far had a good word to say for Mee. They called him lots of names as imaginatively as they could, but the consistency of the terms used made Old promise to himself that he would try to swear less if that was the effect it had. Rather than add emphasis, it gave a smooth consistent texture to their language, like Campbell's soup.

Already with flagging commitment to Mee, he resolved to keep an eye out for a loophole. Every one of the men he had seen so far had said the same. They wanted to 'get their hands on the fucking slag. Give him a fucking good kicking. Fucking kill him if they got their fucking hands on him.' One of them had a habit of using consecutive *fucking*s in a kind of verbal tic. A trick Old had not heard before, even in the Army.

The last thing he wanted was to get involved in a manslaughter. He might have to consider, if he ever found Goodman, trying to force him, if that was possible, to pay off at least some of the money. It wouldn't be easy and Goodman would want to know why he was doing that rather than handing him over.

If he guessed then his bluff could be called and Old assumed that making that kind of assessment of intentions and calculating when someone's bluff can be called must be the kind of skills a conman must have to survive in the job. Another consideration which had not occurred to him before was Davida Goodman – the henchwoman, as Old had become used to thinking of her. If he handed Goodman over then she was surely in a deal of trouble, and Old had very firm views on women and violence – the views he had explained to Dougie Owen. He had to start looking for a loophole before he found Goodman; if he started thinking on the hoof there was a good chance Goodman would be ahead of him. He had the numbers of the other five suckers in the consortium – with Mee he had seen half. He guessed that that was a good sample and decided there was nothing new to learn. After all, they had met him only the once and all heard the same lies. He had seen more of Mee, who knew the most about Goodman. He decided to call it a day, maybe call Norton, spend some time on the computer, chase the names he had, see if McCreery could help check the names for criminal records.

This was getting to be a pain in the arse. Here were Mel and Kevin, elected representatives of the other pains in the arse who he had done nothing worse to than try to do a favour and here they were trying to lean on him. Mel and Kevin, of course, eye on the main chance, were after being courted a bit like the last time. He still wasn't sure whether that was the right way to go about it – see how things go and go with the flow. Mel said that they'd tried to tell the lads he was in the same boat, that he felt bad, and that he was trying to do something about it. They said a few of them had seen this guy came round asking about

Goodman. 'Building up a picture,' he said he was. Asking the same questions of the lot of 'em, they said.

'Well if they're the right questions then of course he's going to ask the same questions,' Mee observed.

'Right,' Kevin said. 'Yeah, course he is, I was just saying. He asks the same questions.'

Mee had heard of this kind of thing. Some people will do anything rather than disagree with someone, especially if they think they're in a position of authority. He knew about it because he got a letter, signed by over a dozen women, all doctor this and professor that, saying that the stories in his magazines encouraged blokes to harass women at work, and they might even get away with it because the women were usually under the authority of the men and didn't know how to say *no*. They were conditioned – that was the word they used – to agree and do as they were told. Mee wasn't too sure about this, so he had someone go down the library, they got some sheets photocopied from some textbook and there it was. They said if you sit some people in a room and hold up black or white cards and tell them to say which is black and which is white, they'd say what everyone else said, even if that meant saying black was white. There was a word for it, if he could only remember what it was, and that was what Kevin was.

Another word was weak.

And fucking stupid.

Then again, Mee thought guiltily, Kevin had only got involved because Mee had egged him on. He said he was skint and he shouldn't, but Mee pushed him, and all the others were doing it, so he went in with them. Same went for Mel, really, he had the least spare cash of any of them. Flogging snide perfume was good money for the work involved but it would never make anyone rich. They probably all went in for it for the same reason at the end of the day. Because the others did. Sheep! Hopeless, he thought. Give them the same treatment again, but don't waste time showing them around. Just be blatant about it and give them a hard on and a full stomach. Hard to be a hard head after someone's just given you the two things you spend your life trying to get.

'There's a shoot in the studio if you want a look. I'm free for lunch, but I've got a meeting for an hour or so first. If you've the time, Debbie'll show you up there and I'll call them and tell them to expect you, not to give you any grief on my say so. Mind you,' he grinned lecherously, 'it's not newsagent stuff today – cling-film-wrapped sex shop stuff. The real thing. Just about as far as you can go without getting the police in. Which is as far as I want to go, of course.' The grin again. 'So if it's a bit much for you lads, just say so.'

He buzzed his secretary and passed them the remains of the bottle of Scotch they had been drinking, which was almost three-quarters of the bottle.

'Take a top-up with you.'

Debbie came in and they were led away, mutely trailing off to have their hard ons delivered.

Like porn or leave it, Mee mused, it gives you a stiff. After their little adventure, the two of them would go off and sing his praises to the others again. Eventually they'd get fed up with Mel and Kevin coming back with their lame defences of him and send someone else and he'd try the same trick: stiffen their pricks and feed their bellies.

It worked every time.

He knew it was a valuable tool in business. He'd seen these fancy companies – PR agencies and ad agencies and what not. All the secretaries look like models, they all bend over the table, give a bit of leg. Give the clients a bit of glamour. Mee took it further. He had other business outside porn but he always worked the same way. Don't just give 'em a flash, buy them a lay. Better still if they don't know it's a lay. Let them think they're so damn irresistible the slag of a secretary can't resist giving them a quickie while he's out of the room. They never notice the girl's not there next time, never suspect she's bought-in talent.

Thinking like this made him mad. If he knew all this, why didn't he notice when Goodman pulled the same trick? Simple. Goodman was a hundred times better at it and now look at the fucking mess.

He didn't know if there was anything behind the chumps' veiled threats and demands for action. He knew what they really wanted was for him to make good their losses. But that wasn't going to happen. He might be a millionaire now, but he didn't get that way by handing over a hundred grand every time someone got a bit peeved with him. Just string them along until his man found Goodman and then let them at him. Then if they don't get their money, he's out of it. 'You did business with him,' he can say, 'so sort it. You know where he is, get your money or do him. It's between you and him. I've spent a fortune finding the slag so you can get straight. So do it, I'm not your nursemaid.'

He had just about written off his own money and Old's fee. He wanted revenge. He suspected the others were after the revenge and money. It's going to get ugly, he thought. Be nice to see the guy in hospital, but I'm not going to end up in the dock. He decided that when he found out he would take a holiday, pronto. Pass on the information on Goodman over the phone. Go somewhere with good lines like the States. He could do with a holiday. That way he couldn't get stitched up. And if the chumps didn't know where he was, so much the better. Could be at work for all they knew. Why help them out? He was sure they would as soon do him a disservice as Goodman. Fuck the lot of them. He was only giving them Goodman's name as a hands-off way of doing him. Do yourself a favour and watch your own back. Two mottos to keep life sweet.

McCreery was as co-operative as Old had ever heard him. Either he had just had a major collar or he had discovered the Buddha. And he wasn't the type for the Buddha. Unfortunately, what his co-operation entailed was checking the records for the names Old gave him and coming up empty. Still, he gave a cheery apology, said 'Any time,' and wished Old good luck with his search.

Now it was time to hit the keyboards. Once, his practice in a situation like this was to call an old friend who could, he claimed, get in just about anywhere. Eventually though, he did Old a bigger favour. He let him into the secret of computer detection, which is that most of the information you want doesn't need a hacker, just a chequebook. He linked up Old's PC with a good-quality modem to connect him to the telephone network and gave him the numbers for the most important commercial databases and away he went. Since then, Old got a good part of his business done without ever leaving his chair. He paid almost two thousand pounds a year in subscriptions but he estimated this brought in at the very least sixteen thousand in fees. Once the subscription was paid, he needed only to pay for line time and, like all detectives, his telephone bills were astronomical anyway.

He smiled when he thought of the electronic tagging schemes being introduced as a replacement for prison. As they were generally used for white-collar crimes, there was a good chance that these were crimes committed entirely over the telephone, solved by telephone, and now the villains were imprisoned by telephone.

The work he did this way was mostly tracing skipped bankrupts and debtors. The trouble with these people was that usually they liked to spend other people's money in preference to their own. As soon as they did, they were Old's.

First he ran the names on his list through a credit rating agency. They all came up triple A. This was not what he expected – he thought there would either be no record or records on only one. That all three came up meant at least that Silvester's information was good, that there was someone using these names, and that they were not just throwaway alibis used for quick bar scams, like the one he had done in the Consul – or, apparently, like Goodman, which he had checked out this way as one of his first moves and come up with absolutely nothing. The question now was whether any of these seemingly hot names would lead to his man. All of the names on the credit agency files, naturally, were attached to addresses. He checked the addresses on the council tax registers for the relevant boroughs. None of the same names came up – each was a rented property with the tax paid by managers on behalf of the property company. A dead end, or not. It probably meant he had used these addresses, renting them for the duration of the scam. But they had to be names of long standing to get a triple A rating. Usually the top rating would only go to a homeowner. Maybe Goodman had the entries doctored; but credit ratings are fiercely protected, that was unlikely. Old tried the land registry for the properties. Again, they were all registered company properties. But things were improving. All the same property company: Marchlane Hope.

Big coincidence.

On to the database for Companies House. The company had no named directors, an accommodation address and the information that Marchlane Hope was wholly owned by an Isle of Man company, Marchlane Holdings, about which no more. Once in the tricky area of offshore tax shelter companies Old was lost – his databases did not cover that far. But the information was out there. Someone was trying to hide something; Old wanted someone who was hiding and the two were connected.

He called Toby Norton.

'Fucking miraculous,' Norton said. 'I was just about to call. Dinner tomorrow night. Can you make it? I know it took a while coming but I've got a guy knows lots: techniques, names, everything, and he loves to talk, so long as he knows it stops there, and I've assured him I trust you, which makes you fine. He has plenty invested with me and thinks I'm the business, so he's smart, too.'

'I'm a bit past background, Toby, but thanks.'

'Come anyway. I'll be there. It'll be worth it. If not now then later. He'll tell you things you like to hear and he's a useful man to know, good name to drop in the right places.'

'OK, so I'll go. I need a favour. I'll fax you a sheet of information about some names I have so you know what I know. See if you can find out some real names attached in the Isle of Man. I've got Companies House data but no foreign stuff. I've got subscriptions for occasional user, US and EC, but the offshore stuff I wouldn't use enough to justify it.'

'You're creeping into the eighties now we're in the nineties, Gumshoe.'

'You'll help?'

'Well, you're assuming I will, I see – the fax has just come through. If I don't call within the hour, call back.'

EIGHT

Old grinned at the fax from Norton. Angelo Tapley. The name was there, clear as day, on a digest of Marchlane Holdings' accounts. They were scanty accounts; all that was required under Isle of Man law, but they had the name he wanted, and they had an address. Old had a good feeling about the address. No one wants to buy good property and lose it. He had hidden it behind a paperstorm, but there was a clear path with clean legal provenance. He didn't want to hide it so well its ownership could be disputed. It was in Arkley. A pretty little commuter village in Hertfordshire, just past the furthest reach of North London. Old knew it vaguely as he had twice visited it with a friend considering the move, but who had eventually decided he was paying too much for the location, leaving too little for the house itself. It was the kind of place where people bought horses then hired people to ride them.

He had three hours. Just enough time to give the place the once-over before he had to pick up Sam. He changed into a plain blue business suit, dug a clipboard out from a pile of assorted rubbish in his office, clipped a customer service questionnaire onto it that the bank had sent that morning and dropped a false market research ID into his pocket. Really, he thought, the difference between me and these cons is only the result. In working methods we're virtually interchangeable. As if to confirm this, and while his mind was on a criminal tack, he threw his burglary kit into the boot of his car. It comprised a pinched head steel tube, a cordless power drill, a set of professional lock-picks that had set him back a hundred and fifty pounds, and an electronic gee-gaw that was supposed – and it had worked twice so far – to neutralize most alarms and, more importantly, to tell you whether or not it had succeeded.

It had taken him some time to learn to use the tools, especially the picks. At first he had tried it on his own front door but he had so quickly attracted funny looks that he bought a mock-up door from a double glazing firm going bust – it was a half-height door with a free-standing frame, and he had it fitted with a Yale and four mortice locks. It took a week to learn to get through all but one with an average under a minute. The fourth, with six independent cylinders, he could not predict. Sometimes he lucked through in a minute, other times it defeated him utterly. Still, so long as he remembered to practise regularly, this meant he could be in most houses in little more time than most people took to fiddle with their own keys.

As he expected, it was a comfortable-looking place. It was on a wide street, perhaps a quarter of a mile long, and with twenty-two houses on each side. Each was set well back from the road. A newish development, ten or so years had given it time to settle in, and from the look of the gardens they had been planted with mature trees and shrubbery. They were all different to a significant degree, choice is what comes with big-ticket new houses, but looked like four bed, two bath, two garage was about the base line, the bulk being around the six bed, three reception, two bath and half-acre lot mark. Money. It wasn't the kind of area where he could expect a response from quizzing the neighbours, no matter how tangentially.

He knew there was a limit to how long he could park before someone came to check him out or called the police. He drove a Mini convertible and in a place like this even the second car would be a late model sporty Ford or an antique Merc – for fun.

He watched for ten minutes and saw a movement through the half-closed venetian blinds in the front room. So no burglary. Today. He clipped the false ID onto his jacket pocket and headed for the house, clipboard purposefully gripped in his left hand, pen poised in his right. He knocked on the solid hardwood door. It was answered by a girl, around nine or ten years old, in a smart pale blue school uniform – which reminded him he had a little over an hour before he was due to pick up Sam from Barney – and long jet-black Italianate hair – another pointer towards Angelo Tapley being maybe a real name: with a name like that likely an Italian mother and an English father. He asked to see her mother and she strolled off, without a word, down a long hall with doors off both sides. She entered the kitchen at the back and her mother returned. It was not the Davida he had seen on the photos. This was not necessarily important. Just because the woman was presented as his wife, she might have been no more than a business partner, though it would take an extraordinarily patient or ignorant wife to tolerate such a partnership.

She had striking looks. Long black wavy hair, like her daughter's, a slightly too long and straight nose and prominent cheekbones. She reminded Old of a young Angelica Houston. Not the look he went for, but he couldn't deny she was a very attractive woman. Sexy too. She had very distinct eyebrows – not plucked – and she raised one in a silent interrogative sentence. It seemed that parsimony with words was a family trait.

'I'm here to offer you a free financial survey and free advice. I'm not selling anything . . .'

'And I'm not buying anything.'

Summarily dismissed, Old had no chance to reply before she shut the door.

Given that the connection with an Italian background was no more than the dark hair of Tapley's daughter, and given that that could equally have come from her mother, Old knew no more than he had when he arrived except that the house was occupied. Probably under a completely different false name, and rented again, from himself, through some kind of paper trail: Peter paying Paul. He was sure, though, that this was the right house, the right family. He knew most people were short with door-to-door salesmen, but few were so efficiently brusque, and he was sure that verbosity, other than when professionally required, was not a good thing for cons and their families. Besides, again, he had a *feeling* he had his man, and he would find out.

They sat in the back of the Mercedes and watched London flit by as they listened to Art Blakey and his Messengers pound out a terrific rhythm.

'If there's one thing about this line of work,' Old said, 'it's that it doesn't suit single parenthood. I mean, if you're going to bring up a child alone, you need regular hours, so that if you do manage to get regular trustworthy babysitters, you can use them to give yourself a life. I use them to work.'

'And by work I guess you mean getting driven out to Virginia Water to go to a dinner party, drink yourself silly, be told a few interesting tales and get driven back to your door,' Norton muttered.

'Honestly, that's exactly what I mean. It's not what I'd be doing on my own time, and I'll not see Sam at all, and that in itself means my night's ruined.'

'You're a martyr. You'd admit it's better than going down a mine or stocking shelves at Safeway though?'

'Sure. And it's better than the Army too, for the most part, but it's still work.'

The house was a house like Liz Taylor's rings are rocks. It was a solid, four-square Addams Family House, turreted, with a steeply angled roof and more windows than Old could count. He couldn't see the whole of the house for the heavily wooded grounds and he couldn't even see the grounds until he was through the double gate in the ten-foot stone wall. A property like this would be clearly a rich man's place even in the wilds of the country, but here in finest stockbroker-belt Surrey it was stinking.

They were greeted by a young woman who was wearing what seemed, after a fashion, to be a maid's uniform. She spoke with an impenetrable Geordie accent. She had clearly been told to expect them as she ushered them into the house and into a sitting-room, where she offered them – they were fairly sure that was what she said – a drink.

Warriner kept them waiting a few minutes and Old was getting impatient.

'Is this a dinner party or an audience?'

'He's doing you a favour, Pat.'

'He's doing me a small favour that he wants to do for his own reasons and he wants me to be duly aware I'm having a favour done me.'

'Cool it. What do you want? He'll be here.'

'Five more minutes and I call a cab.'

'Are you going to be like this all night?'

'Like what?'

'Like a grouchy bastard. Like a spoilt kid. I offered, you accepted, with ill will but you accepted. Now pipe down and listen to what the man has to say.'

'When he's good and ready, I get to listen.'

They bickered pointlessly for a few more moments until Warriner joined them. He apologized profusely, opened a bottle of champagne as he spoke and launched immediately into a rambling and extremely funny explanation of the background to the telephone call that had kept him. Old, despite his inclinations, found himself liking Warriner, who insisted, curiously, they call him Den. Unfortunately, Old, knowing his own sometimes contrary character well, knew a part of him, a large part, would stick to the original anger and resist the soothing of Warriner's easy charm.

They were shown into the dining-room by the Geordie maid, whose figure Warriner inspected as if it was entirely new to him. After she had poured the remaining champagne and left to get the first course, Warriner shook his head wearily.

'I make no bones, I hired that girl for her looks, her body, and because I thought I could have her. I hired what I thought would be an easy lay. I knew I could keep it from the wife – I'm a professional liar remem-

130

ber – but I've not had a sniff. Either the wife's put the fear of God in her or something I can't figure.'

'Couldn't be because you're fifty, fat and very nearly bald and she's young and pretty, could it?' Old asked, risking a black glare from Norton.

'I could make her very comfortable and she knows it,' Warriner replied.

'But that'd make her a tart and maybe she just prefers being seen as a maid, even if that does mean she has to dress up in that damn silly, frilly outfit just so's you can get a wank instead of getting the real thing.'

Warriner flushed.

'I invited you here, son. I don't need this at my own table.'

'You brought it up, how you couldn't make a whore of the girl, get in her pants with a few lies and a wedge of cash. I thought that made it up for discussion. If we're taking turns with monologues instead, just let me know.' He paused.

'You still doing Maxwells then or what? We going to talk about that?' This was cheeky. He had guessed from what Norton had said that this was the line of con Warriner covered and, by letting slip the fresh nickname for the con, he showed that it was nothing new, that he would be unlikely to slump backwards in shock at the audacity and brilliance of the con, which was unlikely anyway as a Maxwell was, despite its size, a very crude con: run up a big bill, do a runner and keep a few lawyers riding shotgun.

If it was a line designed to annoy Warriner, it succeeded in trumps. It was a professional necessity that he be able to conceal his emotions. His professional standards were slipping. He drummed his index finger tensely on the table-top and the muscles in his cheeks tightened and loosened in rhythm. His eyes, without exactly glaring, acquired an off-putting fixity.

'You know about Maxwells, there's not a lot I can tell you, old son,' he said, with as near an approximation as it seemed he could manage to calm affability.

'Is a Maxwell once every couple of years the extent of it then?' asked Old. 'Or do you have a few sidelines? I mean, Toby obviously handles the financials, do you do any tricks on the side?'

Warriner grinned. 'I keep my hand in.'

Old made a flowing gesture to Warriner, inviting him to carry on – the floor his.

'Best not to say too much,' he said, with a very final tone.

He's lying, Old thought. We came here so he could talk about what he does. Now he wants to keep it under his hat. He's a one-trick wonder. Made a pile out of it but still, he's got the one thing he knows and he's stuck to it.

From then on, after a very poor start, things went quickly worse. They all three drank too much too quickly. Warriner bragged, unsubtly and badly, about his wealth, more about the maid, about whom he made nasty little innuendos without coming out and saying anything in particular, his stuff – he was in love with his stuff – and back to his wealth. Norton sat and fumed, silently taking out his aggression and frustration on his food and feeling especially annoyed because, whether through thoughtlessness or malice, Warriner had not thought to provide him with cushions for his chair, and he, through sheer blockheadedness, wouldn't ask for one, which meant he was sitting peering up at the others, unable to reach the table with his elbows, like an awkward nine-year-old. Old concentrated on sinking the juice, which was of uniformly high quality and very well chosen, he admitted, even out loud to Warriner. The rest of the time he amused himself by encouraging Warriner's bragging, seeing it as a far better put-down than he could ever manage, and also a lesson he would always remember in how not to regard wealth if it ever should come his way.

They had ordered a car for three hours after they arrived. When it was pushing two hours, it already seemed long enough. Old had long ago decided his life had too few hours to waste in small-talk. He made his excuses and called the car company, asking them to get a car as fast as they could. It was there in five minutes. It was a flat night and the driver who dropped them had been waiting a little way down the road, hoping for an airport job, with no luck.

Norton's face was a mask of suppressed anger. As soon as they were seated in the car he let rip at Old, attacking him for his behaviour with one of his clients, and when he was doing him a favour.

'Who cares what he thinks about me?' Old asked. 'He wanted to brag about being a thief. He wasn't even a particularly imaginative thief, and he wanted to brag about his maid's body. Like she was one of his bloody paintings. He got on my wick and he had nothing worth saying, so forget him. He came to you because he thought you could get him the best return around. He likes his money and you still offer the best return, so he won't be leaving you, so what's the sweat? Maybe he won't hang on the phone chatting so long, so I've done you a favour.'

'I don't think so. Just drop it and we'll pretend it never happened and that way maybe we can stay friends.'

'It just wasn't that big a deal, Toby . . .'

'Drop it.'

They continued the rest of the way in a silence that they both kept just about bearable through a succession of inane comments on the level of traffic and the behaviour of other drivers.

It was still only ten when Old arrived home. The sitter was a niece of Satya. She was fifteen and she was supposed to be doing it as a favour to Satya, and to get out of the house and have a place to study in peace, but it seemed it had not been the evening she planned. Old knew how she felt. When he asked if Sam had behaved himself, she said yes, but she shrugged her shoulders, undermining her own words.

'What time did he go to bed?' Old asked.

'About half an hour ago.'

'But you put him to bed before that, didn't you?'

'Half seven. He just wouldn't stay there. I didn't know what to do with him. I read him stories, I tucked him in, he just kept getting up. He wasn't naughty or anything when he was up, but he just wouldn't stay in bed.'

Old apologized. 'You could stay and study now I'm home, if you like, if you need the peace, but I expect you'd rather be off.'

She nodded. Old insisted he call her a cab. She tried to refuse payment with more vigour than he expected, but when the cab came, he gave her a twenty, saying the cab would be five – though they both knew it would be three at the most – and that he had nothing smaller. She certainly didn't want to pay for the cab herself and finish the evening down, so she took it, repeating that it was too much.

'We'll call the difference a down payment on the next time then,' he said. 'And I'll have words with Sam, make sure he's better next time. And thanks a lot. I really appreciate it.'

Ras lay back in the bath, his legs bent at the knees, his feet resting on the taps and his enormous mass of thick black hair swirling at the other end of the bath, while Satya rinsed the soap from it.

'You know, when this is stretched with the water, I bet it'll come past your bum.'

'No kid.'

'Really. It's thicker than mine and longer as well. There's a lot of girls'd give a front tooth for hair like this.'

'They don't have to wash it.'

'Neither do you these days.'

'I just let you do it because I know how much you like it.'

Satya took hold of a thick hank of hair and swished it, sending out a parabola of foaming water, thwacking onto Ras's face where she left it covering him. He dipped his head below the water and it floated gently away.

When he came to the surface, he looked at Satya out of the side of his eye.

'I've been thinking about Pat.'

'I was nice and relaxed there and you've wound me up again.'

'I think you're being a bit hard on him about this porn thing. He doesn't like it, you know.'

'Then he shouldn't have taken the man's money. He was keen enough on that.'

'You can be very hard. He made a mistake. He said he had misgivings at the start, now he sees it was a mistake.'

'So why doesn't he drop it? Don't tell me it isn't the money.'

'It isn't. Not really. I mean it's part of it. You know he's not short of a few quid any more, but you also know what he's like about Sam – how he has to provide and all that. How there has to be enough for anything. He really goes for the money since Siobhan . . .'

'Well I think he's got to the point where he uses her as an excuse. It's always "if Siobhan hadn't gone", "if Siobhan was here things'd be different", "I love her and I can't forget her". He needs a woman.'

'I think he's got one,' Ras said.

'The woman with the kid at Sam's school?'

'Yeah, her. Anna, Hannah, one of those kind of names.'

'She thinks she's something. Walks around like she's only visiting. It won't come to anything.'

'Pat seems keen.'

'No. It won't come to anything.'

'You know you mother Pat. You'll be suggesting an arranged marriage next.'

This earned him another faceful of soapy water.

'You do. Half the time you act like a friend. When

he's not there, you cluck over him like he needs his life keeping tidy by someone who knows better.'

Satya waited for a moment before replying.

'Maybe I do, but he does need it, you know he does. You even do it yourself and encourage me to do it. His parents are gone, grandparents too. All he has is Barney who isn't really family, and he only helps to keep him moping about Siobhan – they can sit grizzling about their precious wife and daughter and how bloody perfect she was.'

'She was a lovely woman,' Ras put in, defending the woman he had always secretly wanted while she was with Old, a fact which still gave him slight jabs of guilt, as they had flirted for years – playfully but openly. It was nothing to do with her leaving – no one knew what that was all about – but it still made him feel a little uneasy, even though he could not pin down quite why.

'Who walked out on Pat and Sam, him only two at the time? Can you imagine that? Walk out on your husband, it happens. On your two-year-old child, no goodbye or nothing? The woman must have a heart of stone.'

It was a hard action to defend. Ras shrugged his shoulders under the water. A particularly pointless gesture, he thought. Sitting up, he twisted his hair into a pony tail as thick as a man's arm and reached for a towel to wrap it up.

'That's why you're so bothered about him working for this Barry Mee.'

'The pornographer?'

Ras nodded.

'I suppose it is. Whether I mother him or not, I care

137

for him, I like him, I suppose in a kind of way I love him.'

She ignored the squinty-eyed look Ras gave her as she knew it was meant facetiously. He knew what she meant and how she meant it because she knew he felt the same way. She, Ras and Pat Old had been close for years. Siobhan had interrupted without at all breaking the bond, and since she had left Pat had effectively joined the family: he attended their functions – which, in a large Sikh family, were many – and was accepted by everyone. The size of Sikh families meant they were usually less claustrophobically exclusive than European ones. They found it easier to take people in and they had. As for Sam, he would be furious if anyone dared to suggest that they were not family. He had even picked up fair-to-middling Punjabi from the amount of time he spent playing with the kids belonging to Satya and Ras's brothers and sisters.

'So if someone I love makes as big a mistake as I think he is making, whatever his silly excuses, then I'm going to be upset, and if I'm upset, he's going to know about it.'

'What if I could find a way out of it?'

'How? You know what he's like about finishing what he starts. Same as you; the two of you are from the same mould.'

'I'm not sure yet. It's still hazy – kind of a notion without the details filled in yet, but there could be a way he could finish this, if he finds his man, and keep his honour.'

Satya smiled.

'There's not many men left can use that word in that sense and keep a straight face.'

'You wouldn't want me if I couldn't.'

'No. I wouldn't.'

'And you expect the same from Pat. That's what all this is about. You're mad at Pat because you think he's acting dishonourably. He's not working for the man in a professional sense, but the money he is paid with will have shame attached and so it would not be acceptable for a man of honour to take it, or to earn it.'

'It's all true. You might think you've had some great insight, but as far as I'm concerned, I knew all along that was precisely what was upsetting me. You go and think about your little plan, and see if you can't both end up doing the right thing.'

NINE

The van was starting to get chilly so Tandy turned on the engine. Normally he would be reluctant to run the engine just to keep the heater going, but he wasn't paying for the petrol, so what did it matter? Now it was dark it was easier to keep watch. No one was going to arrive at a street like this without a car, their own or a cab, so he could read, listen to the radio, whatever he wanted, just so he didn't sleep. Whenever anything arrived, the light would alert him. Not that it was so difficult during the day – just a little more attention to be paid. The pattern was regular enough. Mid-morning, when he arrived, there was a steady stream of mid-size cars, a few soft-tops with the roofs up, nothing old or tatty apart from an old Beetle and a 2CV – old but with character, they probably had names for them – obviously going shopping or socializing. This was a street with a lot more than the average number of women not working. This trickle in and out continued through the day. From six to eight there was a stream of flash cars, mostly men, though some houses had two cars pull in, and more than a few cabs. There was also the usual trickle of service vehicles – Post Office, BT, electricity, with this or that to do. But no through traffic. The road went from nowhere in particular and looped around to within a couple of hundred yards of where it started. During the late evening the flow came to a standstill, maybe a car every ten or fifteen minutes, suburban socializing, and by late night and early morning there was nothing at all until around six when the hotshots got on the move and the cycle restarted.

Tandy was now in the second half of the second cycle. Nine at night on the second day. He hadn't slept so far – he had been snorting amphetamine sulphate to keep going. Not enough to get him wired but sufficient to keep him awake. Normally, though, speed was a social drug – talk the night away. The lack of anyone to talk to, combined with the slow build-up after he had first missed a night's sleep, then had to stay awake and alert all day, and now looked as if he was going for a second night, was combining to make him feel very edgy. His scalp was itching, his dick, as it always did with speed, had shrunk almost to nothing, which made pissing in a bottle awkward, and he was talking to himself. It was lucky the police hadn't been round. He expected on a street like this they might have. He had been told to drop a name: 'McCreery knows, working for Pat Old tell him, it's OK.' Sounded like a lot of bollocks, he thought, but at least if you go dropping coppers' names, it's not so likely you're out on the blag. Besides, checking out, doing the recce, that's one thing. But a day and a half? Please. And it was his own van. Who goes out on the job on their own wheels?

When his brother Andy's boss Ras said his friend Old wanted a place watching – he had done this kind of work for him before – he said it could take a while and he had best find someone to help him and they could sleep in shifts. He paid him for two men. But times were tight and Tandy decided to keep it to himself, make a few quid. 'Seventy-five quid a day each,' he said. 'The first day's pay up front. Any part day paid as a full day.'

'That's not a lot,' Tandy said. 'Not for a full twenty-four-hour day.'

'Not bad for sitting on your arse listening to the radio and chewing the fat, though,' Old said. And he had a point. And to show good spirit, he gave him another tenner. 'Get some drinks and sandwiches,' he said. 'And take a few wide-neck bottles to pee in. Use a new one each time. Don't empty them out the door. That'll have the neighbours on the phone in no time, the van starts to stink.'

Sure enough, it was easy money. And at a hundred and fifty a day it was sweet too. But if he'd have known it was to take this long – which to be honest he did – so if he'd known how long a day and a half could feel, he'd have got Andy along for a few hours, give him a couple of score, get some shut-eye in the back of the van. Tell him not to come in his Andy Pandies. Your average chef, he's so glad to be off shift, he's in his street clothes and out the door before the clock's stopped striking the hour. Andy, he was so pleased, so proud of being a chef, he had this nasty habit, when Tandy met him after work, of turning up there in his work clothes. True, he'd done well for himself, and his boss Ras had given him a chance, and Tandy was glad he had. Tandy had sat on the dole in Govan. Andy had got off his arse and ended up in London. But the first year he ended up on the streets. A common dosser. He worked in kitchens like a lot of them do, but after a while he got lucky. He was keen, and instead of going through the agency, one of his bookings took him on the books, trained him up. That was the Sikh guy, Ras. Andy thought the sun shone out of his arse. Tandy didn't know him well enough to know one way or the other, so he'd not trust him until he had reason to. Best way. Andy let it slip one day what the work clothes were called. Tandy nearly wet himself. It seemed strange to Tandy that he had a perfectly good name – Mick – and yet he was always known as Tandy. That was just the way it was. Some guys get called by their last name. Like this guy Old. But if anyone in the family should have been called Tandy, it should have been his brother – hide his fucking silly first name. I christen you Andrew Tandy. Hadn't even given the poor sod a middle name he could have used. That's parents for you. What was it someone said – probably someone in *Viz* magazine – 'They fuck you up, your mam and dad'? Never a truer word. Could have forgot the fucking Scotland's beloved St Andrew for a moment and thought what he was going to be called. Andy Tandy. And now he was Andy the chef. Andy Tandy in his Andy Pandies. What a fucking hoot. Ha fucking ha.

Whatever, though, Andy was a diamond. As soon as he was on his feet, he sent for Tandy, put him up, helped him get a bedsit in the same street. And he knew his way about a bit. Tandy got a few bits of work – this and that, ducking and diving. Keep it the right side of the law if poss; life's complicated enough without getting in wrong with Larry Law. But Andy was touchy. Didn't like getting the piss taken. And as any piss-taker knows, the most fun to be found in piss-taking is when someone doesn't like it being taken. So finding out the trade slang for kitchen whites and checks was manna, pure manna. It had got so Andy thought Tandy was taking the piss if he just said Andy. He had something important to say, he had to say Bro', which sounded posey, but Andy liked it and so did Tandy. Well street. They were a real team when they went out on the bevvy. They'd had T-shirts done with JWA in big letters. Anyone asked they said it was because they were Jocks With Attitude. Then they'd smile at each other and say: '*Respeck.*' He had to say it was the brothers – the black guys – he liked best in this town. Yuppies were scum, most of them. Your average working guys, half of 'em were under the thumb, the rest were so fucking full of themselves, taking the piss out of anything that wasn't a fucking incomprehensible cockney drawl. Your black guys though, real attitude, but with some style. Playing a part, knowing it and doing it right. Not many blacks in Govan, so it was new to him, but he felt right at home. And he had history too. Nearly six thousand singles from Stax, Motown, Philly, Northern Soul, right through to House, Rap, the lot. Probably not fifty white singles in there. Guys looked through that lot, he got '*respeck*' for that alone. He was earning some money with it now, too. Home, he'd tried D Jing, but they wanted all this wankey patter, all these stupid DJ party games. Fuck that, DJs should play records. He got down here and that was what they wanted. He knew his collection. He knew how to get the folks on the floor and dancing, skip from one style to another but keep them dancing. He could get them on the floor like Graeme Souness could get a man on the floor. They were both artists, him and Graeme. What was the old joke? Guy goes in a pub and asks for a

Souness. 'What?' the barman says. The guy says: 'Quick half and I'm off.'

DJing though, pays well, but outside Thursday, Friday, Saturday, not much action, and without his own system – though he had a few quid away he didn't want to splash out until he could get what he really wanted – it limited his openings, so it was still only four or five bookings a month, so he still needed the ducking and diving if he was to pay the rent, eat, have a few jars and still put a bit aside.

Wittering again, Tandy.

He turned on the courtesy light in the van, then turned it off again as it seemed more conspicuous than he imagined it would. He had already read three books and four magazines since he had been there, and he had not been reading in the middle of the night. That was the really difficult time. Flicking round the pirate soul stations trying to find someone who liked the music better than the sound of their own voice. He pulled out his mirror and razor blade and his little – and increasingly empty – packet of speed. He took a little scoop with the end of his blade, dropped it on the mirror, folded up the packet, dropped it back in his pocket. This would be the perfect time for the police to pay a visit, he thought. He was finding it hard to keep the stuff together as he chopped it in the dark; it was more than usually crystalline and bits kept skipping off to the side. He wanted it as fine as he could get it. He estimated that this was his ninth line so far, and though each was only tiny, not half what he would use if he wanted really to speed, the lining of his nose was getting sore. It was getting nearly right, just about fine enough. He was scraping the mirror from the edges to the centre, assuming, as he couldn't see, that there would be something there, when a car came into the road from behind him. He was facing away from the house he was watching – he faced it by day, when he needed to see it, but by night, when the headlights would let him know something was coming, he didn't want anyone suspicious accidentally shining headlights in his face as he sat waiting for them. A big Mercedes pulled into the drive of the house he was watching. There had been a few ins and outs so far, a good-looking woman, mid-thirties. And she might have been going somewhere, it would have been worth his while knowing. But that wasn't what he was hired for. Wait for a man, follow him and see where he goes. Now he was in there, he would probably be there until morning.

Tandy took the cheap pen from his pocket and again took the plastic ink tube and tip out, leaving a clear plastic tube. He lifted the mirror and looked at the ragged line of speed in the street lights. Not very tidy but fine enough. He stuck the tapered end of the tube in one nostril, put the other end to the mirror and took up half the line. He removed the tube, put the mirror down and put his head back as he sniffed, first deeply and then a number of short blasts. Good. It was nice and smooth. Not too much pain, and he could already feel a short rush. He lifted the mirror and as he looked down the length of the tube into the mirror, his eyes caught the door mirror and saw a sweep of light coming out of the drive. He quickly snorted the rest, threw the tube and the mirror to one side, checked the lights were turned off and popped the van in gear, thankful it was already started. He edged it backwards and forwards a little so that the wheels were as fully turned as possible, so that the moment the car went out of sight on the curve, he could flip the van round and get after it. Some of the roads round here were lit, others not. The road they joined as they left this road was not and he thought of risking driving without lights to avoid being seen, but the Merc had big tail-lights, and the brake-lights were dazzling. If the car braked for a corner and he was seen driving without lights, even though he might be taken for a drunk, he would certainly attract attention, and he didn't know how far he would have to follow the car. Old had advised that he fill the tank and keep a couple of gallons spare, just in case.

The car swung out and sped off. As it rounded the corner, Tandy kept his lights off as he turned round in a clean sweep, well inside the kerb. He slipped forward, not too fast. The road they would join had no turn-offs for a quarter of a mile in either direction, apart from the other end of this road. When he was sure it would have pulled off, he drove to the end of the road, still no lights, and saw the Merc, a good quarter of a mile away to the left. He pulled out. He put his foot down a little, glad the speed was rushing round, as it was hard concentrating on staying on the road. He would wait until the Merc rounded a corner, then put his lights on. That way he could have come from anywhere, needn't, indeed probably hadn't, come from his road, but there would be no surprise at seeing the lights pop on, the van appearing from nowhere. A gentle curve appeared, the Merc disappeared, on with the lights. Aahh, relief. The concentration level dropped. He followed round the bend and there it was. No problem. Unless he suspected he was being followed, and why should he, it should be a simple matter now. Of course, the further they went together the dodgier it would get, but he suspected there would be no problem. The first turn they took led back to the main road back to London, so if they were both going the same way, what surprise was there in that – all roads lead to London. If he didn't overtake, fine, the Merc was a big fast car. If the Merc put his foot down and the van tried to keep up, fine, cars do that kind of thing on quiet roads and van drivers are always the most macho on the road.

It went pretty much according to plan. The Merc soon hit the A1 Southbound where it joined a fair amount of traffic and climbed to a steady ninety miles per hour. Fast enough but not exceptional. It did it in the outside lane, but Tandy maintained the same speed in the middle lane, occasionally pulling out to overtake. An approach only likely to attract attention because legally it was the right way to do it. Soon after they reached London proper, the London borough of Barnet, the Merc pulled off, Tandy followed. As they had been unlit before the A1 and he had been one among many once on it, Tandy thought it unlikely the Merc even noticed it was the same van as before. Especially as there was a car between them, which would most likely take a different exit on the roundabout they were waiting to join. It did.

Now they were off the A1, which could have taken them right into the centre, and had come off it before the North Circular, Tandy guessed they were going to somewhere fairly near. They were heading through Woodside Park, still in Barnet and on the Northern

Line, when the Merc pulled off the main road. Tandy hung back, not wanting to crowd, but he was nervous that he would miss it if it turned again. Just as he started to reach the bend, he saw the tail lights of the Merc round another bend. He gunned the van to catch up. As he reached the next bend he saw a sign for a dead end. He stopped the van and got out. The road seemed to be a dog-leg. He lit a cigarette and casually strolled round the corner. He nearly stumbled over the man – nearly forty, slightly above average height, good-looking in a well-groomed kind of way – as he took a briefcase into the house.

'Sorry guv,' he mumbled and continued, without looking back, to the end of the street where, as he expected, there was an exit, but footpath only. He jogged back round a couple of blocks, noted the street name and the house number and headed for home, just wishing he had snorted a little less speed, so he could have flaked out in the back of the van.

Mee glared at the telephone sitting idly back in its cradle. No one is ever just not in any more. Every call has to be paid for. They're either in or it's a machine, or worse, they've forwarded the call to somewhere else they're not. He had just left a short message with Old, his man on the revenge detail. Last time he'd spoken, he'd got, 'working on some leads', whatever that was supposed to mean.

If anything.

His friends, co-conspirators – except, they weren't sharing the bill, so any results he saw as his alone – and co-suckers were giving him more earache. When he moved out to leafy Essex, he made a big deal about how most of the neighbours had their noses in the air, like there was something wrong with his money. How he wasn't going to lose his mates, just because he'd moved out a bit. Him and them, salt o' the fucking earth.

Wrong on all counts, M'lud. They were a bunch of small-time, small-minded, small-all-over losers. All this had woken him up to that sad little factoid and it was time he started to make up for lost time and made a few friends locally. Started to hang about with a bit of class.

The losers'd got fed up with hearing Mel and Kevin making excuses for him. Now they had a new idea. Which was a miracle in itself. Hassle him on the telephone. He could hear the conversation: 'If we all call two or three times a day, that's over twenty calls. Even if they all stop at the secretary, she's going to get on to him, he's going to know it's us, going to annoy him enough he'll get back to us, cough up some dosh, at least remember we're here.' And they were right in that last if in no other regard. Slags. Made him sure of one thing, if nothing else: when the man Old found Goodman, the thing about being in the States was on. Get over there, sitting in some nice hotel in San Diego or somewhere, clocking up recordable items on the room-service tab, but make the call from a call box. Let the slags know where Goodman is, and what happens happens. Let them do him, give him a kicking. And if it goes wrong, like it has every chance of doing with amateurs like them, so be it. No tears shed, and Barry Mee, I'm All Right Jack, alibied up to the fucking eyeballs by the pool in Southern California. Probably a good idea to suggest the man Old does the same. No good to have him getting questioned. Keep him out of it, seeing he's a direct link. Just let the revenge be the Slags' Annual Outing, then kiss them goodbye. They come out with any more crap about the money, tell them, you had him, I didn't. What d'you do about it? Nothing. So get off my fucking back. And if Mel and Kevin came back, they could take a long walk where they chose. His hospitality account was closed. The snappers in the studio had started to complain they felt like they were running peep-shows. Told them if he heard any more, he would be and they'd be on show. They had a point though.

He tried Old again.

Machine.

He hung up.

Old had to work hard to hold back the urge to drive his fists into the fascia of the car. He was stopped on a double yellow line, at least a hundred yards before the next left turn, he was equipped for burglary and the car was broken. Again. After the previous night's drinking, there was also an outside chance he was over the limit still. The day had started badly and got steadily worse. After waking with a thick head, he shook that off with a couple of aspirin-codeine and a scaldingly hot shower. Sam was fine, dressed himself and ate all his porridge. Then, just before Old took him to school, he thrust his hand at Old, asking him to explain what was the object he had found on the floor next to Old's jacket. It was a jade figurine. Drunker than he thought, Old vaguely remembered pocketing it at Warriner's house, so maddened he was by the bragging about the number and quality of his possessions. Another stuff-junkie. The shelves were littered with tasteful trinkets, statuettes, boxes, thises and thats. Now he had the figurine, Old couldn't think how to get it back without looking a complete fool. But if, and more probably when, Warriner noticed it was gone and contacted him, or worse, Toby Norton, then he would be in an even worse position. He resolved, half-heartedly and with little passion, to cut down on the juice. Meantime, he had other matters to take care of. He pushed the car round the corner, fighting a small incline the whole time, hardly blaming the pedestrians who strolled by without helping, as his face looked hostile and angry: a clear window to his feelings.

He felt worse because only a couple of days before, Ras had tried to persuade him again that, especially working as a detective of sorts, he needed a blander and a better car; and last week he had paid ninety pounds for a new head gasket and his mechanic, Yomi, a gloomy Nigerian, had told him the Mini was about to start costing him more money.

He knew he had to let go. He kept the car from sentiment alone – he had bought it while Siobhan was still with him and he was broke. Buying a convertible had not been prudent, but he knew she loved Mini convertibles. Now he had the money to buy a better car and he was also learning to put Siobhan behind him. Time to put the rattles and draughts behind him too.

He consoled himself that he had the money in the bank to get a better car and didn't need to wait until he could sell the one he had. He parked the car up, called the AA to come and pick it up, called a cab to take him home and called Barney to say he was taking the day off and he would pick Sam up after school, Barney didn't need to bother – though he knew Barney wouldn't see it as a chore cancelled but a treat withdrawn.

With any luck, he could get a car before school closed and take Sam for a spin.

'No!' Ras said. 'No, no, no. You're missing the point. You want a car that goes, but you want one that's inconspicuous. So a Saab convertible is as bad as the Mini. Besides, they depreciate like a bastard and they have dodgy alternators. Listen. Vauxhall: Cav or Carlton. Ford: Granada, Sierra, Mondeo. Rover, 2 or 8 series. None of your flash sporty jobs with spoilers either. Cost you on the insurance and get you pulled over for being flash. Omega's still too new, cost you and still get looks. You'll say you'll look like a salesman, I know you, don't say it. That's what you want. Other people don't notice them, police don't notice them. What you need is to grow up, stop thinking of cars as a pose, seeing a ragtop Mini is a pretty lousy pose in any case, and think of it as a reliable way, if not a very fast one, of getting around. Slower than the tube but you can play your own music without annoying the rest of the world and you always get a seat.'

Useless arguing with a man with a strong opinion, thought Old. He thanked Ras and promised to think about it. Trying to reach a consensus, he called Yomi and asked his advice.

'Anything Japanese,' was the beginning and end of his advice, which dovetailed neatly with nothing Ras had said. He tried Barney who said Mercs were the only truly reliable cars on the road, with Vdubs and Volvos trailing in the distance.

With his collection of reasoned and consistent advice, he took a cab to the Romford Road, which had one stretch almost exclusively made up of second hand car dealers, looking for whatever took his fancy for under five thousand, and terribly afraid that, most likely to upset Ras, it would be the first odd-looking, idiosyncratic car he saw. So no one was more surprised than he when, fifty minutes later, he was cruising down the M11 testing a high-mileage Carlton, hence the low price, less than two years old, for only six fifty on top of his five grand absolute max. It was better looking than he remembered standard executive cars being the last time he looked, it was more comfortable than the most comfortable chair in the house, the stereo was better than the one in the house, and keen to be duped by the entirely irrelevant, he suspected it was the in-car CD player that finally persuaded him. It felt solid, handled like a dream, was as bland as Ras could possibly have wanted, had a five-speed manual box, and so many bits of it were entirely electric or power-assisted, he was mildly surprised when he found he was actually expected to drive it himself.

Another day, another chance. He parked the shiny new Carlton round the corner. If there was a problem, he wasn't about to lose the car – he could say he came by public transport. The registration documents would take a few days to come through with the change of ownership and he didn't want his new toy impounded as evidence before he'd even had the thing a whole day.

Old guessed the house would be a rental property. Tandy had given him the address but also described it to him, and given him the lay-out of the road. There were two locks, as usual, one mortice, one Yale. On his first pass, Old knocked on the door to check if there was anyone in. If there was, the day was dead. His luck was in. While he was there, he checked the mortice with his knee, giving it a firm push.

No movement. Damn. Still, if there's any justice, Old thought, it shouldn't be too hard. He had spent a couple of hours the previous evening, getting through the dummy door in his cellar. By now, if he was really pushed, he could make a decent living as a burglar. A straight Yale normally took him no longer than someone with a key. The mortice though, he saw on his second pass, was a five-pin Assa. Old had one on his practice door. He pulled the right pick from his set. Two years for that alone. The courts looked very hard at professional lock-picks. They knew most burglars were opportunists: in through the window, either one left open – summer is high season for burglary – or smash or force the thing, get the video and the CD player, a few CDs if possible, and out. They'd flog the video for forty, the CD for twenty and they'd go and buy a quarter of blow and a bit of speed. Professionals go through the door, and lock it from the inside: nothing worse than being disturbed on the job; that brings the risk of violence, and that might mean getting caught, as you never know who is good at violence. That was why many burglars now carried a shooter. The chances of being caught on the job were slight, especially with the door locked, but you had to leave some time. A gun would paralyse almost anyone with fear and a man could leave the job, lie low a bit, and go on to burgle again. Most of these precautionary guns were never even pulled, though they upped the stakes because getting caught carrying was a dangerous thing. Old knew that if a burglar who was carrying set off an alarm or the neighbours noticed something or for whatever reason the police were called, the gun would be hidden on the premises rather than risk the extra time. Old knew all this, and still he was carrying a gun. The situation for him was different. As an ex-member of the Army and with his background in security, for his own safety he had a firearms licence and was allowed to carry a concealed weapon. Further, he knew that his only chance of police involvement was if he was reported by a stranger, which made it doubly important that he get in fast. Whoever was working from this house, Tapley, whether or not he was Goodman by another name, was unlikely to go rushing off to the police. Old knew he would rather get in, find out what he could and get out to plan further, but if Tapley turned up, so be it.

He held the pick in his pocket as he rounded the corner. He had it facing the right way, his fingers warm. If aligning the pick in his hand took a second, as well to have it ready – seconds were the measure for a lock-pick. Once minutes came in, it was time to walk. The pick was a fine surgical steel bar with a sprung rod attached to the centre, coming off at an angle, and with a little flare at the end, like an italic *y*. At the bottom of the down stroke, the pick was slightly flattened to allow a better grip. About three inches long, the thumb could control the movement of the sprung half-section, while the main rod held back any pins already pushed back or turned. It was mainly a pick for a Yale-type sprung lock, but Old found it was also the best for this type of mortice lock. He strode confidently to the door, put the pick in the lock and closed his eyes. He counted time to check himself.

One, two, three – *one!* One, two – *two!* One, two, three – *three!* Going well. One, two, three, four, five, come on, seven, eight, please, ten, eleven – *four!* One, two, three, four – *five.* He withdrew the lock and checked by pushing against the door with his knee. Done in under twenty seconds: he knew his was a slightly fast count. He pulled a long, slim piece of sprung sheet metal from under his coat – two seconds – and slid it through the door frame until he found the Yale – two seconds. He pushed hard – under a second and in. He closed the door behind him. This time he didn't lock it from the inside – the only person who could disturb him was someone he wanted to meet. The door was secured with him on the inside, less than thirty seconds after his arrival, no damage. That was a good time. He had done better at home but pressure counts. A good burglar could now hit the place for jewellery and money and be out in under ten minutes and if he was professional enough, it might not be noticed he had been until the next time the jewellery or cash is needed.

And Old, not being a burglar, good or otherwise, could do whatever he wanted.

He strolled round the house first, getting a feel. Whether by accident or design, to Old it felt absolutely typical. Typical of how he expected a just-about-suburban, fairly large, turn-of-the-century terraced house to feel. It wasn't a cheap part of London and to afford it, the occupant would either have to be doing OK or have been there a long time. It was furnished fairly expensively, but without any real character. No one had thought too long or too hard about the decorations, all rooms being professionally decorated in pastel colours, sofas upholstered similarly. The house was rented, Old had already checked, and probably from someone entirely innocent of Tapley's schemes, it seemed. In a few weeks' time they would be pleasantly surprised when he skipped, rent up to date, leaving rent in advance and a deposit. Tapley would want to leave no trail. The landlord was the only person aside from Tapley who would come out of the deal on top, and he wouldn't even know he had been involved in a deal.

Old checked the cupboards. There was enough food to look plausible if anyone opened them looking for a glass or a cup, but not enough to stand a good look from someone checking the place out thoroughly. Lots of tinned tomatoes and dried pasta, plenty of chutneys and sauces; Old guessed that whatever eating went on there would mostly be take-away, and this was confirmed by the kitchen waste-bin, which had empty Chinese cartons and pizza boxes folded and crammed in, topped off with empty cans of Marston's Pedigree Bitter. At least they can pick a beer, Old thought.

In the sitting-room, which Old guessed would be where the business took place when the guys were invited round, or when they were invited round to socialize earlier on in the sting to assure them of Tapley's solidity, the obvious-looking stuff – the electronics – looked expensive and flashy: like the target marks. There was a large-screen stereo TV and video and a NAD stereo with enormous speakers, and above it a rack of perhaps eighty CDs which could have been selected by the computer of a commercial adult-oriented rock station, right down to the almost unexpected bits – a bit of Miles Davis and Stan Getz, and a tiny smattering of popular classical, some of the more media-hyped performers, leavening the main diet of Steely Dan, Fleetwood Mac, Luther Vandross, Terence Trent d'Arby. It looked plausible enough as the record collection of a mid-thirties baby boomer, and it was probably just that. Why fake it when you can just bring a few of your own CDs?

The room was tidy enough – not show-house tidy but not stake-out untidy either. There was a pile of magazines by the sofa; a TV guide, a soft rock magazine and a couple of car magazines. Old picked up the most read-looking of these and skimmed it to see if it wanted to fall open. It was too thin for that but there was a well read section on mid-range Mercedes.

Bingo.

Old lifted the sofa cushions, home of spare magazines and half-interesting junk mail the first world over. Under one of the cushions was a pile of Mercedes brochures: ones for the whole range, ones for different models, in both English and German. Now there was no doubt. One way or the other, Goodman or not, Old had found someone doing the scam – the scam he was after. That was a big step. And under threat of being shopped, there was a good chance that, if he knew how to find Goodman, he would spill it. Old decided to confront Tapley mob handed – less risk of any mishaps. He would come back with Ras and Tandy. If Tapley was in, fine; if he was out, Old could break in again and they could wait. Grand. One way or the other, Tandy being free most of the time, it seemed, they could come whenever Ras could get away. Tapley would really have little choice. Three to one, and besides, they could break up his little game, now they knew who he was and where his family lived. Just the threat of blowing the con should be enough.

Assuming it was exactly the same con, now the house was rented, he had presumably bought the Merc for the lead mark and was waiting for him to reel in the others. Which meant – assuming Old was right and Tapley had bought the first car – that Tapley was now around twelve thousand down on the cost of the car plus whatever expenses there were in snaring the lead mark, whether it be on a flash holiday, in a flash bar, whatever.

It was better if there was no sign he had been there. Apart from the cupboards and the bin he had touched nothing but the cushions on the sofa. He patted and smoothed the cushions, assuring himself that they were as he found them. He gave the room a last look, checked his pockets to be sure, though he knew he had taken nothing out, that he had everything with him. He raised his hand to the lock and immediately saw a shape through the mottled glass in the window. The shape grew as it walked up the front garden path. Two shapes.

Old hurried into the kitchen where there was an island unit he could hide behind – to climb the stairs would be too noisy. He had to hope that Tapley was irregular in his mortice fastening habits and would not think it too strange that his was unlocked. At least not so strange that it would stop him entering the house.

Old heard the mortice turn, then the Yale, then a muffled curse as the door didn't open. He had locked the mortice, and would probably assume he had simply failed to unlock it properly. Old was often surprised by the number of people who seemed to be completely unable to master locks, even ones with which they were familiar and with their own keys. It seemed Tapley was one of them. He waited until they were inside the house, the door closed behind them, before he made a move. He had at first intended to wait until they both came into the kitchen, but if only one came in, as was fairly likely if Tapley came in to make a drink, then he had the two of them in separate rooms. And he didn't know if the person with Tapley was a mark or not. Or what name he was using. Whatever he did, he decided, it would be best if he could find out a way not to blow Tapley's scam away, at least, not until he had what he wanted. That way he could get his co-operation. He wanted first to get a good hard look – past the cosmetic details of level of tan, colour of hair, style of clothes. He wanted to be sure his man was or wasn't Goodman. When Tandy had trailed him here he got only the briefest of descriptions, from a brush past on a poorly lit pavement by night. But it hadn't sounded quite right. There had been superficial similarities – hair colour and general square-chinned good looks – but Old put the good looks down to natural selection. So many cons, from what Old had learned, picked up their trade as gigolos that the looks came with the job for the most part. He was fairly hopeful, given the match in scam, that this would be his man, but there was not too long to wait.

The two men were in the hall and were making general disrobing noises as Tapley offered to take the other man's coat and there was a vague puffing and panting.

Old was still half planning his next move, half panicking. No matter how much a situation is planned, no matter how experienced the person, there is still bound to be an element of blind fear and panic in being found in someone's house, clearly having broken in. It was important to seize control of the situation. He decided to confront them, whoever they were, just as they both came into the kitchen.

Old held his revolver loosely as he rose, but as he and the two men saw each other, he brought his gun up, pointed it at a space between the two of them and remained silent. A few more seconds: he could find a line on the back of the response, which, hopefully, would tell him whether the man with Tapley, who looked for all the world like a dim film heavy from an old Shepperton thriller, was a fellow con or a mark. It was very unlikely that he would be neither – this was a place of work for Tapley and socializing was not on the agenda. As for Tapley, he was certainly not Goodman. Still he would be useful to talk to. In the meantime, the silence stretched, and the situation made a slight shift from the silent and terrifying to the terrifying, surreal, not quite under control and worryingly unpredictable.

It seemed Tapley had made the same calculation – that he would see who was threatening him before he built the lie for the defence. The big man looked panicky as his eyes flitted from the gun to Old's face, which was as impassive as he could manage, and across to Tapley, still and silent, but with beads of sweat beginning to form at his hairline which was, as Frankie Silvester promised, beginning to grey.

'The fuck's the crack here, Bob?'

The relief at the broken silence was palpable. And the silence could stay broken. Bob, not Tapley. Silvester said one of Tapley's aliases was Bob Gold. So here they were, Tapley caught on the job with a mark, which meant he should go some way to keep the scam intact: time to blow it up later if he had to.

'*Wer ist das?*' ('Who is that?') Old barked in a clean, accentless German that he had picked up while training as an intelligence officer in a base near Hanover – supposedly home of the purest German.

'*Sollte ich das nicht fragen? Wer sind Sie? Was machen Sie hier?*' ('Isn't that my question? Who are you and what are you up to?') Tapley/Gold replied, quick on his feet.

Old looked at the fat man who was now looking entirely lost. He pointed the gun straight at the man, who visibly shuddered and tried to take a step back, banging into the kitchen door. The man was blinking furiously.

'What is your name?' Old asked the man, in a not too heavily accented English.

'Terry Craig!' he blurted, 'it's Terry Craig. I'm a mate, a friend of Bob's, we're just doing a bit of business, no, I popped round for a beer, I'm a mate, I've no money on me. The fuck are you? I want to go. Can I go? Who the fuck is he, Bob?'

He was gabbling, and Tapley had begun slowly to shake his head when Craig mentioned he was there to do business. Old kept the gun pointed at him.

'Lie!'

'No mate. This kind of thing's not my style, not my speed at all. I've never had a gun pointed at me and I

163

don't like it. I wouldn't lie to you mate. What was that, Kraut? You a Kraut? German I'm sorry. It's about the Merc, isn't it? I bought a Merc off of Bob and he was going to get me a few more. I knew it was too sweet.'

Tapley's face now wore a mask of the purest contempt. He was still forced to crack a smile when Old spoke again.

'Herr Craig, I meant lie down. Lie on the floor, face down.'

Almost before he had finished speaking, Craig had done as he asked.

'*Sie auch!*' ('You too!') he said to Tapley, in what was plainly an order. Tapley obeyed, but with a little more decorum beside the mad drop to the floor of Craig.

Old took two pairs of plastic wrist-ties from his pocket. He secured both men's wrists, then put his gun away. He turned Craig over and sat him up, leaning him against the kitchen wall.

'You should be more comfortable that way, Herr Craig. I will speak to you later. I can assure you that you will come to no physical harm. I am employed by Mercedes as a security consultant. They have had trouble with Mr Gold before, but he is hard to shake off. Like a disease,' he said, smiling wanly at his unfunny little witticism. 'I will speak to you later.'

Tapley looked at him quizzically. Old knew he had him confused now – as in reality his scam wasn't anything to do with Mercedes. Which meant Old knew his scam but was willing not to make Tapley out a liar. When Old said Tapley was hard to shake off, he was leaving the chink of light for Tapley to believe he could still keep his man in the scam.

Old pulled Tapley to his feet and waved him towards the front room.

'*Und jetzt, sind wir daran,*' ('And now it's our turn,') he said to Tapley. He turned to Craig. 'A little privacy. We cannot have the world knowing Herr Gold's little tricks. Bad for business.'

In the sitting-room, Old helped Tapley down on to a comfortable chair. He selected a disc – *The Best of Sam and Dave* – and put it on a moderate volume to cover any conversation that leaked through the two closed doors between them and Craig.

Tapley nodded his appreciation and Old knew he meant thanks for the protection from his mark's eavesdropping, not thanks for the choice of music.

'*So, was ist los?*' ('What's going on?') Tapley asked.

Old replied, keeping his clipped German English: 'You would prefer we conduct our exchange in English. It is comfortable for me. How is your German?'

'*Warum ist es nie verstandlich das Auslander kann Ihr echtes Deutsche spreche egal?*' Tapley asked.

'*Warum verstehen die Deutschen nie, dass es Ausländer durchaus möglich ist, Deutsch zu beherrschen?*' ('Why can Germans never understand that it is possible for foreigners to speak their language properly?') Old replied.

'Isn't that what I just asked?'

'It's what you meant to say, but correct.'

Old switched back to his English with his own native East London, not a strong accent, after his years away, especially as an officer, but still recognizably London, if without the usual glottal stops of his neighbours, and a million miles from the lifeless perfection of the German English he had been using.

'With grammar like that, it's no surprise Germans want to speak to you in English. Still, be enough to fool the punters, eh? Get you by if you do try to hook anyone speaks proper German. I was you I'd invest a grand on a Goethe Institut course.'

Tapley smiled and shook his head.

'Very good German, yours. Perfect is it? Mine's not good enough to say for sure how good anyone else's is. Or are you going to turn me round again, say you're German, can speak English well enough to do regional accents?'

'No, but to tell the truth, my German *is* perfect,' Old said immodestly – he was very proud of his languages, too proud to cover it up when praise was offered. 'And I can do a few accents – my natural one, the one I just used, is *Hoch*; I can do *Mittel*, *Bayerisch*, and the yokels up by the Danish border. Business?'

'I can't wait.'

'I've been hired to find someone who does a clever little scam with flash German cars. You know the one.'

Tapley smiled.

'You sure? How do you know what I know?'

'Sorry, wouldn't want to make any assumptions. I could always ask your man Craig, see if it rings any bells with him. I thought we were being friendly. So far I've gone out of my way not to foul your pitch. One word and that's all gone. A word like 'con' would probably do the job, don't you think?'

'That's the first thing I want to know. Why haven't you blown me out?'

'From now, I'm going to ask the questions, but so's you know, I want answers. You and I both know your man Craig is going to be scared and angry, but you've already got him in, and you'll probably be able to convince him to stay. I might even have helped you – knowing Merc are on to you but they still leave you alone, having to resort to sending heavies round, all that, shows you're a few steps ahead of them, smarter than Merc. That's smart. Then you swear the guy to secrecy, say it looks bad a firm like that, despatching hired heavies, but if the police get involved it queers it for everyone. You know you've got your pitch half worked out already, so give yourself a chance to use it. Tell me what I want to know and I'm out the door. Lie to me and I'll fuck it all up, just like that,' he said, clicking his fingers.

'Get on with it, then,' Tapley said, sounding far chirpier than Old thought he had any right to be.

Old sat on a sofa facing Tapley.

'I said I was working for someone who had a scam like yours worked on them. Obviously it wasn't you or we'd not be going about it like this. I need to know if there's anyone else runs the same scam. The scam I'm after was BMWs, he worked under the name Goodman, had a woman, called herself Davida, worked with him, whether it was his wife or not I don't know. Considering the way she fitted into the scam, I have to say it seems unlikely.' He looked at Tapley expectantly.

Tapley shook his head.

'It's not like there's a blagger's union you know. It's a hard crime to trace.'

Old raised his eyebrows.

'OK, so you're a smartarse, but cons on the whole don't get caught. Any I've heard of in the nick, the whole place wants to hear their story, it's all so damn slick and there's so few get caught. But without getting caught and meeting people inside, you really wouldn't get to know anyone except completely by chance, if someone tried to scam you, and the chances of that are just about non-existent. It's just not the kind of work where there's a whole lot of networking goes on.'

Old scowled.

'Is that it then? You can't give me any more than that?'

'Look, I can see the position I'm in, I've got no levers. If I had anything, I'd give it to you. I just don't. I can't tell you what I don't know. Matches up my fingernails and I wouldn't be able to tell you any more. I just do my scams and keep to myself.'

'You haven't helped me at all then.'

'Sorry.'

'So you've no one to tip off, telling them I'm on my way. Part of the reason I wanted you sweet, I wanted to be sure if I got a name from you, you'd keep schtum if I did. There's no name, I might as well fuck you up.' He stood. 'Herr Craig awaits.'

He watched Tapley close his eyes and flinch.

'No, wait a minute. All this networking, kind you get inside, never know when it might come in handy. You might be losing out. And you'd certainly be more useful to me in the future if you knew a few names. I know a way you can get to meet a few people in the crime game; failures mind.'

He picked up the telephone and dialled McCreery's number, dialling correctly so that if Tapley decided to check if his bluff was being called, he could check last number redial and see how close he had come. Old wasn't bluffing, which Tapley couldn't know, but if he turned out to be useless, he was perfectly happy to have him go down.

'D.I. McCreery, please.' He waited a few seconds. 'Hello, Pat Old here, yeah, about that con thing I was talking to you about . . .'

'Des Silvester,' Tapley interrupted.

'Yeah, I got the appointment, talked to the slag, I just wanted to let you know the crack. He was pretty useful, in a slimy sort of way. I get anything positive out of it, or any useful names, I'll let you know, OK?'

Whatever had happened to cheer McCreery up the last time Old spoke to him had, miraculously, not gone sour. Normally, he would have chewed his ear off for daring to call with anything so insubstantial as a thank you. But he thanked Old and said he was looking forward to the results. Old thought it must be a woman, a promotion and a big collar at least. He gave a beaming smile to Tapley as he hung up on McCreery.

'Des Silvester?'

Tapley nodded. 'He's a good operator. Has a dopey brother, nearly got him in trouble last year, been bailing the guy out for years. But the one thing you can say about Frankie – that's the brother – he can keep his mouth shut.'

'So where can I find my man Des Silvester, or his brother?' He knew as he asked that this was no wild goose chase. After all, he had been so near on his very first call, seeing Frankie Silvester, and it was he had sent Old chasing shadows, and placing a friend, an associate, whatever, at risk. Old again thought about honour among thieves. It always amazed him that such a chimera could be so widely believed, given that nine out of every ten collars come from bought information.

'Frankie's in the nick. Last I heard about Des, he'd retired, been doing this scam for three years or so, said it was pushing it to do it any more, he was going to take a nice break, look for something new, try and work up a new one. Maybe the big one that'd let him out for good. Course, we're always after the big one, it's what gives us a stiff in this game, but Des is good. And it's not impossible. If anyone thinks one up, it'll be Des.'

TEN

'So I guess one way or another, after I cut them loose then linked them through the arms of a rocking chair, they got to know each other a bit better. I mean, I couldn't have Tapley charging down the street after me, I expect he knew I wouldn't get the gun out in the street, still less use it, and the last thing I wanted was him clocking me getting in the car. I expect he's got damn near as many ways of finding out what's what from a bit of something and nothing like a car plate as I have. So if it only gave me a couple of minutes, it was enough.'

Ras was trying to look down his nose at his moustache and beard, trying to flick bits of crisp out that he had missed when he combed his fingers through. Eventually he shrugged and left it.

'Now there's the same palaver, I guess, to find your man, except this time you're sure it's actually your man Goodman, right?'

'About the size of it.'

'Then . . .?'

Old paused, looked Ras in the eyes, held the look. They both knew the other had reservations. They understood the dilemma.

'Hand him over is what I'm paid for, but I don't like it, and I don't want to do it. There's a couple of good reasons why I shouldn't, but only one of them is a good business reason.'

Ras raised his eyebrows, urging Old to say what he

had to say. Old glanced at his empty pint, Ras's an inch behind.

'Directors again?'

'Sure.'

Glasses full apart from the introductory swallow, they had time for an undisturbed attack on the problem. Late in a session, arguments and discussions interrupted by a trip for a round have a nasty habit of resuming on some wild tangent from where they were unwisely left.

'First is, be honest, he's a slime. I don't like being involved with him, but that's dishonest. The case is damn interesting, it's challenging, it's fun. I'm enjoying the whole thing. Beats missing spouses hollow and I know, I've looked for enough. So if I didn't want his money, I shouldn't have taken the job.'

'Which is what Satya said to a T.'

'And, of course, she's right,' Old added.

'So the real reason, the honest reason, is?'

'They're amateurs, and you know how dangerous they can be. Mee can afford it. He sees it as a bit of dirty business and his pride was hurt. But he knows it was more to the others. He lost his face and he wants to get it back by handing them Goodman on a plate – when he also puts himself back as top dog, because they all want to get their hands on him but it's Mee makes it happen.'

'Good old Bazza.'

'*Genau.*' ('Exactly.') There were few ex-servicemen who did not know a few words of German, and Ras had a gift for languages with French, German, Hindi, Punjabi and Arabic. There were few of Old's and Ras's common friends who did not find it intensely annoying when the two of them made little asides in German, occasionally lapsing into whole conversations if they thought no one was listening or if they thought someone might be listening they would rather didn't. For them it was a simple reminder, a renewal of their common bond, their history. They didn't serve together, though that was what they had planned, but their paths crossed, and most importantly they both served, and that would never be just one more bit of the past among many.

'Which means if I hand Goodman over – this is all assuming I find him, assuming again that Tapley keeps his mouth shut – then Mee will hand him on to his mates. He's not as daft as he looks. He might not be brilliant but cunning is another thing and he has that in spades. I'd say as soon as we hand Goodman, or his details, over to Mee, he'll be off the scene, and his soft-headed mates get their hands on Goodman and he's mincemeat. They'll all want to get a couple in, no one will want to be seen holding back, one or two will want to show off their especially bull-sized balls, and before you know it, this relatively harmless con is maimed or dead, and everywhere you look for the last month my name is crawling over the scene. Have the best alibi in the world on the day itself, I could be having lunch with Elvis in front of the world's press and it won't stop them having me up on conspiracy.

'Win or lose, I lose. McCreery is useful to me, and a few of the others I met at Bramshill, and he'd not come near me. Besides which, if the punishment is to fit the crime, that's not right for taking a few quid off a few greedy bastards who were only in it for the money, who weren't hurt at all.'

'You want the punishment to fit the crime, that's what you want?' Ras asked, beaming widely. Old nodded and waited as Ras took a deep swallow of beer and wiped his mouth and the surrounding hair with the back of his hand.

'Good. Listen.'

ELEVEN

Old had suggested that they meet for dim sum again but Norton insisted they meet at Now & Zen. Old knew that this meal would be on him, and given the importance he knew Norton placed on money, and knowing how willing Norton was usually to flash it about, stand him meals, that the bill would top a ton, very, very comfortably; Norton would make sure of that, hear those lobsters squeal. He reasoned that this was Toby force-feeding him humble pie, with langoustines in ginger, but that it meant that he was also forgiven.

He had an hour and a half before he was due to meet Norton and he had arranged a quick get-together with Barry Mee. He was not looking forward to the meeting but it was unavoidable. Mee had been pestering him for results and, whatever his reservations, his qualms, Mee was paying and he had an obligation to tell him what he was getting for the money. What made him more apprehensive about the meeting was that he intended to warm Mee up, give him a few hints about what was to come, or more to the point, not to come – Goodman. He wanted to get him used to the idea that when he found Goodman, and by now he fully expected to find him, he would not be handing him over. He did not anticipate a sunny reaction.

Mee frowned. He took a small sip of his coffee and peered across the top of the cup through half-closed eyes.

'You've been on this a fortnight now, right?'

Old confirmed this. It was thirteen days, but who wanted to quibble.

'That's impressive. When you say you're sure you'll find him but you can't hand him over, you mean you've already found him, but you want to see my reaction when you say I can't have him. I'm right, aren't I?'

'No, I'm afraid you're not. What I said was about the size of it. I've found what I need to find, which is a name. It shouldn't be more than a couple of days now before I have him. I did need to see your reaction, though.'

'You're right. If I had him, I'd be forced to hand him over to those clowns who've been giving me nothing but earache for weeks. And if they got their hands on him, there's no saying what would happen.'

'And, as I'm sure you know, however far we both were when he got the kicking that was coming, we would both be linked in. Soon as the police got a good look, I'd be in the picture, and there's no client privilege attached to this job. Officially speaking, there's no such thing as a private detective, no licence or anything. You're just paying a fellow citizen, or subject, I should say, to do a job. I have no more client privilege than a plumber. So your name'd be in the picture pretty sharp. Even if I kept my mouth shut, they'd be into my records, the whole big thing. Soon as look, we'd both be in as deep shit as your idiot mates – maybe worse – we'd be in line for conspiracy, and it's one of those quirky things in the law that it seems to be worse to conspire to do something than actually to do it.'

'I could take offence on their behalf but you know something? I really can't be bothered.' Mee said, in a quietly amused voice. 'So first thing, I'll pay the bill so long as you find him, no worries there. And don't lie, I knew you had thought about that, same as you'd thought about you don't like the idea of taking my money in the first place – think I don't know when someone sits there like there's a smell under their nose, like someone's farted and they're trying to pretend they haven't noticed but they can't act for shit. Frankly, I don't give a fuck. There's no kiddy porn, nothing weird, they're straightforward fuck books, wank mags. Pictures of nearly-sex and stories about sex. I know you wank, I know you imagine stuff while you do it. I know that because you're a man. All I do is get people to pose and write stories, save people the trouble of all that imagining. Give a wank a bit of spark. So don't be so sickly prim and invoice me for the work to date.'

Old couldn't find the words. He knew most of what Mee had said was true enough and that it was a prudery that was not normally in character that led him to think the way he did in the first place. It was probably the fact that, though everyone masturbates, buying a magazine was like planning it, giving body and recognition to the fact: everyone spits now and then – if you have to run unexpectedly, there's often the need – but that doesn't mean you buy a spittoon. The magazines, the deliberateness, the planning, the whole industry and finally the purchase were solid evidence of the fact: men are wankers – Old, Ras and at least the male section of the telephone directory – and by despising the industry, it was possible to pretend the fact was not exactly there. He had gone to see Mee feeling defensive and found nothing but agreement and understanding from Mee at his most amenable. Now he felt chastised for a belief which he had felt was on firm ground.

It was all a bit heavy, not the kind of thing he would usually worry about too much – one of the side effects of working for a pornographer, he guessed.

Mee broke the atmosphere by pouring more coffee. If he drank it the whole time the way he drank it whenever Old met him, the only way he would get to sleep, Old thought, was with the Scotch he drank almost as copiously.

As if he read Old's mind, he put the coffee pot back under the drip filter on the sideboard in his office and pulled out a bottle of Knockando.

'Too much coffee can lay heavy on the stomach, do you not find?' he said, pouring two healthy measures, without bothering to ask if Old wanted one. Old was not about to get picky; he had only tasted Knockando a couple of times, had never got round to buying a bottle – so many to buy, so little time – and he found it was one of the subtlest malts available.

Mee shoved his nose deep into the glass and inhaled deeply.

'Nose as fine as the best cognac and home-grown to boot. Life is sweet.' He took a small sip, smiled and looked Old in the eye.

'Now the question is, given that you've taken my money to find him, and assuming you do, what happens next to make me feel better about the money I spent and the money I lost to him, and the face? Not forgetting the lost face.'

'The revenge factor.'

Mee patted the table, like a snooker player silently applauding his opponent's shot.

'On the button. I didn't employ you for nothing then, did I? You have your eye on the ball, I like that. What are we going to do that's going to make me smile and make Goodman sick? Where are we going to stick the knife, and how are we going to do it nice and legal?'

'There's two ways to go about it that I can see. One's simple, the other's not. One's vicious, the other's subtle. One'll hurt him straight off, the other will hurt his pride, his face, and his wallet. And I think we can be sure he's fond of his wallet.'

'I like the second, already. Run me through them both, though – I'm paying; I may as well see the menu.'

'First is quick and easy. Gets me off your payroll, does to him what's never happened before and it's legal as can be. We shop him. You press charges now. Tell the boys in blue the truth – that you thought you'd seen the last of it, so what was the point in reporting it? You can prove at least part of the story – you must have reported your money stolen on holiday for the insurance, yes?'

'Yes.'

'And you can get the rest of the lads to press charges along with you. If any of them are nervous about the funny money, it doesn't matter, I'm positive it wouldn't come up, but if they want to stay out, fine. The cleaner the money stolen, the worse the crime, in a jury's eyes at least. That's the only problem with it. He wouldn't get bail – too easy for him to disappear. We could give them evidence of all his false names and stuff. But when it came to trial, they'd be sure to ask a good few questions about you. You wouldn't look good – you know that, right?'

Mee nodded.

'It's been known for juries to dismiss just because they didn't like the victim,' Old continued. 'It's a risk. The jury went that way, he's looking at maybe three months in a remand nick, wearing his own clothes, then he's on the streets. Even convicted, he'd be looking at two to three years tops. Could be out in a year with a low sentence and good behaviour.'

'It'd fuck his career as a conman though, wouldn't it?' Mee said. 'All the false IDs in the world are no use to you once your prints are on the record. You can't do a con wearing surgical gloves.'

'True, but looking at a guy I was talking to couple of days ago, works in the same business, he had to have assets worth over half a million, just the ones I traced, and he said Goodman was better and had been at the game longer, so if he's fucked up as a conman, he could retire. Or he could move into long cons.'

Mee raised his eyebrows in question.

'It doesn't matter, financial cons, done at arm's length, with lawyers all over the shop. Chances are, though, he'd just relax, spend the money. That's what he'd be looking at – that's the punishment. It'd take away his clean sheet, give him a year inside, but that'd be about the size of it. Quite a bit of pain, but is it what you want? It's not like we'd be hurting him too badly, and you'd get revenge but little else.'

'I know what you're getting at. Whatever you think of my business, it's legit. All above board. Has to be or the boys'd be down my neck. It is possible to make lots of clean money in this game. Look at Paul Raymond – supposed to be the richest bloke in the country. Might have made a lot of it in property but this is where he started and believe me it's where he still makes plenty.'

'Did I miss something? I thought we'd got over that.'

'I'm getting there. What I'm saying is, I'm legit. So there should be no reason why I don't like that option. But there is. I was brought up grassing was wrong.'

'So was I,' Old interrupted, 'but I grew up. I got over it. I learned villains are a real problem. Grasses might not be very nice on the whole, but villains are worse and grasses keep the numbers down. Besides, this wouldn't be grassing, it'd be reporting a crime. You're the victim. Grassing's a different matter.'

'True, but like you said it's not going to hurt him too hard. And it just doesn't feel right. Let's hear the other.'

'I think this is the way you'll go. You need to bankroll me a bit, give me some large folding for effect. Let me explain. It's a peach.'

Toby Norton had the good grace to be open about the apology he expected. As soon as they were seated, he cleared the decks.

'You were a wanker the other night. So is he, but I already knew it about him. You were a pain, and with a client of mine, when both him and me were doing you a favour. Which means today, the treat's on you, shitface. Now what do you want; what's the favour of the day?'

'Seeing it was the financials gave me a lead on the last guy, Tapley, and he's given me the name I need, could you do the same job as before? I check Companies House records on my machine, pass the results over to you if his name crops up, and if it's all the funny offshore stuff that comes up, like there's a good chance it will be, you put all that through your machine, OK?'

'Fine. In fact, seeing the Companies House stuff is on my machine as well, I can just do a universal search, ask all databases to look for the name, and save you a bit of time. That's it?'

'Not quite. Once I know where he is, I don't want to go barging in on him all young, dumb and full of come. I want to do it with kid gloves. I need to meet him, nice and business-like, put a proposition to him.'

'You're going to try and con a con.'

It was a bald statement not a question.

'Not quite, though it is a nice thought. Ras has kind of fallen in love with these cons. He's been doing a lot of thinking and he's come up with the sweetest thing. The deal is, we go in with Goodman – Silvester, got to get used to the new name – on this gorgeous scam. It needs him as the front, me playing a part. Ras is in the background, kind of executive producer, setting up the scenes. If it works, there could be a few hundred grand in it. If it doesn't, there'll be gore on the floor.'

'Your man the porn king went for this? I thought he had something a bit more dramatically vengeful in mind.'

'He did, but he's not as daft as you might expect.'

'As *you* might expect. I don't worry myself about the morals and the attitudes, I'm willing to think well of the abilities at least of anyone who can make themselves worth over twelve million before they hit forty.'

'He's not!'

'He surely is. I did a bit of checking, even punted him on the phone. Not this time, but I think he's warm. I think he might try me out with fifty or so, let me play a few games with it as a warm-up for something serious.'

'Grand?'

'What else?'

'So why all the fuss about whatever he lost, twenty-five grand or so?'

'That's what twelve million's made of. Just short of five hundred of those. That old saw about watching the pennies, comes true every time. When it comes to twenty-five grand, you can expect anyone to watch as close as can be, at least when it's their own money. And then there's that pride thing, and you know about that as well as anyone: you and Ras and your overdeveloped sense of pride, face, all that male stuff.'

'And you don't get testosterone-pumped over the size of your margins?'

'Maybe I do, but I don't come over all macho about it. It's the job. One way or another, you're a private detective, and you've let too much of the bullshit attached rub off. Either that or it was always there and the job lets you let it all hang out.'

'Back to it. Whatever you're up to, Mee's putting up some money. So he's certainly up for a risky punt. The idea is, he gets the payback he was after originally, right?'

Old nodded to confirm this.

'So aside from everything else, if he's up for that kind of a punt, he's a warmer prospect for me, especially when he learns I've had my finger in this pie and helped you pull this off.'

'Assuming we do pull it off,' added Old.

'When I've helped you find him, how do you suppose you're going to get the head-to-head?'

'I want you to sell him a hot deal.'

Norton paused, soaking this in.

'You want to explain the con to me, then I sell it to him, me who's never met him and he doesn't know from Adam and he jumps up and says, "Okey Dokey, I'll be right over with a bag full of money"?'

'That's not it. I'm going to be straight with him. Straight*ish* anyway; straight up to a very precisely defined point. Tell him I'm from Mee, how Mee wants him to get the crap beaten out of him then shop him, tell him how I was hired to find him, which he probably knows already from his brother, and tell him I don't want to get involved with any of this beating-up crap, so to prevent it I won't give Mee the name, instead I want the money. Then I tell him, also true, that I know he's going to be reluctant to just cough up some hard-earned, but that I've got the prettiest scam that will, if it works, give him enough to cover Mee's losses, plus a bit for the face – that again – including his stooges – up to him if he passes it along to them or pockets it – and there should still be enough in the pot for him to make as much as he would on a few BMW scams, because this scam is big. His only real alternative to paying up out of his reserves – an idea he's naturally predisposed to loathe – is to sing for his supper. And the reason I want in on this is, I tell him, because doing all the hunting for him, I just found the whole thing so damn exciting, it gives me a hard on – and that's not just telling a story, it's the way it was.

'I tell him how I did a little bar scam and it was the most exciting thing since combat – which he likes to hear, because it makes him the big vet of a thousand scams and me the admiring novice. But also I have the muscle to make him play – the threat of shopping him. It's a classic carrot and stick. Also, cons being a big front thing, he's got the experience, and between the money we can find between us, the con we've got and his background, we can do it. Any of the parts go missing and we can't.'

Norton, as Old expected, skipped right over the pitch, which he understood first time, and went for the hook.

'You went and did a bar scam? You cheeky bastard. How'd it go?'

'I couldn't explain.' Old bit his tongue and tried not to smile as Norton as good as volunteered to take over the bill which he had already boosted to the extent Old had expected – heavy on the fancy seafoods, abalone and lobster, and two bottles of Pol Roger champagne.

'So show me.'

'You know learning a con you didn't invent carries a rent?'

'You mean you lose you pay, sure, a bet's a bet. Remember though, I'm half way sober and I'm smart. You know that for sure, you didn't with the poor sucker you tried it on in the bar.'

'More than once.'

Norton smiled with what could not be disguised as other than admiration for Old's bottle.

'Just don't bank on winning, that's all.'

Old wanted to laugh. Norton was the perfect scam victim, if only he knew it. All scams depend on the greed and self-confidence of their victim. Without the greed, the victim doesn't bite. Without the self-confidence, they stand back and check the details again and again. Norton was sure of himself and he would go down like a stone. Some cons depend on knowledge as well. With this one, being smart was no advantage. The self-confidence alone would sink him.

'What's the stake?' he asked.

'It'll emerge.'

Old stood and pulled some change from his pocket. He pulled three pound coins from the jumble, put them on the table and put the rest back. Then he picked up the three coins and put that hand back in his pocket. He pulled it out and sat. He put two coins on the table.

'How many?'

'Where's the other?'

'The other what?'

'The other coin.'

'The world's full of coins. We're watching these. Eye on the ball, Tobe.'

'Don't call me Tobe.'

'How many?'

'Two.'

'You sure?'

'Sure.'

He shuffled the two coins around like a street huckster playing 'Find the Lady'.

'Now how many?'

'Stop messing about and get on with it.'

'You want to do the trick?' asked Old, pushing the coins towards Norton. 'Or find out how it works?'

'Find out,' Norton snapped.

'So how many?'

'Two.'

He shuffled some more and went through the routine of shuffling and asking, asking Norton if he was sure of his counting ability, asking him to check up his sleeves, asking him if he was watching, for almost five minutes and until he was absolutely certain that Norton was thoroughly fed up with the trick and absolutely sure there were two coins before him.

Time for the punchline.

'How many did you say?'

Norton wearily held up two fingers.

'Sure enough to bet on it?'

Norton perked up, an end in sight, his opportunity to overcome a simple scam.

'I'm sure as I can be. How much you want to bet? A ton, a grand?'

'Let's just say whoever's right pays for the meal.'

'You were paying anyway.'

'And a bottle of vintage Krug for afters, that should add another ton.'

'Fine.'

'So whoever's right pays?'

'You know, you can be very repetitive.'

'Was that a yes?'

'Yes.'

Old nodded at the coins, gave them a last and lengthy shuffle and looked at Norton.

'Now how many?'

'Two. As ever.'

Old gave Norton a wide grin as he hit him with it.

'OK, you're right. There's two. Whoever's right pays.'

He called for a waiter as Norton sat, blankly, soaking up the whipping he had taken, and on the rare occasion of his sticking Old with a beefy bill.

'If you have an '85 Krug,' Old said to the waiter, whose face immediately brightened at the addition of at least another fifteen pounds to the service charge, 'I'll have it. Otherwise, I'll have another look at the wine list.'

Norton shook his head.

'You dirty fucking scummy bastard.'

'No, you don't really think that do you, pet?'

Norton shook his head in exasperation.

'Look, you know you'll have that back within a couple of hours, knowing you, and then it'll be all profit. You just bought into a con. The only problem was that it only usually costs a couple of pints of bitter and you had to ask while you were sat in Now & Zen with a lobster inside you. You'll get it back.'

'Yeah, but does that mean I have to like it? Let's forget about it and crack on; it's giving me a headache. Ready then, the scam: you give it to him straight, I'm nothing to do with the scam proper – that the way to go, is it?'

'Not unless Ras thinks of some sweet little touch to add a bit of authenticity – some fancy money-juggling trick to give it a bit of surface sparkle, help stop the mark from looking at the basics too closely.'

'Who's the mark?'

'Better you don't know. The point is, what do I want you to do?'

'Why better I don't know? I like to know what I'm involved in.'

'That's just the way it works. You don't get to hear the whole deal. It involves a ludicrously subtle subterfuge – looks that way when Ras describes it – and it's easier to deliver your part properly if that's your whole truth, if you're not aware of any underlying strata of deceit.'

Norton nodded, reluctantly accepting the logic of the line.

'Another insignificant detail is, what do I get out of it?'

'I thought that might pass unnoticed. Should have known better. First, you get involved, one way or another, with a major scam, which – I wasn't lying – is one of the most exciting things after sex. And like sex, when it's great, it's bloody wonderful. When it's not so great, it's still pretty damn exciting. Believe me, the only problem you're likely to get out of this is you'll be distracted from trading through trying to think up the rinky-dinkiest scams. And I've thought of another *in* for you, which would mean I have to invite you in as a full partner, which would mean you come in on the meetings with Silvester but would also mean you putting up a pile of money.'

'A pile?'

'We need to talk about it, but from what Ras was saying, I would guess two hundred thousand, tops.'

'That's quite an exposure, Pat.'

'It's virtually risk-free.'

'I'm trained to watch out for words like virtually.

Risk is risk. It is its own price. Don't take risks unless you're prepared for events to come out either way.'

'Sure, I see that, but if you didn't want in, you could lend me the money on a formal basis – you know I'm good for it, sooner or later, it'd be clearer if I could explain the scam, but most of the money would just need to be seen. We would never even let go.'

'So explain it. I'll practise my lying, I promise. But I won't promise to say yes. Cash on the streets is inherently unsafe, it offends my caution.'

They took a few moments to let the waiter uncork the vintage Krug, and a few moments to admire its golden, light-absorbing hue, its honeyed nose and its tantalizing, fragrant taste.

'You get to pay for it,' Old said, as he put his glass down, 'but it's not all loss. How often would you taste a glass like that? The nearest there is to perfection in a glass.'

'Are you going to explain the scam?'

'Gosh, we're hard-nosed today. I said I have to talk it over with Ras first, but I'll confirm within a couple of days. The job I had in mind, though, before I thought how we could bring you in, was to tempt Silvester. Once we find him, you need to think of some quirky, sexy little investment angle you can interest him in enough to get him to a meeting. That's a good reason why you should be in – he understands why you called him in once he gets here, doesn't feel too resentful. For that, you get five grand.'

'Not a percentage of the proceeds?'

'The expenses could be fairly high. Five grand is good for a finder's fee. Especially as I did most of the finding, you only have to talk him into a meeting.'

'I only asked.'

'You never *only* do anything,' Old said, smiling. 'Every waking action of yours has side, one way or another.'

Norton waved for the bill, waving off the remark casually as if it didn't matter whether it was true or not.

'I guess if I want to find out how this scam works, we'd best find the man. That's got to be a first. If we go back to my office, I can make a few trades and you can hit the databases.'

TWELVE

Old felt the fat seats hug his body as he pushed the car through the tight bends on the country road. He was going a little faster than he would normally have driven, but the car was capable of far more than the Mini, seemed to thrive on the pressure. He had expected to miss the Mini. He did. Like you miss a hole in your shoe.

Hannah seemed perfectly happy with his driving, seemed not to think it too fast. She was idly gazing out of the window as the North Essex countryside flitted by, the long shadows of trees darkening the road as they passed through broken avenues; flashes of intense light as the warm autumn sun broke through. Sam and Jimmy, bored with the electric windows, tired after a long day tramping the hills, and a short and, for them, intensely boring hour browsing expensive antique shops (where Old suffered a pang of remorse as he realized that Warriner's jade figurine still stood, guiltily, on his mantelpiece), slept soundly in the soft-cushioned, near silent fastness of their child seats.

Though no one had spoken for a while, it was a warm silence, Hannah and Old each comfortable with the other's presence. Old realized they were near the M11 and a choice could be made about how quickly they should get home. He invited Hannah to share some cold meats and cheese and she accepted. He took the motorway and, hitting the outside lane at a shade over ninety, they were home in twenty minutes.

The kids were undressed, pyjama'ed and bundled into Sam's bed, barely opening their eyes throughout the process. The meal was quiet and easy. They no longer had the need for the slightly anxious conversations of earlier meets – each keen to find common ground. The food went down, with it the wine and later port. They slid from the food to each other without effort and kissed lovingly. After an age of the softest warmest kisses, Old started to unfasten Hannah's blouse. She stiffened, almost unnoticeably, but Old was in a position to notice whatever impulses and vibrations were there and, for the first time, an element of self-consciousness entered their kisses. He slipped his hand through the gap his hand had made in her buttons and cupped her right breast in his hand.

'Not here,' she said, and flicked her eyes up to the ceiling.

Old felt as if he should be pleased; a clear invitation to bed from a woman he was attracted to, he cared about and wanted. But the invitation to bed was not, he felt, an invitation to a better arena for their love-making, more a redirection to the *appropriate* venue.

Perhaps he was being too sensitive to non-existent or merely misleading nuances. Perhaps not. He had learned that you could not be too heedful of the micro-tones of nuance, feeling and shade in a relationship in which sex and love were even in sight on a distant horizon. Love and care are not made of concrete, steel and rivets, they are lighter than the wispiest cloud. The twitch of an antenna, the prickle of a goosebump, are as reliable indicators as the sight of the most obvious signal. Nuances in unconscious signal are the nearest there is to substance and Old knew to take heed. But of what? Intuition might be real, but it is not easy to read.

Old was sure Hannah was asleep. As sure as he was that he would not sleep. His heart felt like lead and he could feel a headache building from the tension in his shoulders. He wanted to get out of bed, perhaps go downstairs and read a book, stare at some mindless TV.

Did Hannah think that was how sex was supposed to be? Really? When he had taken her out, it was her personality he had been attracted to, though she was also a good-looking woman, and that always plays a part. But the one thing they had not talked about was their Catholicism. Old had assumed – assumptions, tut tut – that this was because she was like him, a Catholic by birth and upbringing who had let it go for one reason or another, in his case a profound lack of ability to believe what they required a Catholic to believe, and that he simply used the fact of his nominal Catholicism to get Sam into the better schools of the Catholic diocese. Sure, this meant that to make his Catholicism at least a little convincing, he had to take Sam to Mass now and then. So looking back, he realized, it was unfair to think that anyone else should have known the depth of his cynicism.

When she invited him to bed, that confirmed her lapsed status to him. But he assumed too much again. Catholics are no more saints than anyone else: the church can't make them behave better. What it can do, though, and does very well, is ruin their sinning.

Hannah made love like a Catholic in a crippling state of mortal-sin-induced guilt.

She made love like a Victorian matron.

She made love like a log.

Sex might not be everything, but it was certainly a fairly substantial something, and that had been a rejection of affection as clear as a slap in the face and a spit in the eye. His hopes had been high, on that slow walk up the stairs, that their lovemaking would be as subtle and powerful, soft and strong, straightforward and inspired as their kissing. But then the kissing was clothed. Once they were in bed and doing whatever it was they did, she kissed like someone who had just read a book on it. Old had hoped for passionate lovemaking. He had been one half, instead, of a cursory fuck. Perhaps she thought that, by divesting it of feeling, by acting as if it was something being done to her, that she was doing no wrong. Tell it to your God, Old thought. But don't tell it to me, I'm not interested.

The only aspect of the affair that bothered Old now was that, if he walked away, he would be acting like the walking proof of every Catholic mother's advice – probably every mother of every religion or no religion. They only want the one thing. Get it and they're off, not interested any more. Not exactly a universal rule, but right this time, Mother.

And yet Mother wasn't exactly on the ball, there was *something else* – a strange aspect to this, that he didn't understand at all. He was depressed by what had happened, put off, but he didn't want to let her go. He wanted to get close to her no less than before, despite feeling different. He knew instinctively that there would be no notable improvement in the sex – it was ingrained, knee-jerk Catholic sex, so that wasn't it – but he still wanted her around. Confusing. Demanding of attention.

Sex. So good, such a pain. Such a fucking pain.

Ras was pleased. He wasn't hiding it. He was so pleased that twice his huge grin actually crossed the line and he burst into spontaneous laughter.

'This is just so damn sweet. With Toby as a money man, if he wants to come in, it looks that bit better. It's fucking unbeatable.'

'We think.'

'It is. What's wrong with it?'

'Nothing I can see, but it's not our business; not our regular line of work. There could be any number of things you could see were out of kilter if scams were your life. It could be as old as the hills and looking it. We just don't know.'

'Well if it is, Silvester'll let us know soon enough. He's not going to sink his dosh if he thinks it smells that bad. When's he coming?'

Old laughed.

'Tomorrow. It was a bit of an anti-climax after all that. I chase all over London and the Home Counties, have houses watched, cars followed, break in, threats, guns, all that crack with Toby and his bent friend Warriner, searches, more favours from McCreery, visits to the nick: all that and it nets me a name. Just that. I get the name, spend ten minutes at the keyboard and I've got the bastard. Alderney. Jersey companies, living in a flat in Alderney. Any bother and it's that much harder to nick him. And it means he's doing OK. They're strict as hell about residency permits down there. He can either prove he's worth over half a million – which I doubt he'd want to make official, whatever he's worth, or he's there on the never never, not quite official, on long-term holiday lets. They turn a blind eye to a lot of that sort of stuff, so long as you don't work on the islands. Brings money in, rents go to the islanders, no questions asked.'

'So what did you tell him? How'd you get him to agree to come over?'

'Toby.'

'Yeah, so how?'

'That little guy knows how to talk. I don't think he was even putting it on. If the guy wanted to invest with him, he'd take the cheque. Once he gets on to money, it's just start it off and let it go. He can talk up a storm. And believe me, he's convincing. If I didn't already have most of my money with him, I'd be thinking about it seriously now. The way it went, I wanted to be sure, anything Toby said, any wicky-wacky details he threw in, I had them off pat. So I taped it.'

He popped a tape in Ras's machine and threw the switch.

'*Desmond Silvester?*'

'*Who's that?*'

'*My name's Norton. Toby Norton. I'm an investment manager. Independent.*'

'*Where'd you get my number?*'

'*Business. I'm sure you get a lot of calls like this; everyone of independent means does. You may protect your name and number but these things get into circulation. Yours starts here. I hope not to pass it on. If you give me your fax number, I can show you my results for the last three years. I'm sure you will be impressed. Average*' *return nineteen per cent. And you understand a lot of these are very conservative clients. I have a special high-risk category. Last year, for a small and select group of clients, those willing to take a risk, I made forty-two per cent. I believe you could be one of those willing to take a risk, considering your line of work.'*

'Who the fucking hell are you? What d'you mean, my line of work?'

'Toby was talking on the receiver but he had it fed through the loudspeaker, so though it was being taped, I could hear what was going on as it went on. He gave the guy his number, said he had nothing to hide, but seeing they might have something in common, why didn't he ring back, check him out? Then he hung up. It was sweet. He sounded like what I suppose he is. An incredibly pushy, self-confident money type with something risky to offer and good information on the type of people who might be interested in it. We both knew Silvester would want to know how Toby knew about him. He didn't call back for ten minutes and I thought my heart was going to stop. When it rang, he gave it six before he answered.'

'Norton Technical Investments.'

'That's you I just spoke to, right?'

'Alistair, is it about the five-year Daewoo paper?'

'I thought, "Don't be too clever." I thought he could blow it with one wrong word. He kept it together like an angel though.'

'No, Desmond Silvester.'

'Beautiful. Now we were sure in case we weren't before. Out of the horse's mouth.'

'Good. I presume then that you're interested.'

'I'm interested in how you know who I am. Say your piece.'

'Thank you. I presume it's the high risk, high return you're interested in. Do you know much about options?'

'Don't you worry what I know, say your piece.'

'OK, consider this an opening pitch. Like what you hear, we'll meet, set things up. This is how it works. Stock represents a piece of a company. Buy it, you own a piece of the company. Overall, the price of the share is governed by the fundamentals, by how well the companies perform, and how well it is perceived to perform and to be about to perform. That's two indices: reality, and traders' perception of that reality. Options add a third. Time. You can buy an option at a given price in the future. It doesn't look like much of a change, but it is. You don't normally take up the option. You sell it before it matures. But when? That's where the options trader has to act as a trader, take a real risk. From the moment he takes the option, his envelope of time is diminishing. He has to choose the right moment to let go, and at that precise moment he has to find somewhere to put it. If you know maths, you know that every time you add another factor into a calculation, its complexity shoots up. With predictive sciences, that's even more so. Which makes options-trading a big game of skill. And it is a game. For me it's fun, and I use other people's money to get my fun. My own too, but mostly other people's. The other options-traders make money too, the ones with the big institutions. But they daren't lose. They work for cautious institutions. And in the options market, caution is no help. I could make you money.'

'I'm interested. But I want to know where you got my name. Make no mistake, I'm genuinely interested in your

*options thing, but I'm a private man. Where'd you get
my name? I need to know.'*

*'A fact you may not be aware of. All international
calls go through GCHQ. They're scanned by computer
for key words connected to certain guessable subjects.
What happens on one computer has a way of finding its
way onto others. Information is there, it's around: you're
not invisible, you exist, you're there and here I am
talking to you. I work in options but I have an occasional
partner who works in even more high-risk, high-return
areas. He's interested in punting an idea to you too, but
he's also a private man. Too shy even to say hello, though
he's on this line. Between the three of us, options or no,
we could make sweet music.'*

'And that was it?' Ras asked.

'That was it. He was in. I'm sure as much as anything he wants to know just what it is we're up to. He
won't trust us at face, so before the meeting you can
bet he'll be having someone check Toby over, look at
the office, watch Toby, see he's nothing to do with
Lily Law.

'Toby says he's had a couple of calls about nothing
in particular, touting for details about what he does
but non-committal about who they are and he says he
barely ever gets that kind of call. Says he has to hunt
up his own business.'

'What was all that crap about GCHQ, did I miss
something?'

'That's what I said to Toby. Basically it was a red
herring. He said it was out before he knew where it
came from. Still, did no harm, threw the notion of
spooks and Big Brother, all that paranoid cods.'

'He's a devious little toad, your man Toby; I'm a

long way from sure just what I make of him. What'd he fix up with the where and when?'

'You'll like this bit. Tomorrow, Porchester Road Turkish Baths. It's the only municipal Turkish Baths in London. The only decent-sized Turkish of any kind. I don't know if it's there because that's the Arab part of town or if the Arabs settled there for the baths, or if it's just coincidence, whatever, but that's where they are, and that's where we're meeting.'

'Strange.'

'Maybe. No bugging or anything in a place like that – water, steam and marble, there'll be more echoes than you know and with the three of us, me, Toby and Silvester, with three towels between us at best, I can't see we'll have a lot to hide. I suppose that's what he's after. The symbolic thing as much as anything. A case of what you see is what you get.'

'You think Toby'll come in on it?'

'Sure of it. He loved the baths thing. Real cloak and dagger stuff. He likes all that stuff; don't we all? He'll be in on it, I just hope he doesn't ham it up.'

Another busy night at the Star Inn. The car park was full of dark-windowed, ageing BMWs and lumbering Granadas with minicab aerials clipped to the boot, and inside, again after re-arranging half the furniture in the pub, was a group of angry-looking men shouting disagreement at each other. The barman gave them two trays to transport their collection of large Scotches, bitters and lager tops back to the table and shuddered at the thought of any poor soul who might call which-ever of them was a minicab driver, and any pedestrian who might be unlucky enough to try their luck on the roads. They each came in their own car, not a one was drinking beers without chasers and they were getting angrier with each successive round, the current being the fourth.

Eventually, the noise, and the language, rose to such intensity that a customer complained, and the barman realized he was going to have to ask, as the manager was skulking in the cellar on one of his twenty-minute barrel-changing episodes. He strode across, as assertively as he could manage, and asked them to keep the noise down in what he remembered as a landlordly and adult tone, hopefully sounding at least twice his nineteen years.

One of the men turned and scowled at him.

'Do what?'

His confidence vanished, especially as he could hear, now he was here, talk of grassing, shopping, and how it wasn't the done thing. He was already suspicious that they were not the pub's usual suburbanites, like himself. Now he was sure. They were dreadful criminals and he was about to be the victim of a terrible random stabbing for having the audacity to ask the Star Inn Mob to pipe down. He remembered the barman in *Goodfellas*, which he had only got round to watching on video the previous weekend: the lot of the barman, shot in the foot for some equally minor transgression.

'The noise,' he muttered through his parched throat.

The man shrugged and turned back to the table. He shouted above the racket.

'The kid says keep it down. You're shouting.'

All eyes followed him as he returned to the bar, but the noise level subsided and stayed that way until they all left, after reaching no apparent agreement, when they drank up. A few words, such power. So many of them, him alone, the mob quieted. The barman thrust his shoulders back and paced the length of the bar, surveying his empire.

THIRTEEN

Old read somewhere that people who sweat profusely are more likely to be able to be good at sport. Something like that. Especially power and speed sports, like his own sport, wrestling, though he was less and less able to call it his sport. He hadn't visited the Olympia for over a month, and it was almost three weeks before that. He blamed marital bliss. Ras's. If Ras wasn't up for it, it was so much harder to get it together and go down. And when Ras wasn't being the perfect husband, he was running the perfect bar, and making a perfect packet.

Whatever the reason, Old was sweating like a pig in a sauna doing clapping press-ups.

He was leaning against a wall of the Turkish bath. The wall was marble and it was sweating too. Old wiped his face with the big white towel that came with the entrance fee. He had entered with it round his waist, but that hadn't lasted. A few of the younger men kept theirs on – he couldn't figure out why it was all the younger men with the towels, but there it was. He kept having to wipe his face and that wasn't practical wearing the towel. Besides, the heat and humidity seemed to relax his genitals. His penis looked like a turkey's neck, swinging, hot, relaxed and free. He saw Toby getting a few funny looks. He was in good shape, and showed no signs of dwarfism, despite being only four feet ten. But he had a heavy stubble and was obviously a fully grown man. Only fully was still not so much.

The social mix of the place, though hard to guess once naked, was still possible to work out, and it was possible to cheat by checking out the guys in the changing-room. It was the usual communal changing-room, except the clothes were handed over to a cloak-room attendant rather than being put in lockers. Probably because there was nowhere obvious to put a key.

Old guessed that a half of the men were Arabs. As he had expected they would be. A good number were unplaceable. Which is to say they were just guys taking a Turkish bath, guys who would not have gone out of their way to find one, but as it was there, at their local baths, used it. And the rest, a solid quarter, were gay. No point pretending, he thought, that there's no know-ing, because there is. And, logical to the end, if he was asked what the way of knowing was, what the evidence was, then he would have answered, like anyone else, 'Well, you just know.' And to back him up, all the gay men he knew concurred, and he knew many, as wres-tling had become a popular gay sport and a good part of the membership of the Olympia was gay. They all agreed that they could tell, just about every time. He wouldn't have said he could always say whether a given person was gay, that would be silly – to say he is and she isn't, and to expect to be spot on. But some people took up the popular stereotypes and played them for all they were worth. And for what it was worth, they were the gays who were here.

He dipped himself again in one of the giant plunge pools, then laid out on the marble floor to cool off a little more. He saw Toby sitting tight, sweating slightly, occasionally dipping his feet and calves into the water but no more. Old wondered if he always found it hard to let go. He had never seen anyone look as uptight and business-like, sitting, naked, in a room full of flesh, sweat and steam. He mused for a while longer on this and that, the ways of the world and the rolls of dirt the sweat was forcing out of his skin. He thought about Hannah and let his mind wander.

He stepped into the kitchen to check out what was for dinner. Hannah was in one of her usual summer prints. She reached to the top shelf in the cupboard and he dress stretched deliciously against her body. He cupped her breast and she pressed against him. She smiled and reached behind, took hold of the zip and in a moment, the dress was lying on the kitchen floor, Hannah gorgeous in a pair of white panties and nothing else. She took hold of him and whispered in his ear. 'Now.'

Old noticed that one of the pacing bodies was standing in front of him, fairly near, the swinging prick and balls at a level with his face. Six foot one, perhaps – hard to tell from that angle – brown, trim, square-chinned and undeniably good-looking, he would have known in an instant it was Silvester, if he had not already met his brother. As he had, he would have placed his life savings on it he was so sure.

But he wouldn't let Silvester hold the bet.

Silvester looked him up and down and Old suspected he knew why they arranged to meet where they did. He was gay too. Camping it up in here where he was in company. Not that it made a jot of the difference to the scam, but it was something else he knew, and knowledge is power. All knowledge. Impossible to know what would be needed until it *was* needed.

'You're Patrick Old,' said Silvester, without a shred of doubt in his voice. 'And I can see you're pleased to see me – a fine reception.'

Old had his towel draped over his knee, and in his reverie it had made an obvious tent which was attracting more than a few stares. Old flushed and the tent subsided instantaneously.

'Shame,' Silvester muttered. 'But there's always later.'

'Should I call you Desmond, Des, Mr Silvester?'

Silvester smiled.

'Sir? No, Des is fine.'

'How's Frankie?'

'We keep in touch, one way and another.'

'I guessed. You're here to see Toby Norton, then?'

'And you. I especially want to see you. I need to hear the deal. I know there's blackmail involved, from my conversation with Frankie. I need to know the deal.'

Old winced.

'Blackmail's an ugly word. I want us to do business together. If you think the deal sucks, we can look for a better one. Maybe. If you don't want to do business at all, then I'll threaten you, maybe even do something nasty.'

'How nasty?'

'No need to be crude, we'll see how things go, eh?'

'How nasty?'

'Auntie Lil.'

'That's more dirty than nasty, wouldn't you say?'

Old shook his head.

'You knew Barry Mee was loaded.'

'Him!' Silvester groaned. 'Didn't get along with him

at all. Tough one that, I might have guessed he'd be a first-degree grudge-holder. Quite a fan of one or two of his titles, mind you. Broad-minded sort of chap, our Barry.'

'Can we get on?' Old insisted. 'The bunch Mee dragged in on the deal, I don't expect you had reason to know too much about, or care. Some of them could take the knock, some of them, a couple at least, it hurt them pretty badly. None of them were in the same league as Mee financially. Worse, from your point of view, they're the type of guy sees black and white, and they're not liberals. They'd like their money back, but as realists, they don't expect to see it. They know I was hired to find you, and they expect that when I do, like now, I turn you over and they get to beat seven shades of shit out of you. I don't like that kind of stuff. Not my way at all. It's dirty and nasty and ugly and brutish. And it's the wrong way. My way is clean. Turn you in. Not the harshest punishment in the world, but you'd hurt; we both know that. And the alternative is, you talk to me, we see if we can do business, and even after you pay Mee what you owe him – I'll tell him I argued the case, you paid up; the thing's between the two of us, I can't see Barry Mee trusting you with his money in any kind of scam – even after that you should make an easy six figures, and even after expenses, which should be fairly rich, the thing being perfect, it could be most of the way to seven.'

'Seven figures?'

'A million. Just so we know we're talking about the same thing. Seven figures, each one of them to the left of the decimal point.'

'Who doesn't want to know how to make a million? Sure we'll talk. Do we talk here? I saw the little guy over there. One who looks like he thinks he's still wearing his business suit; that's Norton, yes?'

Old said it was.

'He's cute. We can talk here, take a few dips, when it gets to lunch, we can head down to one of the Lebanese joints. Eat some lamb's bollocks. Give you nerve in case you need it. That's what the Arabs say, makes sense to me, eat balls, get balls. Work as a con, you've got to have balls.'

'Toby won't stay for the lot. He's no experience with the police. His part of this is he'll come in and do some financial chatter when it's needed, and he may not even do that – he's very identifiable. He won't have all the details of the scam – less he knows, less there is to tell – need to know and all that. He's not on full share, but he'll contribute full share to the expenses – so he gets to take less risk.'

'So what was he for?'

'Won't make a lot of sense until I explain how the scam works, but a large part of it was getting you here. That was a must. I got interested in all this, thought up a scam. Since I thought of it, Barry Mee's been a sideline. I've been researching the scam. This could make us. Mee was the stick to get you here; the million, obviously, the carrot. Toby was the best person to sell the idea. Are you going to stop swinging your kit in my face and sit down while I whistle Toby over? I'm getting hoarse with keeping my voice down.'

Silvester grinned and let loose a flash of his perfect gleaming array of teeth. Even, capped, unmarked, privately and expensively cared for. What Old always thought of as American teeth.

'I thought you might be getting to like it. You look after yourself, you look good. Since we're going to work as a team, I'll tell you now. You ever fancy fooling around a little, just say the word.'

Old gave a slightly feeble laugh which failed manifestly to cover his profound embarrassment. However many gay friends he might have, however much he enjoyed their company and their often filthily ribald humour, he could not get over the way most could so disarmingly offer sex to men they had no idea were gay or not. 'Nothing ventured,' said a friend at the Olympia, with a casual and unconcerned shrug, after Old had just rejected a proposition made precisely as he had submitted to an expert pin Old had on him, which had them entwined in a way that off the wrestling mat would have been seen as highly intimate and possibly compromising.

'Thanks for the offer, not me, not my style. And don't tell me I won't know till I try. Just let it lie.'

'We'll get Toby, get off somewhere we can talk. It might be a good place to meet incognito, but it's a lousy place to talk about a scam, and so's a Lebanese restaurant.'

Old waved to Toby. The three of them headed off to change, and Old told Norton they would meet in a couple of days.

'What about planning, what the fuck is this? I sit there, sweating and getting the eye while you chat to your man, then it's: "Off you go now Toby." Are you taking the piss?'

'Cool it. The man's a professional earwigger,' Old

said, casting his head back at Silvester. 'We waited an hour, talked for ten minutes. He wouldn't have come if it wasn't for you. Now he feels more secure with a small, tight scam, I told him you had a limited role. If you want to play, that's fine, but I'm not changing the rules for you. Ras designed this thing, he says what's what. And never mention him to Silvester. This is between me, Silvester and the mark. And you, if you're in. Ras doesn't exist. He's executive producer, doesn't come on set.'

Norton agreed, however unenthusiastic he was about being left out of the planning. He was introduced to Silvester, who at least had the sense not to mention his height, and left quickly, promising to be in touch when the time came.

Old and Silvester sat in the sitting-room of Old's house. If they were to work together, they had to be able to trust each other. Old already knew Silvester's main address, his real and false names, and enough about him to put him inside for at least a while. It seemed only fair that Silvester should see his house, visit his home, see he had nothing to hide. It was clear also that this was no dummy home. This was where he lived. Old watched Silvester with half an eye, listened to the music – Astor Piazzola playing accordion tangos, picked by Silvester from Old's rather too quirky collection – and waited for him to finish reading the clippings file. From the way he flicked the pages backwards and forwards, it looked as if he was taking it all in. This was not a cursory glance – he was studying the folder.

'Now I know about Prince Faruk Ibn Fahad. He can only be the mark. Tell me the story.'

He held his mug of tea in two hands, taking tiny sips, and settled into the chair, ready to hear and digest the scam.

Old stood. He wasn't sure why he did it, but it felt right. He was making a sale, giving a presentation. The customer didn't have much choice, but it was important to him that Silvester thought it was a good scam. To be convincing, they each had to be convinced.

'Before we start on the detail, I don't want you to think you've seen through it, I'll tell you the punchline first. The mark gives us a pile of loot, for all kinds of reasons connected to the bullshit we threw at him for the rest of the scam, and we disappear. It's that simple.'

'They're all that simple,' Silvester said. 'That's how cons work. You get someone to give you their money, for a week, a day, sometimes even a fraction of a second in some of the financial market scams, and you fuck off. That's all there is. That's confidence in a nutshell. Convince someone to hand you a big pile of their money and steal it. I have no illusion and neither should you: confidence is theft. I steal money for a living. I just don't use a blackjack. The only thing separates a good con from a bad one is the subtlety of the scam. If they're too wrapped up in the detail to think about the basic issues of trust, then you're away. So there's no need to apologize because your scam looks like a flat-nosed, stocking-over-the-head blag. It is. Give me the detail.'

Old ran through the scam and after Silvester's lecture it looked simpler than it had. He described it in as much detail as possible and was still disappointed at how thin it looked, worse when Silvester summarized it.

'You found the mark, you made sure he wanted what we could provide, we prove we can sell it to him, we prove our credentials by displaying you like a baboon's arse presenting to the world, we give a demo, negotiate, we get the money, I piss off and you and the Sheik stand around shaking with indignation. Except his is deeper felt than yours, which is choking on a king-sized wedge.'

'You make it sound very blunt.'

'A blag's a blag. Some people pull silk stockings over their heads, we use silk ties and double cuffs.'

FOURTEEN

The speakers all faced away from the foam-padded booth that surrounded Tandy, his decks and his stacks of records. It was possibly the only spot in the room where it was possible to hold a conversation in near conversational tones. If the decks were exposed to too much of the noise, it set up vibration and could lead to distortion. The crowd was older than usual, and so the volume was a little lower than usual. It was a retro night upstairs in the Dog and Bone in Vauxhall, a new pub which was named as seriously as it expected to be taken. The crowd was dressed in a terrific selection of flares, penny-round collars, open shirts, skinny-rib sweaters and lurid cheesecloth tie-dyed shirts with flared sleeves. All kinds of anachronistic and energetic nineties gyrating was going on which would have raised eyebrows from Sly Stone and probably from all his family too.

Tandy popped Sly off and segued neatly into the tasteful obscurity of a William Bell and Judy Clay B-side.

'Keeping busy?' Andy asked his brother.

'This crowd like a bit of variety – no following techno with techno. It's a bit like working a Wigan Casino crowd, you have to keep the tempo steady enough so as not to shock them out of the beat, but they like a wide range. It's fun to keep them happy and they appreciate the effort.'

'What are you up to, apart from this?'

'Why apart from this? This is what it's about. The rest is padding.'

'Tell me about the padding, then.'

'Not much to tell.'

'I thought Patrick Old had been keeping you busy.'

'Aye?'

'You mean he hasn't?'

'No.'

'You've not been working for him?' Andy asked, puzzled, and then repeated the question as Tandy cupped his hand to his ear.

'Aye.'

'Is that a yes you have or yes you've not?'

'It was an "Aye I have, not enough to keep me busy but enough to know whatever it was and whatever he has lined up next I'm to keep schtum." '

'This is your brother. I think I should know. They've been involved in things people could get hurt. C'mon, whassa game?'

'I couldn't say.'

'Somebody should say. Just in case, you know, just in case.'

'A bit of following and tomorrow a bit of driving.'

Andy waited, a little exasperated, as Tandy flicked out of the disk, teased them with a quick few bars of Erasure before sliding, beat perfect, into late Isleys.

'And that's all you trust me with?'

'It's all they trust me with.'

A couple of long moments dawned while Andy realized his brother had been teasing him with a puzzle neither of them had tapped.

'You kept me hanging for that?'

'That's what brothers are for.'

Silvester eyed Old.

'How is it you're playing a part in this that more or less is you and you look like a shop-window dummy?'

'Thanks.'

'I mean it, it's a problem. You don't look like what you are. You're playing an ex-military intelligence officer, which you are, and you look like a pastiche.'

He was dressed in a pair of sand-coloured trousers with a lovat green tweed jacket. He had to respect Silvester's eye: he had decided his normal clothes didn't look the part and had bought these deliberately dowdy rags as his attempt at a disguise.

'They're too much,' Silvester said. 'Go and change into whatever you'd wear for a normal business meeting.'

Old came back in a mid-grey, single-breasted suit, with just enough weight for the time of year. Looked at not too closely, it looked like a straight business suit. Middle manager stuff. A closer look and it hung a little too well. It was a Kenzo, and even on the day he had bought it, final reduction day of a sale, well over half off list, it had cost him over three hundred pounds.

Silvester didn't miss the cut.

'Perfect. Beautiful. You wore those other . . .' – he paused while he thought of the muddy green tweed – 'that stuff, and you own that. It's a peach. Nice tie too.'

Silvester was in a black Conran suit with a white shirt and an Etzdorf tie. When they had had quite enough of admiring their good taste, they called Tandy. They decided a driver was a good thing. Gave their operation a little gravitas. They told him nothing except his rate of pay, which was generous, and that he was to do as he was told. Like a soldier, they said, without actually saying he was to pretend he was a soldier. The last thing they wanted was impromptu method acting.

Old sent him off to Marks and Spencer the day before to get a blue blazer and grey trousers, white shirt, black tie. Driver's clothes. He gave him two hundred pounds and asked for receipts.

'You don't trust me or something?'

Old glared at him.

'I'm already paying you a hundred a day plus a thousand bonus. The first rule was don't question me, do as you're told, instantly. The first thing I tell you to do, you question me. You know what "carrot and stick" means?'

Tandy nodded, somewhat meekly.

'I just added five hundred to your bonus. That's a carrot. You question me, on anything, you lose fifty. You disobey, a hundred. You louse up, you lose the lot and you never work for me again, or for Ras at the restaurant. That's a stick.'

'You speak for Ras now?'

'Hope you enjoyed asking that, it cost you fifty quid. We agreed on terms?'

'Sure.' Tandy offered his hand and Old shook it, firmly.

'And one more thing. You only speak in response to a direct question. OK? Imagine you're being paid in crystal, and it's all piled on the back seat.'

The Jag was a few years old but in beautiful condition and they were getting it for less than the price a decent Ford would have cost them from Avis. Good old Yellow Pages. They rode in silence for a while, then Silvester spoke, a worried edge to his voice.

'I hate finding problems at this stage. We know what they want – arms. They know what we want – a sale. But how are we supposed to have come to them? I mean, if we were established arms dealers . . .'

'Then we wouldn't touch Ibn Fahad, we'd say piss off up the Northern Frontier and get some stuff made, a few hundred AK47s, a few of the Afghanis' leftovers, rocket-launchers, Stingers and what not. But he wants the fancy electronics. He wants Patriots, he thinks. He mentioned Patriots, he also mentioned offence, so he's not straight in his own mind, seeing Patriots are strictly defensive. We can make a sale, and we can be straight. We couldn't stand up as arms dealers, not from anyone who knew how to look, we wouldn't last five minutes. We're opportunists. You said it to me: the nearer you can keep it to the truth, the less there is to get wrong. I'm reassuring you, you're the professional. I'm supposed to be the one in a flap.'

'You're doing fine, hon.'

'So why are my palms sweating?'

'Panic verging on hysteria. Don't worry, that's normal. That's the buzz. The adrenalin's kicking in and it won't lay off until this is over.' Silvester rested his hand gently on Old's thigh. 'You'll be fine.'

Old brushed the hand off, noticing as he did that it seemed like the action of a shocked old maid, and then couldn't help smiling when he knew he should be annoyed as he saw Tandy's eyes out on stalks. One more person thinking about the wrong thing is no bad thing, he thought, sure, he detected a similar idea in Silvester's sly grin.

Shawaz had booked a meeting-room at the hotel. It was, as it was fair to expect, well equipped, heated perfectly, spotless and clinical. There was a sideboard on one side of the room equipped with fax, overhead projector, pens for the flip charts and pads and pencils, all marked with the hotel name and logo. On a matching sideboard at the other side were soft drinks, a coffee-maker with a full pot of coffee, a vacuum flask of hot water and tea bags for lousy tea – as it must be without freshly boiled water – biscuits and a bowl of fruit. Bowls of fruit were also prominent in the artwork on the walls. Shawaz stood to greet the two men. Ibn Fahad remained seated.

Silvester busied himself for a moment distributing coffee and mineral water. Ibn Fahad took an orange and immediately became engrossed in peeling it, making long strokes around the orange with a giant clasp knife he pulled from within the folds of his gown. Once the peel was removed, he busied himself with the pith. The room was silent as the three men waited for him to finish. He was very particular about his pith and he seemed not to be in any kind of a hurry. When eventually he finished, Shawaz cleared his throat, Old and Silvester sat up, business to begin, but Ibn Fahad's head remained bent. He started to peel off the clean, pith-free orange crescents and to eat them, slowly, one at a time. Old watched the clock on the wall. A good idea, a clock in a meeting-room. Saved people the effort and embarrassment of the surreptitious glance at the watch. From reaching for the orange to finishing the last crescent took eight and a half minutes. Now they all knew who was boss; and whose time was worthless, able to be squandered waiting for an old man to eat an orange.

As they waited, Old had time to realize what he was doing. He had been swept along with the whole thing, one step had seemed more or less logically to lead to the next. His and Ras's enthusiasm for the adrenalin of the whole thing had brought them to this point and now he was to start on a major confidence trick. A grand theft. His little trick with the coins in the hotel bar was one thing, this was quite another. But it was too late now. He had convinced himself, he had invested money he normally guarded fiercely, seeing it as the future for Sam. He was committed. Ras had planned, Silvester had signed up, Tandy was employed, and he was here. His mind raced. It was the adrenalin, he was sure, that was making him like this, but still the facts were there. He had got himself into something serious and with some of the calls he had made, processes they had set in motion, it was set to get more and more so.

Ibn Fahad looked up at them with complete indifference. He waved a hand at Shawaz who seemed to take it to mean that he should make the meeting happen. Shawaz stood.

We are to be formal, then, Old thought.

'Gentlemen. Thank you for agreeing to meet us. We know a little about you, later we shall give you the opportunity to tell us more.'

His English was perfectly clear and lucid but with a curious slightly American and very middle-Eastern lilt. Very Henry Kissinger somehow, Silvester thought.

'I am Houssain Shawaz. I am personal assistant in all matters to Sheik Faruk Ibn Fahad. I expect you did your homework before you approached us. I also

220

expect you used the newspapers as your source. A dangerous move, if you seek the truth. I will tell you who we are so you can be sure where we stand, what we want, why we want it. You may ask questions and do not bother to wait until I am finished. The right time to ask is when a question arises.'

Silvester nodded, sagely.

'Good,' Old said and relapsed into silence.

'The Sheik is a very wealthy man.'

Great opener, Old thought.

'His wealth is based on land – and oil, but primarily on land. The oil provides the money, but the land provides the people and the power-base which prevent the wealth from being stolen from him. The Sheik is the richest Saudi subject. There are many richer Saudis but they are not subjects, they are all in the Royal Family.'

This brought the first reaction from Ibn Fahad, who gave the slightest curl of the lip and narrowing of the eyes at the mention of the Fahd family.

'The Sheik is unrelated, and they resent so much wealth being held in their country outside their hands. They do not charge themselves taxes, they tried to charge them on the Sheik. He refused. They would not dare arrest him. He and his people are from the south of the country, near Yemen. He owns over one and a half million acres. If you are not familiar with land, that is a little under two thousand four hundred square miles.'

He saw Silvester's eyes widen.

'I can see you do not understand land sizes. That does not mean an area the size of Texas. The land is roughly rhomboid; a squat, leaning rectangle roughly

221

forty-four miles by fifty-three though it is fatter at the eastern end. It used to be deeper, but a three-mile strip which runs into Yemen was seized by the communists when it was still South Yemen. We are negotiating for its return. That southern strip, it contains no oil, which is all in the north-east corner, but it is important to the Sheik, and to the people who are based there who owe him their loyalty. There are eleven thousand people in the Sheik's territory. It is better endowed with water than most areas, it is rich in oases. A few small parts are under cultivation. The Sheik is as a father to those families – nearly two thousand of them. They would die for him and Riyadh knows it. But the Sheik needs protection. Love and enthusiasm are no longer sufficient. He needs to know that he can fight if the need arises, either with Riyadh or with the South, if the communists should return. He is a maverick in the region, and that makes him a target. There is much fear of a genuinely popular figure, not a way it would be possible to describe the King. There have been mutterings about democracy in recent years. The Sheik's name came up as a man who could lead. He has no ambitions in this area, but the thought scares Riyadh and makes them more wary yet of the Sheik. Though an outright attack is unlikely, there are other options. They could give money and weapons to the communist rebels awaiting their return in Yemen. The Fahds hate the communists but fear makes strange bedfellows. You have seen the film of your politicians smiling, shaking hands and exchanging presents with Saddam Hussein while you were arming him during the Iran–Iraq War, so you understand this idea. My enemy's enemy is my friend.

'There you have the background. What we want is modern weaponry. Our people are spread out. On land, they are at home. Anyone attacking them by stealth would have to be impossibly lucky to get within ten miles. If they came by force, they would attract the attention they do not want. The way, we believe, would be to worry like a wolf. Sneaking attacks here and there by helicopter. The Fahds are allowed to patrol their own skies. The settlements are too small to attract the press – no press centres with satellite, and no international hotels. So we want anti-helicopter weapons. Smart weapons that can overcome the electronic defences of the helicopter. We know the way the West sells its weaponry. The best goes only to its friends, and that is usually the best of two years ago, so the seller can be sure he always has the edge: "Attack me, but remember I made your weapons, I know how they work, and I have made better for myself." We want the newest and the best available. We can get it out of the country, but we need to buy it somehow. You say you can arrange it. Believe me, we can pay well. Now tell us how you work and what you can do.'

Old and Silvester exchanged glances, Old nodded and Silvester rose to speak.

'Mr Shawaz, sir,' this last bowing towards the Sheik. Immediately Silvester spoke, Old was impressed. He was not speaking, he was projecting, though there was no boom in his voice, it was warm, inviting, enveloping.

'Gentlemen, we are here to give you what you want. Without disrespect, the immediate fact of your need for weapons is not our concern. Our concern is to give you what you want. We are not men of principle, we are opportunists. Once, we would have been described as adventurers, when that was not a term of praise.

'This,' he gestured towards Old, 'is Patrick Old. He is an experienced soldier with a past in military intelligence. This is important, as it means he knows many people, is owed many favours and knows the secret desires of important men. I am Andrew Noble. I know how to bring people together, deals together, how to make money change hands. I can also, if it becomes necessary at a later stage, again of course for a price, arrange for any purchases to be delivered wherever you wish.'

Ibn Fahad spoke for the first time, a guttural sound that was over before it had begun.

'This will not be necessary,' said Shawaz. 'We are interested in purchasing weapons. For transport, we have our own means.'

Silvester bowed slightly, acknowledging Shawaz's contribution.

'As you wish. Getting on, all we want is to give you what you want. Like the genie in the lamp. And we can. Patrick.'

He sat, and again gestured to Old, who stood, taking his turn on his hind legs. Old could still not get rid of the idea that, though he was playing himself, he was required to act a part, and though he was genuinely ex-military intelligence, he was no less susceptible to film and TV clichés than anyone else, and felt obliged to ham up the part of himself. He didn't hit the character acting too hard, but put himself back in the role of officer, out of civvies, his speech a little clipped, less relaxed.

'My colleague has given you the facts and is largely correct.'

Silvester scowled at him. More hamming – they each knew what the other was to say to the letter. They had scripted their parts as far as was possible without knowing what questions there would be. Both were sufficiently glib to be able to ad-lib, but the script gave them a fluent start.

'Of course, we cannot supply absolutely anything you might wish for. We cannot, nor would we want to,' here he again looked at Silvester as if he had wilfully overplayed their lack of conscience, 'not even all conventional weapons are within our remit. But from your description, we can supply the weapons you need, and in good faith. If your opponents, your enemies, if they are supplied with weapons from the great flea market that the Red Army has become, they have fallen at least three years behind in R&D, and anti-helicopter weapons can be obtained relatively cheaply that will beat their outdated electronic defences. Three years is a long time in defence research. It would be worthwhile for you to buy your weapons in two halves – a cheap half for the rebel threat and an expensive half for the Riyadh threat. Riyadh poses, of course, a much greater threat. As a friend of the West, it is supplied with top-quality weapons, but not as readily as you might think. The purchasing process, the supply of export licences, all this takes time and, as you rightly pointed out, we like to keep a year or two lead for ourselves. You will have seen the Patriot missiles in your country and Israel. But the US did not supply those weapons for anyone's use. They offered Patriot protection under the control of US personnel. As an offshoot of SDI – Star Wars – the Patriot is the only usable piece of weaponry developed from that program so far and as such, if the cost of Star Wars is counted as the cost of its development, is the most expensive weapon ever made, far exceeding the notorious B2 "Stealth" bomber. So, before you ask, nothing quite so smart is possible. Still, technology has moved on since the Stinger was first seen – it was tested very thoroughly in Afghanistan and development is always faster after proper field testing. I can arrange, if necessary, for you to be given a demonstration of the Stinger in its newest incarnation: a long, long way from its first.'

At last a real response: Ibn Fahad crooked his finger at Shawaz, who put his ear to the Sheik's mouth. They muttered to each other, inaudibly, for almost a minute.

'That is what the Sheik wants. We have met other salesmen, but none have been able to offer us this. When?'

'It is not so simply fixed. I will have to make contact with a few people, see what I can arrange – contacts are the essence of this thing, and it can't be tied down to specifics and delivery dates until I know a lot more about who's doing what and when – questions I wasn't prepared to ask until I knew you were interested.

'It may be almost immediately, it may be a few weeks, and whenever the time comes, we must move quickly. Another point, which I hope will not cause difficulty. A demonstration will cost money. The weaponry costs, the personnel costs, the open doors cost more, and closed mouths are difficult to price. We cannot lay out the kind of money this would cost without either an assurance that the demonstration will lead to a deal – which I expect you cannot provide – if you were so sure now, you would not need the demonstration – or you can pay for the demonstration.'

As he listened without a translator, they knew Ibn Fahad understood English. But they had only heard him speak to Shawaz in his own tongue, which Silvester presumed to be Arabic. When he did speak in English, his voice was quiet and barely accented, though with a little sing-song lilt.

'How much? I want to see the weapons work, I want to see them work, but I do not . . .' He raised a finger and pointed it briefly at each of them, lowering his voice, which encouraged them to lean in closer as if to share a secret. 'I do not want to be taken for a fool. I know many men think Arab money flows like water and can be diverted with the least effort; a scoop here, a culvert there. If I pay for this demonstration, which I fully expect will be expensive – fifty thousand . . .?'

Silvester had said this would be the point of make or break and that maybe they should front the money, remove the obstacle. Old said it was imperative. When they turned up, did as they promised, it proved they were what they said. The demonstration made it final and bingo! Payout. They had not expected the Sheik to confirm his suspicions so openly. This was not in the script. Silvester rose.

'I am not the Queen. You do not have to leave your seat every time you wish to speak,' Ibn Fahad commented, with a wry smile.

Silvester hovered uncertainly for a moment, half in

and half out of his seat, like the Grand Old Duke of York, before sinking back.

'We thought something nearer sixty-five, but if you want to give us fifty and we sort out the difference later?' Silvester suggested. The Sheik shrugged.

'Open doors and closed mouths do not come with written contracts, what difference will later make? Houssain.'

He waved imperiously at Houssain, who pulled a briefcase from under the table and rested it on his knee. They could see nothing behind the opened lid, but after a little shuffling, he started to unload money onto the table. Cash money. Silvester looked at Old, eyes agog. This was not what he expected, not real, exchangeable-for-goods, paper money. It came out in five piles. Four of five-banded packs, one of six. Twenty-six banded packs, each of two and a half thousand pounds; fifty fifties. Altogether it was about the size of a large single-volume dictionary. And it was impressive.

When they had transferred the money to Old's brief-case – Old wanted Silvester to be sure that, although they were partners in this, Old would have the whip-hand – Shawaz spoke.

'There is nothing more to say. Contact me when you have prepared a demonstration. And remember, you have my money, you are indebted to me and you will remain so until the demonstration. Do not try to be amusing with the Sheik's money, because if you do, the debt will be recovered, if not one way, then another.'

Silvester was uncontainable. As the car slipped through

the stream of traffic, he slapped the briefcase repeatedly and laughed.

'If that wasn't the easiest sixty-five grand I ever took off anyone in my life! I didn't believe it. I thought I'd blown it, offering to take fifty, I don't know why I did it. It just looked like the right thing to do and then as soon as I said it, it came out cheap, cheese-paring. I thought we'd lost it. Then he just ignores it and out comes the money. Crispy, fresh, new ones. If this was a scam in its own right, just this far, it'd be a dream.'

'Forget it,' Old said, sharply, leaving no room for debate.

'No, I mean, it wouldn't cover what I owe Mee, it isn't what we planned, and I know it depends at least in part on having someone dependable and traceable to play your part so you can come over as aggrieved as the mark when I vamoose. But it could be, I mean, it has the makings of a first-rate scam, with a bit of work.'

'But you won't be doing it, because if I see it in the papers, years hence, I'll be on to you.'

'Patented it have you?'

'Just do what the man Fahad said and remember what I said.'

'Fine. You know, you can be a real downer. I'm getting a nice rush and you're coming over like the Victorian father, which is rich, seeing you're in this as deep as I am. Deeper – it's your con after all. You manage the next bit, can you? That's why I couldn't do it alone. Now it gets really serious. Now we have to start doing *real* things. Not just conversations, meetings, we have to get the guy in the same place as some missile and blow something up. Which is a long way from convincing some porn king to buy an iffy BMW.'

'*We* have to do that now? So what do you suggest, how do you say we go about it?'

'Forgetting for a moment, you're the star for this part, my bit is blagging the Arabs. Fine. Now, drop me off. Far as I figure it out, you go meeting your uniform types, you don't want me cluttering up the place. I'll just kick back until you have something, tweak the script, look for holes, make sure we can dream up a plug if I find any. Next time we need to meet is when we agree terms with our man, arrange to meet for the demo. That right?'

Old nodded.

'And then', he rubbed his hands, greedily, 'we collect. You're a natural, Pat. This is sweet as a nut.'

The cellar was damp and gloomy. Ras poked through a box of old tools with his toe as he balanced on the back legs of a folding vinyl chair, swinging backwards and resting his turban on one of the supporting pillars. He glanced up at the ceiling.

'What d'you reckon they're talking about up there?' he said.

'Christ knows. Tell me if you know different, but I'd say Satya doesn't think much of Hannah. I thought I must be imagining it at first, but I'm sure now. I don't think Hannah noticed anything, but I caught a few of those Satya signals, you know the ones.'

'Oh, I know the ones. There's more of them than you can imagine. Sometimes I think she should have married a cryptographer. Then she'd have someone who knew what she was at, instead of poor saps like us who're always making a more or less educated guess.'

'Hannah though?'

'Sure, you got the signal right. Satya thinks she thinks a bit highly of herself.'

'She's self-confident, so's Satya, what's the matter with that?'

'Nothing. Absolutely nothing. Except I was being diplomatic. Using straight language, what Satya thinks is she's a snotty-nosed cow who thinks she deserves better; thinks a prince is going to kiss her and she's going to wake up in Hampstead.'

'She's not that bad.'

'My, what a rousing defence. Ardour cooled since last week?'

Old looked around, checking the cellar door was closed.

'Look,' he said, 'I'm sorry about tonight, but it was your idea, and I'm sorry about dragging you down here with this pretend "men looking at some DIY whatnot" performance, but I had to get away for five minutes.'

He paused, looking sheepish before he strung the words together.

'I got her to bed the other night. I suppose I should say, we made love, but the other is more what I meant.' His tone dropped at the end of the sentence.

'And she's a package of sensual delight,' Ras put in. Old frowned at Ras, who had stolen his story before it had started.

'And you can't drop her because you would feel bad and because it would be a problem for Sam who's thick as thieves with her Jimmy. And so, because you were already fixed up to come here, and being the sensitive soul that you are, it would have embarrassed you to cancel or to turn up alone and have to explain to Satya, who would have said: "I told you so" all night, though you weren't to know that, because actually it was me she told at great length that it wasn't a starter. Have I missed anything? Oh yes, the Barry Mee thing has been a bit hyper and you didn't need more complications on your mind. How did Silvester get on?'

'We've moved on, I take it.'

'Looks that way.'

'Do you mind if we don't – move on I mean. Carry on about Hannah. I'm not sure what's happening.'

'Situation hard to get out of?'

'Not even that. I mean, if you'd have said all that stuff, glib but clever, an hour after it happened, after I got her to bed, I'd have said: "Smartarse – read me like a book." Except it's not right. It just should be.

'The sex was lousy. The pits. She probably doesn't even know that, she's still keen, sure that we're closer than we were, that there's something real going on. What I just can't understand is that I see it more or less the same way – despite the crappy sex. Isn't it supposed to be men who see it as the be-all and end-all? Whatever and however, I still want her. It's like, it's not *how* the sex was, but *that* it was. I'm going to tell you something.' He paused again and managed, against the odds, to look even more sheepish and to pick up, at the base of his neck, the beginnings of a blush.

'And I'd really appreciate it if you didn't take the piss.'

'Go on, I'll try.'

Old didn't look convinced, but carried on. Now he'd begun the process of deliberately embarrassing himself, he thought he should get it out of the way.

'I was sitting at home, watching Sam while we were waiting to come over here, he was prattling on like he does, nursery rhymes at half cock, mixed with ad slogans, you know the way he does, and I started thinking about it. I float off, thinking about Sam's crazy rhymes, next thing, I'm knocking verses together. I got a pen and put them on paper. You see what I'm saying, I wrote a poem about the woman, I mean, Jesus, what's going on?'

'You don't need me to tell you that, do you?' Ras asked. 'A big obstacle pops up, this woman thing, you ignore it. You want to be around her all the time. You're writing poetry. Do you need me to spell it out, when you know what's going on? Did you see how much food you ate tonight? Not so damn much. That's hardly you is it? So this is the way it is.'

He put on his fruitiest, deepest Barry White voice, which for a Plaistow-born Sikh was pretty good, but which they both knew, on any kind of absolute scale, was pretty damn awful – maybe only half as unconvincing as a Dick Van Dyke cockney, or maybe an Olivier Othello. But at least not as bad as a Costner Robin Hood.

'Luuuurve, baby. Talking 'bout luuuurve here.'

Old held his head in his hands, took a pull of beer.

'I think maybe you're right. Love huh! What have I let myself in for?'

'Plenty, when you think there's still the scam to take care of. Which we need to do: take care of it. So if we

233

can put the darling Hannah on the backburner just for now, what about Silvester – he OK?'

'He was pleased as punch. Very slick, but he was looking at the possibility of building up the con so far as a free-standing con. Low horizons.'

'You've got the money, though? I mean you can keep up your end of the expenses?'

'What do you take me for?' Old smiled quickly before adding: 'Don't answer that.'

'Have you sorted out this demonstration yet, you have anything going?'

'Not yet, but I know I can sort something. All that bollocks about knowing people's secrets, in the script, it's not exactly the way it works. I do, I know a lot I shouldn't, but I wouldn't use anything. On the other hand, searching here and there, doing this and that, I built up a huge surplus in the favour bank. I'm just going to make a few withdrawals. Maybe even end up owing someone. They won't mind. Everyone knows the game and there's a terrific sense of security in being owed favours.'

Ras nodded. 'You know the strange thing? There's a strange feeling of security in owing too. You can't get too overdrawn with the same person and not have anyone owe you – looks like you're a user. You know the way it works, everyone has to know you understand. But you owe someone a big one, it's the same as being owed – you know you can rely on that person, you know that when it comes to it, they'll be there. And you were.'

He was right – Old was there. Though it was rarely mentioned between them, Old's favour had made its way into the fabric of their relationship. No longer a real debt, if it ever was, now it was part of the bond.

When Ras had gone AWOL, finding him had ended up, purely by chance, on Old's desk. Charged with finding missing Army personnel when they were in possession of specialized knowledge, which meant it was too urgent, too touchy to be left to the MPs, he had plenty of autonomy. It wasn't a job that could be ruled by the book. He was trained as a detective and let loose. He pushed the file to the bottom of his pile and took a couple of days leave. He found Ras in thirty hours, but they were continuous hours without sleep, and he convinced Ras to get back to his base sharpish, as it would be better for him to turn up under his own steam than go after being found. Then he chased around Ras's family tightening up an alibi. Anyone can tell a quick lie, but a good alibi needs to be tight, original and able to withstand a lot of knocks. The problem never got to be a real problem and within the year Ras had gained his sergeant's stripes.

He did have a family problem, but it was one that would have been unlikely to gain him emergency leave – convincing his cousin not to go to fight for Khalistan – and though going AWOL was madness – Ras loved the Army and was deeply proud of his stripes – he knew he had to go. The way Old sorted the deal, Ras got a private and extremely vociferous verbal beating, from his sergeant-major and his captain, a formal but low-grade censure on his record and a three-hundred-pound fine. The Army is very big on fines.

A month later, his cousin went to Punjab to fight regardless.

FIFTEEN

Tandy was driving again. The Jag had been returned; now they were in a Mondeo. Standard rental car. It ate up the miles on the motorway, a steady eighty – no one wanted to get picked up. Official records that you were in a certain place at a certain time: not what was wanted at all.

This time he was not in the uniform duds, he was told to dress casual but not inconspicuous. He tried this, tried to look as invisible as he could, and could see nothing wrong with his attempt – faded blue jeans, old chambray shirt and a stone-coloured cotton jacket with elasticated cuffs and collar. Then he picked up Old who was wearing exactly the same thing. Exactly. The jeans and shirt were standard enough, though they both had Levis and M&S shirts, just to make the exactness of the match tighter, but they had both bought the jackets at the same shop; they had both been introduced to the place by Ras. The effect was too much. Old skipped inside and came out with a black Harrington jacket. Fine, now they could be anybody.

They arrived in Aldershot – a town Tandy had never visited before, but which he knew was the big-gest garrison town in the country, just squeaking Colchester. Aldershot was the garrison, the garrison was Aldershot. Old seemed to know the place fairly well. He directed Tandy through the streets, quickly heading off the main roads and had them park up a narrow alley beside a tatty, unkempt-looking pub, the Dog and Goose.

The outside of the pub, if anything, was flattering. It was not even a spit and sawdust joint. It was just a dump. It had been given the early-seventies red vinyl treatment, and nothing since. Foam puked out from untidy gashes in several parts of all the bench seats. The stools were similarly beaten up and there were missing staves in the backs of many of the upright chairs. The carpet looked as if it might have started off a dark maroon. Beer and vomit had taken their toll on the remaining coloured areas, but the predominant theme was cigarette burn: they were now in the ascendancy, taking up more space than the areas between them. Perhaps the biggest surprise was that the place was busy. Old had explained, as they parked, that it was difficult to find an Army-free pub in Aldershot – city-centre pubs were full of squaddies and the suburbs were full of officers living off-site and their wives. Impossible to say who knew whom. That was actually what he said, which took Tandy back a little, hearing a 'whom' like that, just thrown into conversation without warning.

All the beers were keg. Sad. Old ordered a bottle of Guinness for himself and an orange juice and soda for Tandy, after asking him, pointedly, what kind of *soft* drink he wanted.

Their man had to meet in Aldershot as he could only manage an ordinary lunch hour if he wanted to avoid attracting attention. And as he was a creature of habit, Old explained, who took a regular fifty minutes, and given that it could take ten minutes to get in and another ten to get back, they had a twenty-five- to thirty-minute opportunity, which meant meet near the barracks.

Even a small town has its malcontents, its deadbeats, its half-in and half-out of society types, its conspiracy theorists, drifters and loafers. Here they were at home. This place was well known as a spot where locals and Army simply didn't mix. Others were known as rucking grounds, where the 'ownership' of the place was disputed and machismo could be bared to support the cases of the different sides.

Parks are another possibility for this kind of cloak and dagger idiocy, which works better when it does not have such mundane obstacles as having to happen during lunch. They are too visible, and questions could be asked. Two strangers meeting on a park bench, too many prying eyes. Too Tinker Tailor. The Dog and Goose was the one safe place Old knew, and even it had its drawbacks. Being known to be Army-free, it was openly hostile to those it thought might be Army. The Army was not welcome. It was an original form of niche marketing and not one likely to catch on.

If only the Army knew what it was missing.

Tandy eyed the locals as they eyed him. It was obvious from his haircut that he was not in the Army. It was not long, but neither was it a crew, and his three earrings hardly fitted the part. Worse, they were strangers, and it was not the type of pub where the regulars took to strangers. Regardless of what the landlord thinks: there are certain types of pub where the landlord is only the nominal owner, in charge of the stock, the till and little else.

Their man was due in at 1.20. He was second-perfect.

He was wearing a pair of uniform trousers with a white shirt and a tweed jacket. He would have been recognizable as an off-duty English Army officer by a potato. Immediately he attracted looks. Unfriendly looks, which, being a trained killer, for all his politeness, good breeding and impeccable time-keeping, he recognized the moment he stepped in the bar. Tandy saw it on his face; a distaste for the smell of threat, unbounded by diplomacy and treaty.

'Get you a drink?' Old asked. Tandy stood back, a discreet but small distance away from the other two. Far enough to let them talk, near enough to be clear they were all together. His eyes kept moving around the bar.

It was a shame it had to happen, but he knew it was going to. You don't have a decade and a half of troublesome youth in Glasgow without a self-preserving feel for these things. And though these boys might have a bit of a chip on their shoulders about all these Army types wandering all over their town as if they owned it – which they did – they weren't Glasgow boys. A country town in the Home Counties is what it was, garrison or no. No kind of a place to get an education in street.

Probably start off all Queensbury.

'I would, but nothing doing for at least three months,' Tandy overheard Old's officer friend say in as low a voice as it seemed it would be possible to use without actually whispering. 'You know, if this is anything like what it looks like, I know you well enough to know it won't be, but it could be seen as being well near treasonable.'

'I can guarantee you, nothing's going to change

hands apart from money. If it is any use, there's enough moving around for a fee.'

'That's not what I'm after. And as I said, it simply isn't about to happen this end. What I *can* do is give you a name.' He stopped dead. Old had seen the movement very soon after Tandy and held up his hand to stop the conversation. There were enough people casually moving around shuffling here and there with their drinks, but this one, without a drink, had a sense of purpose, and an audience.

Tandy saw Old give the slightest signal with his eyes. The signal was a clear enough instruction: whatever it takes.

The man approached them and the noise level in the bar dropped.

'Do you need a hand, or can you leave on your own?'

Tandy stretched out his left arm and put his hand in the man's face. His thumb shoved hard in the man's throat, index and little fingers in his cheeks and the other two fingers in his eyes, which closed just in time. He strode quickly forward. The man had to scurry backwards quickly to keep his balance, completely out of control. Tandy bent his elbow so he could walk alongside the man. He kicked one door open and marched through, the next set of doors opening with a dull thud as the would-be heavy's head struck it solidly.

They continued to the kerb. As the man lost his balance as he tipped off, Tandy let go with his left hand and sent a curling right into his jaw.

He had a glass jaw.

He lay, stunned, and probably aware he was in the

safest place. As Tandy turned, he saw the pub doors were still open. The regulars seemed to think they had been about to see a good fight and they crowded around the doors. He saw Old, back at the bar, give a thumbs up. The officer looked slightly shocked but was trying to stay cool. Tandy strolled back through the crowd, took his place at the bar and took a deep drink of his orange juice. He nodded at his drink, as he made eye contact with the barman.

'More ice this time.'

A couple of the men helped up the debris in the gutter,brushed him down and took him off down the street, with what looked like little conscious co-operation from the heroic street fighter. The rest returned to their drinks, the level of noise returning to its old level and past it. Now the whole bar was looking at Tandy, but with furtive, sidelong glances. As if he was not supposed to notice.

Old was scribbling a name and number down.

'I owe you.'

'Not really. Maybe we're even now. Who's counting?'

'We are. But if you need anything, call.'

An hour and forty minutes each way for a twenty-minute meeting, about which he knew barely anything, a pointless bit of aggro and two orange juices. Still, Tandy thought, he who pays the piper . . .

Mee flicked to the Teletext menu and found the share index page. He felt he should know the number, but his most used pages were the TV guide, the weather and the news. He glanced at a number of shares, the dozen which held the bulk of his holdings, and smiled.

They were up, overall. Not by much, but who wants to argue? Up is up. He turned off the TV and pulled a light-box onto his desk. He spread a number of transparencies around.

Of all his magazines, the most respectable, the least gynaecological, the one he wanted to boost to chase the sales of the American edition of *Playboy*, dump the premium telephone line ads and start to pick up some proper advertising – cigarettes, cars and stereos, maybe a few men's clothes – was *Gloss*. He was never sure about the name, but the South Audley Street consultants he had brought in said it had researched well. Maybe, but the research had certainly paid well. This month, *Gloss* had a short story by a young writer who had won some sort of a prize a couple of years back. Still didn't have two pennies to rub together and Mee knew he didn't want to do it, but there was a big fee in it and that means everything. If it was possible to buy respectability, Mee would do it. To a large degree, *Playboy* had managed it. After all, in the most perfect piece of timing, the month Nadine Gordimer won the Nobel Prize for Literature, there she was with a short story in *Playboy*. That was the great thing about quality fiction – from Mee's angle – they could be at it for years and still make no real money. Jeffrey Archer would have told him where to get off, any of the big sellers, but these 'literary' types who didn't have a pot to piss in, well they couldn't take their eyes off the two grand he'd offer. That could be as much as some of them would get up front for a book, and all he wanted was five thousand words, and don't think it has to be sexy.

He looked at the photos. An outside shoot. That was good. Sun. Showed you'd spent some money.

This one was in the Canaries, all that black volcanic sand, black model, chiffon in the wind. Clichéd as hell, but there was no denying it made for a better shot than all that three-foot spread from knee to knee stuff, laid over the boss's desk.

After marking the shots he liked best with a white spot pen, touching the top corner of the tranny, he dropped the shots back in the envelope, put away the light box and called Debbie.

'Those two deadbeats are still outside here,' she complained in what would have been a whine if she hadn't been whispering. 'You sure you don't want me to offer 'em coffee or something?'

'I didn't invite them, let them rot.'

'They're listening in to me, they keep staring at me, they're messing up my reception. Can't you get rid of 'em? Please, Barry?'

'Leave it a while, love. Bring me a cup of tea and when I'm done with that, I'll see.'

There was a pause at the other end, then a whisper.

'You're not frightened of 'em, are you, Barry? I can call someone to get rid of 'em if you want.'

Mee smiled to himself. 'No thanks, Debbie love, I'm just making the bastards wait. They've been an annoyance to the both of us over the past couple of weeks, calling in here every two minutes, the lot of them phoning up, see how they like this kind of thing. The tea first though, thanks, Deb love.'

It could take Debbie ten minutes to make a cup of tea when it suited her. Now it was in her interests, she was at the door with it in under a minute. Lucky I like

243

it weak, Mee thought. As she opened the door, Kevin and Mel pushed it open. Mel took the tea from her.

'I'll take that for you, darlin',' said Mel with a sickly, false sincerity. Debbie looked at Mee with a mild panic. Mee raised his hand and pursed his lips, signalling that she shouldn't worry.

'That'll be all right, Debbie, for now. I'll call when I need you.'

She sidled out behind the two men. As soon as she was gone and the door was closed, Mee rose slowly from his chair.

'What's going on here? Who do you think you are, barging in my office like you own the fucking place?' Mee yelled, taking the offensive. 'Explain yourself and piss off!'

'Talk to us like that, you fat little slag,' Mel started. 'We've been out there for over an hour and you fucking know it. We've had it waiting around after you. You going to sort this slag Goodman or are we going to have to sort you?'

Mee sat back in his chair. He shook his head, resignedly. He thought of the first Brando scene in *The Godfather*, where, as Corleone, he promises a favour, and shows, in his manner, that everything is in his power. It was Mee's favourite film, and he tried to put something of that manner into his demeanour now, knowing he wasn't getting it as he did it.

'You just blew the only chance you ever had of seeing any of that money.'

'Think you can threaten us . . .'

'Shut up!' Mee yelled. Listen to me or you'll never even know how you fouled up. You've been annoying the life out of me, the lot of you. But the one excuse

you had was that you were cut up about your money
and you wanted to know how it was coming. I understand that. But if it's a case of get our money or else,
then I've got to ask: "Or else what?" See, Goodman
got our money and fucked off. *Our* money. Remember,
I got done for two cars. But he wasn't there to be
threatened or to threaten; he got on his toes and off.

'If you threaten me, let alone touch me, anyone
connected to me or anything I own, then I'll get the
police. Don't think I won't. When Goodman invited
me into his little deal I was as fooled as you. I was
greedy, I saw easy money and I bit. I was offered
more and I bit again and I invited some friends in and
they bit too. All by themselves. That's the difference
you see. I invited you in as friends. Now you're here
as enemies, you're deliberately making yourselves into
my enemies. And I have no time for chat with enemies.
Now fuck off out.'

'Listen to me . . .'

Mee pressed a button on his intercom.

'Call the police, Debbie. Now please.'

Kevin opened the door.

'You're going to be sorry about this, Barry. Fucking
sorry.'

'I hope not, Kev. Don't forget I've money on my
side. I could squash you, and if you don't disappear,
I'll do it happily. If my man catches Goodman, I think
I'll keep him to myself; try to get my piece back. You
want your money back, hire your own detective. Now
get out. If I don't see your face again, the phone
doesn't ring again, and you behave like good little
boys, and my man does his stuff, I might just throw
you a biscuit. Go on, get out of my face.'

Always late for Mass five minutes or so, he had made a special effort to be there on time. Normally for Holy Days of Obligation he didn't bother, but Hannah did. She had asked him which Mass he would be at. The assumption was that he would be there. It wasn't time to get into a discussion. Not that one. So he was here and he was early.

The circumstances of the unusually correct attendance at Mass – psychological coercion – didn't help his attitude. Sam as usual was happily soaking in the stillness, coming over like the Boy Buddha. Old felt like a reluctant and sulky teenager sent to Mass by his mother. It sent him mulling over all the reasons why he didn't want to be there, which were linked, like one sausage to the rest, to why he was such a lousy Catholic and such a first-rate hypocrite.

First there were his Jack Horner habits: he wasn't the police, so whenever money came onto the scene when he was working, he stuck in his thumb and saw what he could persuade to pop out into his lap. Ethical? Probably not. Feel guilty about it? Certainly, and more, the greater his success and the juicier the plum. Tried his best not to, but he was trained to feel high-level guilt at the slightest prompt. He knew he did it for Sam, because he needed to be secure, to provide, but guilt doesn't take excuses, not even signed by your mother and your doctor. You feel guilty, then you feel guilty. No way round it.

Then there was the sex thing. Why was the Church (he could never help but capitalize the Church in his thoughts) why was the Church so hung up on sex? He looked around, saw the images. Death, blood, pain and sex. What was the old joke? Play word association with a Protestant, say wine, they say Claret, Merlot, Beaujolais. With a Catholic, say wine, they say blood. And the female images. The Virgin Mary, Mary Magdalene, whatever the stories said, how come the pictures always showed luscious big-hipped women with creamy breasts and deep cleavages? He found himself getting turned on by the image, Mary Magdalene on her knees, washing his feet.

Hannah genuflected at the edge of his vision. She was wearing a Spanish lace mantilla that covered her head and partially her eyes. It made her whole face ravishing. Made her partially visible eyes look as if they held a million secrets. Concealment always does so much more for a man than revelation. In his mind, as she smiled and slid down the pew, his mental image of Mary Magdalene continued, but her place was taken by Hannah. He could feel his face flush red in the gloom of the church. He could hardly look at Hannah straight. This line of thought was doing him no good at all. Sam and James started whispering to each other and almost immediately burst into a fit of giggles. Sam was a little boy again. And a welcome distraction. Thank God.

If there was one thing could be said about Silvester, it was that he didn't need telling twice. He loved a good scam, and once he had been told the details, he knew it well enough that, given the resources, he could have walked straight out and done it. He could do confidence because he had it. He was running over with confidence. Straight, he would have made a brilliant salesman, if he could only be persuaded to keep making the same sale day after day, and if he could get used to the idea that once the punter handed over the money, you had to hand over the goods.

Old was explaining progress, though there was not a lot to explain. One refusal had led to another lead, someone he would be meeting the next day. No, Silvester couldn't come along. Army people were most comfortable with their own.

Once he knew his part – sit back and wait for the next meeting with Ibn Fahad and Shawaz – Silvester was happy to let that be and carry on telling Old some of the best cons he had heard in exchange for Old's 'finding the missing' anecdotes, though he found these lacking the spice of a good con. He was disappointed, though, at the depth of Old's research into the lying game, as this meant he knew a good number of the best cons already.

'Wait then. This one's a gem. Guy goes into a pub, he's got a dog, plug-ugly bastard. He orders a couple of drinks, passes the time with the barman, buys him a couple of drinks, blah, blah, blah. Mobile phone goes. Guy says he's got to go. Is it OK if he leaves the dog? The barman says no. The guy virtually begs, sticks the barman a twenty, says it'll be a couple of hours, tops. It looks like a cared-for dog, guy'll be back. Eventually, barman says OK.

'A while later, another guy comes in, orders a drink, sees the dog, he's off his stool looking at the thing. "Jesus," the guy says, "That's a Strasbourgeoise Waschbärhund," or some such cock. Barman shrugs. "Is it yours?" he asks, the barman says no. He witters on and on about what a wicked dog it is, how he's wild about dogs – some people are football crazy, some are babehounds, he's a houndhound.'

Silvester couldn't help laughing as he delivered the line. It sounded like to him it was the best part of the story: babehound – houndhound, you had to laugh. Old nodded in appreciation. A con is really a short story, and if you can't get the feel for a story, you don't get into words well used, you can get nowhere as a con. Silvester took a sip of water, muttering to himself: 'Houndhound, slays me.' Eventually, shaking his head, he forced himself back to the con.

'So your man, he says he already has two dogs, but he always wanted a Waschbärhund. Paid for a pup once but couldn't get an import licence, blew the money. Talks about how they're really rare, and of course being German doesn't make them any cheaper. He asks, can the barman get it for him. He gets down, looks at the dog's teeth, paws, all that stuff, says he'd pay up to four fifty if the barman could get it for him. Checks his watch, he'll be around tomorrow, see if the barman managed it. "Please, do your best, mate," all kind of bollocks.

'Your man comes back, the guy brought the dog in. Suddenly, the barman's wild about the dog. You see, you know how they all work now, I know you can see it already, he won't just say: "I know a guy wants your dog and'll give you a good price and for a few quid I'll introduce you." He has to be a smartarse and that's the core of the con: you know he will be, because people are stupid, they're greedy, and most important, they think they're clever. *Especially*, most *especially* when they're *not*. So he's telling the guy what a great dog this is, how in the past hour he's really come to love it, laying it on with a trowel. Your man says, really it's just a hangover from a relationship. Good dog and all that, but so what? Not as if it's a pedigree or anything, just a Heinz dog – 57 varieties – for all he knows about dogs, which is nothing. He gets to it: "Let me buy it off you." Suddenly, your man's fonder than he imagined, making out he doesn't want to look a rube, he mightn't want the dog but someone else does, supply and demand. The barman's in "sneaky bastard" mode, so greedy is just what he expects. Eventually they settle, usually somewhere over a hundred, and the barman's just bought himself a hundred-quid, dollar, whatever, plug-ugly dog he could have had from the dogs' home for free that morning.'

'And the other guy's gone.'

'He's sitting pissing himself, waiting for his turn tomorrow when he plays the guy with the dog. You sure I can't come along tomorrow? The chat is half the fun of a scam.'

'I'm sure,' Old said firmly. 'Soon as we've got the demonstration booked, you're in it every step, schmooz-ing the client and throwing all those big numbers at him. I'll just try and look all Military Intelligence; suggesting there's tacit, unofficial approval for the deal, which is how we're getting our paws on the stuff.'

The advantage of meeting in London is the total an-onymity of the place. You can be the most liked, most popular guy in town and walk around in ever-widening circles until you drop without ever passing anyone you know. And being in London, on home ground, Old was able to give Tandy the day off, after warning him that whatever he got up to, he would have to be presentable the next day. No red-rimmed eyes, no stubble, pressed clothes. Ibn Fahad and Shawaz might only see them for a moment getting out of the car but everything had to look right. Tight and professional. For now it was off-duty but smart none the less.

He had taken the name given him by his Aldershot contact and looked it up in the MoD manual. He wanted to find a point of contact with himself; a place, a base, a person, anything. He had been plum lucky. They had both been based in the same area near Hanover, on the same base, and consequently with the same commanding officer, and enough of the regular staff there would be known in common for it to be impossible that he be a fraud, as it was likely, if he had any sense, that the contact would try to trip him up. Once they had sorted out their credentials, the common history would also give them the basis for a bit of a chat. They also had Old's contact in common. Old had worked with him in Intelligence, though he had transferred out to Ordnance. Old suspected, as he had been reluctant to say, that he had met Captain Brayne, his contact today, in Intelligence. As is usually the case, Army people identify that kind of thing by the unsaid as quickly as they would if it was out in the open.

They met in the Hand and Racquet on Whitcomb Street. Roughly equidistant from Trafalgar and Leicester Squares and Piccadilly, it still managed to be in a backwater. Until a couple of years earlier, it had also managed to repel possible customers by being not so much decrepit as seriously untidy, apart from the toilets, which would have given a German tourist cause for a year in therapy. Since then it had been refurbished in all regards bar the two women working the pumps who looked as if they had worked there since Dickens had been turned away for trying to get served under-age. It was only their infinite lack of vim that kept the punters out.

Brayne was there before Old. He was drinking a pale brown drink, which looked like ginger, and as Old could see none of the tell-tale translucent spirit swirl, he was willing to guess it was ginger alone. It was a popular Intelligence habit – drink what looks like alcohol but isn't. Keeps you one step ahead and every step counts. If he turned out not to have worked in Intelligence, all this calculation would look pretty silly, he thought, before he joined Brayne who rose to shake hands.

'Old.'

'Brayne.'

A very typical Army exchange so far.

'How much do you know of what I want?' asked Old, getting straight to the issue, and hoping to avoid the positive vetting as far as possible.

'Before we even touch that, there's a great deal I don't know about you.'

Some hope.

'Whatever you need to know,' Old offered, readying his well-rehearsed mixture of a great part of truth mixed with outright lies at the relevant places.

Brayne was keen. He was willing to help, and Old was sure he was willing to take money. But before they touched on the specifics of Brayne's possible role, they got involved in minutiae that Old would have sworn he didn't know. If he knew how to interrogate like that, there was no doubt he had worked in Intelligence. It was a hard and thoroughgoing investigation, which still managed to seem like nothing more than a casual chat, a hunt for common ground. He still had access to files, presumably, because he knew Old's dates, and who was there at the same time, whereas Old could only make a rough guess at Brayne's dates and potential colleagues. Fortunately, he had nothing to conceal at this stage, so he could submit to the questioning without a qualm.

'. . . side of the officers' garages was the outside hose?'

'Left. South.'

'. . . feature of the last cryptographic civilian staff member to arrive during your stay?'

'. . . 36DDs. Yvonne. I keep in touch, now and then.'

'. . . Hanover bars were forbidden, which and why?'

'Two. Schwabinger Sieben and Trib. Both because there were too many drugs, openly used. I hauled quite a few lads out of there myself. And that's enough. You know who I am, you're just doing it for fun now. I am who I say I am, I don't need a turn checking you out. Your questions tell me all I need to know. You worked in Intelligence before Ordnance for I'd say four years and it was while you were in there that you won your captain's bars. You spent a lot of time in Germany, though your spoken German is still wooden, but I'd say you spent a few spells in Northern Ireland, and if your ability to do accents is as fluid as your German, I sincerely hope you didn't go undercover. Chances are, though, you were an interrogator, briefing and debriefing informers in the protection and placement programme.'

'And before you were put in the missing persons

find and return unit,' Brayne put in, 'which seems rather to have dominated your life since, you were scoring top marks on analysis of raw source materials. A skill I expect you would find useful in your present work.'

Old stood.

'All this is making me thirsty. I'm having a pint. You want whisky in yours this time?'

Brayne shook his head and smiled, pleased that Old had picked up the insiders' trick.

'As it is; ginger, ice.'

When Old returned with the drinks, he decided if he was to make this part of the story – the iffy part – work, he was going to tell it his own way.

'Now you've led me by the nose through a history paper, I'm going to tell you what I want, and I'll let you know now, I won't tell you everything. But I will tell you two important things. Nothing, absolutely nothing will happen as a result of my actions which will affect the security of the State or that of any of our allies. The other thing is that, if you help me, I can pay you a fee. A generous one.'

'And now you're going to tell me a story.'

Old had planned a neat twist at the end of the story which was supposed to explain why no arms fell into anti-Saudi hands. It was another of his sly hints at official approval. But just before he started, he saw that Brayne was too smart. There was every chance he would believe the story completely right up to the point where it turned into a lie and then he would blow it up. Old told him precisely what was to happen. He laid out the scam. And he offered money for Brayne to take part. Ten thousand pounds.

'Now you've got to rationalize it,' said Old. 'I know how it works – there's no good Army reason to do this, but it doesn't harm the Army. There is a good reason to do it for yourself, but unlike the rest of the world, you're not used to that as a motivation. And last, it looks like a jolly jape. It's a bit cheeky and you like the idea of being part of it. It isn't as if I'm asking you to do anything you wouldn't anyway – you just have to let me in on the fringe. The very furthest edge.'

Brayne listened carefully.

'You're very familiar with the processes of rationalization. I'll have to have another look at your files, see where you were acting up.' But he was grinning as he said it. He was going to allow himself to put a toe on the wrong side of the line, Old could see. He nodded and they shook hands.

What Old needed was very very simple, and Brayne could do it on the spot. He had a time. He had a place. The place was precise. He gave him an OS map sheet number and a reference.

'As you know, with that scale, a reference puts you within a hundred yards. It puts you in a small wood on the edge of the shooting range. It is clear there is only one road nearby. The woods are round, like an apple with a dimple on the side facing the action. You will be in the dimple. If you are anywhere else, I will despatch MPs to move you on – lost tourists.'

'Bit unnecessary isn't it?' Old asked.

'Discipline and predictability. The Army needs and loves them both. On the day I'll have a job to do. You are an added factor. If I know precisely where you will be, I can plan the day. Imprecision breeds more imprecision. Be in the dimple.'

'The dimple,' Old nodded, meekly.

'It isn't so important if my men see you – we do get funny types watching now and then. No one asks questions, as you know. The demonstration will go ahead when I said. If you are late you will miss it. Pay me the week before, this time, here.'

Businesslike; business done.

Another piece in place.

Suited and booted, they were ready to see their people and ask the big question: 'Are you in?'

They were back at the hotel, but had been given a different meeting-room. Because the rooms were adjacent and the doors to the rooms also adjacent, the one room was the mirror image of the other. The slight change had a curiously unsettling effect.

Silvester stood the moment everyone was present, wanting to pre-empt another round of pleasantries.

'Sir,' he bowed slightly towards Ibn Fahad, who acknowledged with an almost subliminal flicker of the eyes.

'We have arranged for a demonstration. It is sooner than we expected. Next Thursday.' This was Wednesday. He opened his case and took out a manila envelope. He emptied it onto the table and a pile of money spilled out.

'Five thousand and bits,' Silvester said, visibly suppressing a smirk. This had been his idea. Once he had become used to the idea that the first piece of the money was not the point of the scam, he saw it could be used to purchase extra confidence. They took their genuine expenses – Tandy, the cars, clothes – and Brayne's fee out of the money they kept.

He knew already that it was a sound move. He thought he was becoming quite a skilled interpreter of Ibn Fahad's facial tics and twitches and he decided the flicker he saw when he pushed the money and the envelope across the table was one of approval.

'The demonstration will take place in Wiltshire. We will arrange transport.' He stopped, straightened his back, interlocked his fingers, and, in what Old thought was a very theatrical gesture, cracked his knuckles. Still, Old thought, this is theatre.

'There is one matter we need to settle before we make final arrangements,' Silvester said, 'and as you can guess it is financial. This is a once only deal. You are not ordering from a catalogue. When we supply you, we will supply a full inventory of spare parts, but you must order what you need at the very beginning. You cannot come back for a couple here, a couple there. I will have moved on, I may not be operating in the same field, I may not be welcome in the same places. Mr Old will still be here, plying his respectable trade in consultancy and intelligence, but I suspect he will be denying any knowledge of me. What is possible today will not be possible later. You must decide what you want and abide by the decision. The missiles we will show you have a price tag – negotiable of course – of twelve thousand pounds; that's through official channels – to approved buyers. Governments. We have our channels which lead to a non-negotiable sixteen. There is another slightly older missile we recommend you also use to save on excess use of the good stuff. Reserve it for your Yemenis. This we can obtain for five and a half.'

Shawaz raised a hand.

'As we are being straightforward today, I will tell you what we have decided, in order that you set things in motion with your people, establish commissions, the usual things. We want two hundred of the cheaper model. At your figures' – he paused for a barely discernible moment to make the mental calculations – 'this means we will owe you £1.1 million pounds. For the intelligent model, we expect we shall want seventy-five. Again using your figures, this comes to £1.2 million pounds. This is a total of £2.3 millions. You say your figures are non-negotiable. We say, let the negotiations begin. We are willing to pay no more than £1.75 million for the whole package.'

Old had watched Silvester throughout. Seated while Shawaz spoke, his eyes had blinked perhaps a little more than usual as the numbers came out: the speed with which he had calculated showed both that his mind was quick, and that he was not thrown by big numbers, even when they represent hard cash. When Shawaz stopped, Silvester was cool as a cucumber.

'Gentlemen, when we started, we said we would deal straight. We did so when we gave you a price. Of course the deal includes an element for us. We are taking risks and we calculated the sum we were willing to accept and we abide by it. The same applies all along the supply chain. The sum you stated is very near the price of the goods, but leaves nothing for us. It is for us that we are involved – not patriotism or idealism but money.

'I think it would be a waste if we were to take the agreement we have no further. Remember, the demonstration is next Thursday. It will go ahead whether we are there or whether we are not. You know where to find us.'

He stood.

'Mr Old?'

Old rose slowly. Silvester was looking very positive. A good performance. The two Arabs watched impassively as they left the room.

SIXTEEN

The plane seemed to be hedge-hopping compared to the normal altitude of a commercial jet.

Everything was going exactly as it should. Silvester had lost a stone in weight over three days waiting for the phonecall. Then it came. Full price. Silvester agreed and thanked them for the call without a tremor in his voice.

Thursday morning, dressed for the country in specially purchased, second-hand, beat-up Barbours, boots and cords, apart from Tandy who was still dressed as a driver, they picked up Ibn Fahad and Shawaz from the hotel and drove to a car park in the City. The car park had a direct exit out to the City Heliport. They took a chartered helicopter to a small airfield just outside London to the north-west. There they changed to a small eight-seater jet which took them to Swindon where they changed to a Land Cruiser. It was a forty-minute drive to the demonstration, and less than forty words were exchanged. The entire dialogue in the car trip had consisted of:

'Radio, sir?' from Tandy, and 'No,' from Old, and a further 'This is it, we're here,' from Old, which was especially redundant, as Tandy had stopped the car and was opening the Sheik's door.

Tandy was not used to off-road driving, but he had been practising in the Land Cruiser for the past couple of days and had already taken the trip to the demonstration site from Swindon twice, except he had travelled to Swindon by 125 Express train and stayed one night in a hotel. He took every turn without hesitation, no less when he was off the road for the last two miles and twenty minutes of the journey. It was timed to perfection. They had less than ten minutes between their arrival and the demonstration.

Old checked his binoculars and confirmed that it was Brayne in charge and they exchanged signals to confirm that all was correct on each side.

Ibn Fahad was rapt as the deadly missile coldly tracked and destroyed the model helicopter. As it whipped through the air, keenly and bloodlessly seeking the destruction of its quarry and itself, his eyes were fixed, amazed at such power, there to be purchased, apparently, by anyone with the means, the contacts, and a willingness to bypass the rules. Silvester was also fascinated by the show, but could not help keeping a watchful eye on the Sheik. And he was pleased with what he saw.

Though it was only a demonstration, it was a fearsome demonstration of extreme and controlled violence.

Ibn Fahad for once looked happy and Shawaz confirmed the order.

'We will meet next week to confirm the details, to clarify ways and means.'

The rest of the way back they travelled in silence, except on the plane, when Ibn Fahad and Shawaz sat separately from the rest, as far as is possible in an eight-seater jet, and conversed in a low undertone in their own language, comprehensively excluding Old and Silvester.

Old hardly noticed. The rush he had experienced on

his bar scam paled beside this. The helicopter ride over London was by itself exciting, as was the private jet flight. The off-road driving had its thrills and the demonstration took the breath away with its suddenness and brutality. And overlaying it all was that all of this, the whole elaborate edifice, was in the name of a big, a massive criminal lie. He felt hugely, throbbingly alive.

Old could see, as they dropped Ibn Fahad and Shawaz at the hotel, that Silvester was very tense. They shook hands and promised to be in touch as soon as they had made a final decision. They disappeared through the thick glass plate doors and Silvester immediately launched into a little jig. He skipped and twirled around and the commissionaire glared at him, as if he were lowering the tone of his valuable piece of pavement. Old smiled.

'Very nice, now get in the car. And we still can't talk in front of Tandy.'

Tandy heard this and smiled to himself. He could see a lot of what was going on, could see a lot of funny business. He didn't have all the details yet but he could see someone was going to bend over, innocently as you pleased, and be awfully surprised when they got it, long, hard and unlubricated. He hoped he would be there to see that when it happened.

By the time they were back at Old's house, Silvester was shaking. Old told Tandy to stay away indefinitely but to stay ready.

Inside, Silvester had to put down his Scotch, his hands were shaking badly.

'I always try not to bank the money mentally until I

have it. And I always fail. We've got the bastard. I know it. Two and a half million almost. How much is the little squirt in for?'

'Toby Norton?'

Silvester nodded that this was who he meant.

'Nothing. He'll not be pleased when he learns but he's not in. I thought they might want some tricky stuff doing with the money, and I thought they might not cough up the expenses and he could help us spread the load. But we didn't need him in on it, and when it was obvious he was on the fringes he got all miffed, told me he didn't want in if he wasn't in properly. So he's on a fee basis.'

'Fee for what?'

'Reeling you in, hon.'

'How much?'

'Five K.'

'Nice to know your true value,' Silvester said, his voice dripping with sarcasm.

'But that means it's just you and me and a damn big pile of money.'

'When we get it. Like I said, it's not easy but you have to try. Harder than it ever was on this thing though – this is retirement. Hard to sleep without thinking about it.'

'Follow your own advice.'

Sam was a source of constant wonder to Old. After he complained that he had nothing to do in the house, making a pain of himself, deliberately irritating Old to get a response, get him to roll about and fight on the floor, Old took him out to the park. He wasn't interested. He had always been keen on the park, climbing to the highest point of whatever apparatus he was on and turning Old's hair grey. Suddenly, he could take it or leave it. He clung firmly to Old's hand and wasn't about to let go. Since the park had little to offer if you weren't using the playground, Old took him off to the Wanstead Flats, where there was even less going on but where there were few trees so he could fly his kite. Sam had been unaware Old had the kite with him. It was an ingenious design without any solid struts; it was given rigidity by fabric tubes which filled with air. This meant Old could keep it in his pocket if he folded it well and wore a big coat – which he needed as there was a good, stiff kite-flying breeze. Sam had been utterly delighted.

He stood now, utterly oblivious to anything around him, watching the tiny blue, red and yellow rectangle and its flickering tail over three hundred feet up in the air. Behind him, a number of middle-aged men were grumbling about the kite. They had their model aircraft, big lumbering home-made things for which they had made a small runway, but they knew the skies were open to whoever got to them first. They simply didn't like waiting in line behind a five-year-old boy. They would like it no better when they realized the extent of his patience, Old thought. He could stand and watch it for an hour or more, a calm easy expression on his face, which reminded Old of the meditative look he took on in church. And just as he did when he took Sam to church, to sit in the gloomy afternoon stillness, he found himself running over his life, looking at what was happening, unravelling the mental knots.

But for once, he couldn't.

The Barry Mee thing was all too much. Exciting, dangerous possibly, but too hectic to suit as a resting place for a contemplative mind. He would sum it up for posterity, take a view on it, when it was all wrapped up, which should be no more than a few days by now. As for what passed for a personal life, it was best if he avoided looking too closely. Every time he did, a damp fog of confusion wrapped around him. As fast as he lost focus, Hannah gained it. The more he saw a tangle of contradictory possibilities and meanings, the more she saw a bright pasture, a glowing picture of equanimity, tranquillity and fun. Fun for God's sake! That at least was not one of the factors blocking Old's way to a view.

Was this what passed for not thinking about it? Best was simply to watch Sam watching the kite. The wind was steady, so the kite did little bobbing around. Sam gave it the occasional cursory tug, but he seemed as lost in his thoughts as his father beside him. The model pilots' grumbling mounted, as if someone else's occupation of the skies was only justifiable if they cavorted around as aimlessly and as randomly as they would, if ever they got their planes up. Old and Sam stood, silently, gazing into nowhere, for ever. Until, after the sun started to dip behind the first of the trees at the edge of the Flats, Sam hugged Old's leg and said he was cold, handed Old the fully extended line and reel and fished in Old's pocket for the car keys. Old shouted at his back not to play with any of the switches, but he knew he wouldn't. He was a good boy, he would sit, nose to window, and watch the kite jump around, trying to climb ever higher, the faster Old reeled in the line. It was relaxing work, like winding wool. Not too fast or the kite pulled back, could cut your hand in a flash. Just nice and steady, pull in a couple of feet, wind it round the reel, pull and wind.

He thought about Hannah's neck. The way she wore her hair up when they went to the hotel, her neck was smooth and pale, a few wispy hairs half concealed by the few strays that had slipped down from her French plait. He remembered the way he had wanted to kiss it softly, and thought how, no matter what he knew about her now, he wanted to kiss her neck again. He would see her later. Maybe things would improve. He had thought they wouldn't, but optimism came more naturally to him. Give it time, give her time.

Nice and steady, pull and wind.

Just in from the ear lobe, Old could see the tension in Silvester's jaw, the tightly clenched muscles. He could see Silvester was ready for the order, ready for the words that would finally allow him to believe he was to become a millionaire, a man with over a million pounds of real money all hand-stolen and dearly and individually loved. He had even convinced himself that on this scam, by removing money from a potential conflict, and thus the arms it was meant to buy, he was doing some good. Old suggested that was rather more sophistry than a real motive and he was forced reluctantly to agree and shuck off the cloak of philanthropy he had been trying for size.

There was a breeze outside and they both wore overcoats – Shawaz said Ibn Fahad would not be meeting them this time, it would be the two of them and Shawaz alone, so there was no need to meet in the artificial air of the hotel. He wanted to take in a few sights, he said. He would meet them on the Riverside Walk, next to the Hungerford Bridge and in front of the Festival Hall. He was late. The two men faced the wind whipping across the Thames, wondering idly which way he would approach, as it would have to be on foot whichever way he came. When he did arrive, it was Silvester who saw him first, emerging from the doors of the Festival Hall.

'Soaking up the culture while we freeze,' Silvester muttered irritably, his eyes watering slightly with the chill wind.

'I am pleased to meet you, gentlemen. Shall we stay here or do you wish to take shelter from the wind?'

'Here's fine,' Old said. 'If you want to take in the sights we may as well walk.' They headed east, towards Waterloo Bridge and past the rest of the South Bank arts complex.

'What's the point of this meeting, if you don't mind me getting straight down to it?' Silvester asked, a little brusquely, Old thought.

'Always a sound practice – do what you have to and move on.'

'So?'

'Money. We have agreed the sums to be paid. Where and when?'

'We have to pay for the goods. We're not a whole-saler, buying and putting the stuff in a warehouse, we need to pay up front, and that means you do too. Where is immaterial. It's a lot of money to pay in cash, cash tends to attract attention, but at least once you have it, it's hard to trace. Cash is best.'

'The form of money is to all intents immaterial,

though I agree about the pleasing anonymity of cash. Money talks, but to the authorities, cash offers only name, rank and serial number. I merely wanted to know what you needed.'

'The when: as soon as possible. Where: the hotel again. I'm not carrying any suitcases full of cash on the streets of London. Knowing my luck, that'd be the one time in my life I get mugged.' He smiled. Shawaz frowned.

'Mr Noble, when you carry large sums of money, you need to be protected.' He tapped his chest. Silvester looked at him and looked at Old, guessing whether Old took that to mean the same as he did.

'You're carrying a gun? Did you just say you were carrying a gun? On the streets of London? Is that wise, do you think, Mr Shawaz?' Silvester's tone had risen. He was obviously not happy with this notion.

'You deal in weapons, but you are not happy with them? Weapons for us are a way of life. The Sheik is not loved by everyone and consequently neither am I. The Sheik is like a father to me and we both have our enemies. I would lay down my life for the Sheik but I would prefer not to. This', he reached inside his pocket, 'helps me believe I am less likely to have to.' He pulled out a gun. It was chrome and snub-nosed, flat, which made it an automatic. Old could see it was a Browning. Silvester seemed to be seeing only imminent arrest and started to panic, though, amazingly, he maintained his politeness to the mark.

'Jesus, the f . . ., Jesus, that's, that's, will you put that away please, it's not such a good . . . someone might . . . will you please just put it back?'

Shawaz pointed it towards Silvester.

'We are friends. The gun should not worry you. No one is watching, no one cares. But you should carry a weapon from the point we pay you to the point the money arrives somewhere safe.'

'Tandy, our driver, will be armed. In fact he is already,' Old said. 'And when we are carrying the money, I'll carry too.'

Shawaz nodded approvingly and Silvester's chin dropped.

'Our driver? Tandy? Shouldn't I have known about this?'

Old shook his head.

'When you react like this? I knew as well as Mr Shawaz we were involved in something that meant care was important. The arms business, believe it or not, has a good few arms washing around. Especially the illicit side. Wake up.'

As they spoke, Shawaz holstered his gun.

'We can arrange weapons delivery after we hand over the money. We can have the money ready for Thursday.' This was Monday. 'First we need to meet again once more. Same time tomorrow.'

'Why?' Old asked.

'Oblige me.'

'But I thought everything was arranged.'

'Almost.'

'What then?'

'Tomorrow. Same place and time?'

'Same place as we are now or same place as we met?' Silvester interrupted, trying to placate Shawaz, who he thought looked irritated at Old's questioning.

'Where we met.'

'Why can't we sort it out now?' Old insisted.

'Because tomorrow,' Shawaz snapped, and strode off the Riverside Walk, away from the Thames towards the road.

Perched on a stool in the dingy, smoke-filled Hole in the Wall pub, opposite Waterloo Station and a short walk from where Shawaz had left them, Silvester gazed contemptuously at his vodka tonic.

'What can you say about a bar that doesn't have lemons?'

'You can say you won't be back,' Old said.

'Did you have to go on like that?' Silvester asked. 'Looked to me like you really got his back up.' This was the reason for Silvester's silent walk to the pub, for his moody staring into his drink. He was mad at Old, though, more for not telling him about Tandy's gun than about a few questions to Shawaz.

'Look, they want the missiles,' Old replied. 'They've got the money, everything's sorted. All they need is for the one to be swapped for the other, and I don't know why he wants to meet and I don't like not knowing.'

Silvester took a sip of his drink and grimaced again.

'Bland, bland, bland. Amazing the difference a little slice of lemon makes. The scam, we've been very lucky so far. It's a good scam and the better they are the closer you should be able to keep to the script. You thought up a beauty and so far it's been more or less letter-perfect. If there was anywhere it should have fallen down it should have been finding someone to let us in on a demonstration. Your contacts got us through that, got us a private view, which was what we wanted. Can't ask for sandwiches on the lawn with a field marshal. The next major problem was supposed to be after we scarpered with the money. You call them: "What time did Mr Silvester, Noble sorry, what time did Mr Noble leave?" They say an hour or so ago. "Oh dear, he's done a bunk, what a calamity." You're aggrieved along with them – I fuck off, you're ripped off as well. Now we don't know how they'll handle that, especially seeing him flashing his gun around. That guy is a loose cannon, he's too fucking unstable, but you could finesse that. You're the one with the Army contacts, you're the one lives where he says he lives, does what he says he does, has the right history, all that. I'm the one, it turns out when you look it's a false name, false address, false history. I've piggy-backed on your history, conned you into becoming a partner and stolen your credibility, then I've stolen their money. More or less, we've both been conned. That will be hard for you, but you're getting well paid for it, senior partner and all that.'

'Partner?'

'Sure, more or less. You might have had me over a barrel when you dragged me in on this, but now I'm in, I'm in, and as for taking the heat from Ibn Fahad, well Jesus, at over a million each, we can take a little inconvenience. But we just can't expect the whole thing to stick to the script like magic. He wants a meeting, so he gets it, we busk it, make it up as we go along. Can't be anything we can't solve.'

Old grumbled a grudging agreement.

'Still don't have to like it though.'

★

The next day was important. The days on this thing were closing in, the timetable all compressed into the next couple of days. It was nerve-jangling stuff.

'Sleep well, sleep long.' Words of wisdom from Silvester.

Easy to say.

But here he was in the kitchen, watching the treetops whip in the wind, faint in the dark sky, illuminated only by the dim, burnt orange streetlight from the next street, the light barely reaching over the tops of the houses. What light there was filtered through, refracted by the rain running down the kitchen window.

It would none of it be visible if the kitchen light had been on, but he was sat in the four a.m. gloom feeling four a.m. gloomy.

Hannah had spent the night. Again, the evening had shown promise and he had begun to convince himself that the last time had been a result of nerves – that Hannah had been too nervous to act like a woman and had instead acted like timber. This time had been no different. Passionate kissing followed, in bed, by her inactivity quickly being followed by his embarrassment. They soon finished the chore and fell into an uneasy sleep, Old's soon disturbed by the unfamiliar feeling of a bed shared.

Where would this lead, he wondered. Compatible, fond, he at least in love and Hannah too he suspected, good for each other and good for the kids. All things hard to find in late youth or early middle age. What else was there? Only sex. And did it matter if it stunk? Unfortunately it did, it does and it always will. If he ended up with Hannah, if they made a life together, he was not the type to stray. Hannah would be what sex was.

Was it possible that bad sex would be his lot for ever and that he would opt for this with a smile and an open heart?

Fine thoughts for four a.m. gloom.

He stared into his cooling mug of tea as he tried vainly to empty his head of any thoughts but peaceful, sleepy ones. Thoughts of warm duvets and tired limbs. And again thoughts of Hannah, himself and matters carnal. Where he supposed they both wanted to make love, they had shared what he supposed and knew was meant when men talked about a quick leg-over.

Sleep well, sleep long. Huh!

Old undid the buttons on his jacket as they were pulling slightly. Since he and Ras had stopped going to the Olympia regularly for wrestling practice, he had started hitting the weights in the spare room a little more heavily than he should. In the past couple of weeks especially, he had been working off some of the frustration he had felt over his thing, relationship, whatever it was, with Hannah. Because of all this he had added close to another inch to his chest, and though he had been nearly this thick across the chest before, not quite, some of his clothes were showing it. He resolved to go for more repetitions and less weight – increase strength and tone without increasing muscle mass.

Shawaz was half an hour late and Old was watching the traffic on the Embankment from his spot on the Riverside Walk. He was determined to keep looking this way as to look any other way would mean he would see Silvester who was pacing furiously, flicking his eyes over the National Film Theatre, the Festival Hall, the Hayward Gallery, the Hungerford Bridge, the Riverside Walk and all the passages, canyons and alleyways between, any one of which could deliver Shawaz at any moment. He was as wired as a cat in a microwave. Every time Old looked at him it wound him up. Frustration, like yawning, is strangely contagious. Normally, Old could wait patiently for as long as need be. He was extremely punctual and, like everyone who is punctual, he wasted lots of time waiting for those who weren't.

His job favoured patience. Without it, it would be impossible to stand the drudgery that made up the great part of the work. There was the waiting around for this and that, waiting for someone to leave a pub, waiting for a phone call that never comes. If he knew something involved a ludicrously long wait, or a wait of unspecifiable duration, he would hire Tandy, who was, unfortunately, not so patient, but who was also keen to earn money. But he still got plenty of waiting in on his own account.

Shawaz came barrelling down the steps of the Hungerford Bridge. Old looked over to Silvester who was strolling their way, an equable smile on his face.

'Sorry for the delay. Unavoidable.'

'Not a problem, we were preparing our own excuses when we arrived late – London traffic.' Silvester lied as easily as passing breath, Old thought.

'Now we are here,' Old said, 'can you tell us what this meeting is about?'

'Not a problem. First, I want to tell you some history.'

'Do you have to?' Old asked, abruptly, prompting vicious scowls both from Silvester and Shawaz.

'I do. Listen.

'Both my parents were killed when I was three. A gas cylinder blew up and killed them both instantly. I was outside the tent, in the shade of a tree. The Sheik stepped in, took charge, saved me and made me. He paid for my upkeep, arranged for me to be looked after until I was eleven, provided money for my education. When I was eighteen, he employed me. I owe him everything and I would die for him.'

'Your loyalty is admirable. Can we get on?'

Shawaz continued as if Old had not spoken.

'Let the man speak,' Silvester whispered, harshly, and within Shawaz's hearing.

'But I also learned from him to put my own interests first, not to cling too much to easy sentimentality. Loyalty is a form of self-interest – be good to the powerful. I am good and loyal towards the Sheik. But where it is possible, I look after my own interests and today is one of those days.' He smiled a cold smile.

Old looked at Shawaz and then at Silvester.

'We're not going to like this are we?' It was more of a statement than a question but Shawaz answered it anyway.

'No, I am sure you are not.'

Silvester's mouth opened at this exchange. He looked unsure of his ground. He was so used to having a firm grip on the edges of the carpet, ready to tug it from beneath the feet of his victims, when it looked as if someone was making moves on his ground he was completely thrown.

'What do you want?' Old asked.

'I am glad you understand. Four hundred thousand pounds. Cash. Tomorrow.'

A silence fell on the group.

'Are you trying to rip us off?' Silvester asked. 'You are, you're ripping us off, you filthy, robbing bastard.'

Old stepped between Shawaz and Silvester. There was a number of passers-by and he was attracting attention.

'Calm!' he ordered. 'Calm down, cool down, shut up.'

He returned his gaze to Shawaz.

'Why shouldn't we deal directly with the Sheik?'

'Because the Sheik only, only ever deals through me, so it is not a possibility. I told the Sheik I am carrying out some last-minute checks. If I find something suspicious, I can say anything, he will believe me, the deal will be off. Believe me, you are not the first. This kind of thing happens, and it is happening to you. You will make whatever you can make out of this deal after paying me or you will make nothing. There is no third way.'

Old gazed coldly into Shawaz's eyes, Silvester watching, warily.

'I could kill you.'

'You could try. And what would the Sheik think? I go out to do final checks on a couple of illicit arms dealers, I do not return. He is a wary man. He would be on the first plane home. No third way.'

'It's too much. It's a heist, I can live with that, but it's too much. That wipes out our entire margin,' said Silvester.

'If you remember, last week, we came to meet and started to haggle. You have an interesting technique –

to sit on your price like Allah, eternally patient and unmoved by any petty squabbles. To an Arab it is an unusual approach but I can see its merits. Four hundred thousand. I am sure you will see your way to a deal. You will have to see your suppliers, squeeze them as I squeeze you.' He smiled.

'Try not to be so angry. It is a normal part of an arms deal. See it as a facilitator's fee. It is an attractive way to make money. You have until eight in the evening, tomorrow. I will take a suite at the Consul where we may make our deal. To show goodwill, I will pay for the suite.'

'If we can't haggle on the amount,' Old said, 'let us haggle on the time. We don't have the time to raise the money. If we wait until the following day, we can pay you from the Sheik's money. Just one day can make no difference to you.'

'Every difference, as you well know. Today I hold the top cards. When you have the money I hold none. The Consul, eight o'clock. Ask for Mr Rahman.'

'False name?'

'Does it matter?'

Old looked at Silvester. He was pale, his eyes dead. He had nothing to say. He nodded feebly as Shawaz wished him goodbye, jogged up the steps of the Hungerford Bridge and walked across towards the Embankment.

SEVENTEEN

There was a sweet and slightly sickening smell in the room in the Hayward where Silvester and Old sat, talking in hushed tones. They were sat in a room alone with one exhibit, a block of lard, about fourteen feet by eight by five high, draped with tattered chamois leathers. On the floor, in front of the thing, was a perspex sign:

Exegesis eight point eight
by
Garth Delaney

'Mr Delaney's a better con artist than we are,' Silvester said, bitterly.

'I don't know enough about it.'

'What's there to know? Five tons of fucking lard and a few used car leathers.'

'How do you know he was paid more to make it than it cost him to make?'

'Because why would he do it?'

'Maybe because he's an artist. Or maybe you're right, he's a con artist. That's what I said, I don't know enough about it. I don't like it enough to want to know more about it, I don't know what it is, I don't know why he did it, I don't care why he did it. I care that we're getting four hundred grand ripped off us and it isn't a good feeling.'

'We can't pay him, you know Pat. We can't let him

get away with it. I know this is your scam, your set-up, but we're working as partners, and he's taking the piss out of us both.'

'What do we do, walk away? I don't think so.'

'But like you said, it's too much.'

Old grinned.

'Tell me why?'

'You know why. Like we told Shawaz – it's the whole margin.'

Old slowly shook his head, smiling.

'No it's not. And we can get our revenge as soon as we get paid. We're talking as if it takes up the margin, right, and we can't afford the margin. But there is no margin. Remember? We're too close to the scam. It's a scam. We're thieves, only better ones than him. We get the lot. And as soon as we rip off the money, your man Shawaz is in deep shit, because he's just about to tell his man the Sheik that he's done every background check known to man and accountant alike and we're sweet. So that's his goose cooked.'

Silvester nodded, appreciatively.

'You're right, I get inside the scam. That's what I was doing. I was so deep inside, I was believing our story about losing the margin, the profit. But we're just losing a slice. Sure he's ripping us, but easy come easy go, that what you're saying, yes. We're ripping him more than he is us, and we get the last word. And he's helping alibi us, because why shouldn't you be fooled by my credentials if he is after all his checks. It takes us from £2.3 million to £1.9 million, which puts us fifty grand under a million each, but seeing we're talking about doing it, not wondering how to do it, I guess that means we both have the money, so after the scam, with or without Shawaz robbing us blind, we'll both be worth a million.'

'So we're still in?'

'Damn right.'

Toby handed a heavy black briefcase over the desk.

'I hope you know what you're doing here,' he said. 'That's two hundred thousand pounds of real money.'

'I should hope so, you tell me it leaves me very low, I should believe you.'

'You just don't want to lose it. It gives me the shivers just to think of you walking around with it. It leaves you with fuck-all – under forty thousand left.'

'Toby, thanks for the worry, but for most of my life, until last year, I never had four thousand saved, let alone forty, so that's just fine. Anyway,' he nodded at Tandy, standing behind him, dressed in black trousers and roll-neck and black leather jacket – Old told him to look as menacing as possible, then gave him the gun, 'he's carrying.'

Tandy opened his jacket to show a big revolver in a shoulder holster – the perks of a continuing firearms licence and a sideline as a small arms reviewer for the military press. 'And so am I. It's Silvester waltzing around carrying his money that worries me.'

Norton shook his head. He liked working on the shady side of things, but became very nervous when they turned the corner and became more overtly criminal, and consequently dangerous to the point of being life-threatening. And Norton slept a sweeter sleep with his life left unthreatened.

'Mr Rahman's suite please.'

The receptionist at the Consul looked the three of them over. He looked especially disapproving of Tandy.

He went to the end of the desk and checked the computer – in a hotel like this you wouldn't even get to know if someone was staying there without their say so. He picked up the phone, spoke a few words and nodded at Old.

'You are expected. Room 1633. It's not a suite.'

'Well pardon me for having cheap acquaintances,' Old said, lifting his eyebrows. They walked over to the lift, Tandy carrying Old's case, Silvester gripping his own as if it was glued on.

They got the lift to themselves.

'You know when we were on the river yesterday?' Silvester said, forcing the words out through the palpable tension in his body.

'Like I'd forget.'

'When we were talking to Shawaz,' he spat the word, ignoring Old's sarcasm.

'Yes?'

'You said you could kill him.'

'I said it was a possibility.'

'Was it?'

'No.'

'Why?'

'I couldn't do it to save money. For a principle, a big one, but not just for money. It was a bargaining tool. If he'd been shocked at that, I could have leaned hard. We might have an angle to haggle with. As it was, he looked at me like he knew my game, so it wasn't even useful.'

'But you're still carrying a gun.'

'You can do more with these things than kill. If someone tried to get this money off me, I could do them a lot of damage. And seeing the kind of petty criminals bag-snatching attracts, I could scare the living shit out of them before it ever got that far.'

When they got to the door, they knocked and Shawaz let them in. He was beaming broadly, without even the tact to conduct the robbery in a business-like manner. Old took his case from Tandy and told him to stay outside and watch the door. Inside, Shawaz had opened champagne. Silvester picked up a glass and downed it in one.

'Thanks for nothing,' he spat. 'Rubbing salt in the wound.'

Shawaz said nothing. He opened both cases and set to work. He checked that all the packs were bank-banded, checked three packs, selected at random, and started counting packs. It was mostly in fifties, around forty thousand in twenties. All the real thing. Shawaz counted it like small change, taking handfuls of packs and stacking them in piles of ten. It took him less than five minutes. When he finished, he took three more packs from the top of the last pile and checked them closely.

'Excellent. Four hundred thousand pounds precisely. It is a good deal. I will see you with the Sheik at the hotel tomorrow. The usual meeting-room at three in the afternoon. You may collect your money,' he patted Old's gun under his jacket, 'and I advise you again to bring protection: £2.3 million demands attention, does it not? So, until tomorrow, and no hard feelings?'

Old shrugged and took his hand. Silvester looked at

Shawaz bleakly and gave a cursory shake. Old admired him. You would never guess from his demeanour that he was about to turn the tables, that he had a secret weapon, that he had not just had all the meat taken from his sandwich.

Talking was Silvester's game. It was his life. As soon as you started to talk to Silvester, you were interested, enthralled even. His talking was social, educational, informative, enriching; all these things you could believe. Silvester's survival depended on the quality of his talk and you could appreciate this. What it took a time to see was the reverse side of this coin. Silvester was not very good at all at *not* talking. Silence seemed to irritate him like an itch that needs scratching, a scab that needs picking. For Silvester a silence was a challenge to his conversational skills. In the twenty-four hours between leaving Shawaz and arriving to meet him the next day they had spent perhaps four hours together and Old had spent ten minutes of that time at the most playing an active part. Ten minutes of dialogue, four hours of monologue. Sam talked a lot, but it was an easy, bantering, inquisitive kind of talk. Silvester was constantly coaxing agreement, chivvying and encouraging. He had spent the money, made plans, wished terrible ill of Shawaz, never seeming to see the irony that what he resented Shawaz for was more or less what he had spent his life doing. No matter, Silvester was mad at Shawaz, yet happy at the world and what was to happen in it today, and he had examined every permutation of those two: all possible lives that could follow for him, to the good, and for Shawaz, to the bad.

It was a relief for Old as he asked for the meeting-room at the hotel reception desk, Silvester and Tandy waiting with him, Silvester already itchy – he had a ticket booked and paid for under one of his many false names and was ready to skip the country with his half of the money, the active half of the partnership to Old's fall guy. He was ready and raring to go.

'No room in that name, sorry, sir.'

'Can you check, please?' Old asked, glancing irritatedly at Silvester.

'I have, sir. No such booking.'

'You've checked Shawaz, can you try Ibn Fahad?'

'Sir, none of our meeting-rooms are booked out today.'

'Can you call Mr Shawaz or Mr Ibn Fahad in their rooms for me, please?'

The clerk tapped the keyboard of the reception computer and checked the monitor.

'No such booking, sir. Ever. Mr Shawaz booked a number of meeting-rooms – our facilities are open to our guests and to the general public. He did not stay with us at any time.'

'Mr Rahman?'

The clerk shook his head, then flitted down the desk to attend to a waiting despatch rider handing over a parcel.

Old looked at Silvester, then at Tandy.

'I heard,' Silvester said. He turned and walked out of the hotel, viciously banging the doors away. Old and Tandy followed.

'What do you suppose has happened?' Old asked Silvester.

Silvester stared at Old with a disbelieving look.

'Was that you in there asking the questions? What do you think's happened? This was your fucking scam, you should be able to recognize when the thing dies on you, goes stiff and starts to smell. It's as plain as fucking day. We had such a pretty scam, scurrying about looking for our mark, but we were suckered. Us not them. We asked about for Ibn Fahad when he came over – we knew he was over because we read the clippings – and someone responded. Someone provided a fucking Ibn Fahad. Ours was so sweet a scam, we couldn't stop looking at it. What did we say: a perfect scam involves the conned thinking they are the wise guy, they are so busy thinking they are ripping someone off, they aren't watching.'

'The money?' It was a question in itself, and Silvester knew it was really the only question.

'Our money was the whole fucking point. Everywhere we were clever, they were more so. We thought by asking for cash and bringing it back we proved we were innocent. By handing the cash over in the first place, they made themselves innocent in our eyes. When he stung us for the money, he did it a day after confirming the details. He gave us time to convince ourselves the money was ours. It's a fucking beauty. Sweet as all the cane in . . .' he shuddered and then slowly he started to weep. 'All the cane in Trinidad, all the fucking West Indies. What a wanker. "Don't spend it until it's in your hands." I've got a room full of brochures for villas in Trinidad and St Kitts. Oh what a bastard. Suckered.'

By now he was like a whirling dervish, spinning, shaking his head, banging his arms against a lamppost and spinning off in another direction. He was completely manic and losing all semblance of control, alternately muttering to himself and yelling out loud.

'Are you not going to try to find them?' Old asked, trying to penetrate Silvester's consciousness with a stab at reality, a little action to displace his mounting desperation.

'If you want to spend a few more pennies phoning around, help yourself, but I know a scam when I see one. If you were to bribe a bit of information out of the clerk in there I'm sure you'd find the rooms were paid in cash and a false address given.' He stopped speaking, choking on his words. By now, tears were pouring freely down his face.

'Look at it,' he sobbed. 'Just look. You know how it works. They're gone. That's the way with a con. The mark's all keyed up waiting for the next thing to happen, and it's over: there is no next thing. None. It ended yesterday at ten past eight. As soon as we left that room without our four hundred grand, it was all over. Sure, we covered the expenses out of the money they gave us, what was it, twenty grand? So we're the two hundred each down, they're three hundred and eighty up, less a few more expenses. It's a straight-out killer. You should have fucking killed the bastard while you had him and the gun in the same room.'

Old sat on the edge of an ornamental flowerbed watching the exhibition, waiting for the right moment to take charge and decant Silvester into the car. Tandy stood waiting for the next move, trying desperately to suppress a smirk and not doing very well. One porking in progress, he thought, and hummed to himself a

286

song by Zappa, one of the few white musicians really to get him going. From the 'humour' period: 'Keep it Greasy so it'll go down Easy'.

EIGHTEEN

The house was quiet. Satya was sitting for Sam. Silvester had not spoken for over ten minutes since he had called the *Middle East Economic Digest*, who told him that the Sheik had been over in the UK for three weeks, had purchased an executive jet from Whittle's in Londonderry and had returned, on the jet, with a pilot provided by the company, a little over a week ago.

Old waited, giving Silvester his grieving space. The man cared deeply for his money and it was gone. After an hour of this and similar, Silvester started to shuffle, embarrassed at the silence, Old guessed.

'There's business to sort out, wouldn't you say?'

'Could well be. Tell me how you see it,' Old said.

'I owe someone something. You got in this to get yourself out of a spot – you wanted to keep your client sweet but you didn't want to give him what he wanted, so you cooked up a scheme which gave him his money and took away any entitlement he might have. That suited your purposes because you fancied yourself as an amateur con. I have to say, as a pro, I thought you had a peach and you could cut it. Except by now, apart from your little coin trick, your record stinks.'

Old shrugged off the slight.

'But your man Barry Mee is still left empty-handed.'

'So what does that leave?'

'I piss off, accepting you could give lots of useful

but not indictable information to your copper friends, and you could pass my details on to Mee and his band of merry thugs and that could lead to a nasty accident down a dark alley. Plenty lock-up time for them as prime suspects, bad news for me and probably for you too, given your involvement. No consolation for me lying in a persistent vegetative state until the patience runs out and they turn me off.'

'Rosy outlook you have.'

'It's not a day for a rosy outlook. So another option is pay Mee what I owe him. Not too attractive given I just lost more than I took off him and his silly friends, but maybe better than the third, which is start from scratch, sell everything I own, taking a beating on the price so as to be sure it's all fast and quiet – usually those two are contradictory in a sale – and start new IDs. Frankly, that'd cost me more than paying, but after consideration it'd have to be better than paying. Goes against the grain. And the IDs are blown anyway.'

'So there's no way you'd pay Mee his money back?'

'Not a hope I'm afraid. I was hoping maybe the time we've had, the beating we took together, might buy me a small favour.'

'I let you go?'

Silvester nodded, deep, ponderous nods as if he saw the unlikeliness of the prospect but also its deep desirability.

'Where does that leave me with the client?' Old asked.

'There is that. Shit creek I guess.'

'But you definitely won't pay Mee back?'

'Sorry but I couldn't. Fat little fuck simply doesn't deserve it.'

Old smiled. 'I kind of hoped you'd pay up. Would have been a nice bonus. But it would have been a little hard, too; kicking a man while he's down. You can go. You don't owe Barry Mee anything.'

Old saw the raised eyebrows and carried on before Silvester could confuse things with the wrong questions.

'You've been done, hon. Scammed; ripped off; burned; robbed; blagged; conned; taken for a mug. And before you say it, that's not you and me both, that's just you. I've got a friend, Raswinder Singh Virdi. He's a Sikh, but as he'd tell you, most people just see any old raghead. He speaks a few languages and Arabic's one of them, but him and his uncle speak Punjabi together. He speaks great English – he should, he was born at St Clement's Maternity, Forest Gate, long since closed. Gets a bit pissed off when he's reminded that his dad wanted him called Jasvinder but the registrar didn't hear right. By the time he was a teenager there was a yard full of Jas's but only one Ras, so it stuck. Ras sounded cooler. You'd like him, he's a good guy. He thought up a great scam, you'd love it. Great part for him and his truly horrid Henry Kissinger English impersonation. You should meet and talk about it. And then you could tell him what you were telling me: about the difference between a pro and an amateur.'

When Old stopped he was keenly aware of the big grin he was wearing, somewhere way the wrong side of smug. Silvester was smiling too. It wasn't a happy smile, but it was a smile.

'I guess now's the time to look for positive spin and the best I can find is I've got a clean slate.'

'A big plus against where you were five minutes ago.'

'No point bitching and moaning; a conman conned – like sitting in traffic moaning about the traffic. You are the traffic, live with it. I've been turned over, nice as you like. I'm off. No point hanging around starting a postmortem.'

It was as quick as that. That was the sign of a real pro, Old thought. To take it on the chin and retire gracefully, without recriminations. They shook hands at the door, but before Silvester left, he grasped Old, two hands on his face, and gave him a smacking kiss on the lips. Old started backwards.

'No hard feelings, honestly,' Silvester said. 'You never know when we may be able to do business, now we understand each other, and just how far we can trust each other.'

He turned and was gone.

Ras added the sums. Twenty thousand expenses. They had been right not to do it on the cheap. On top of that there was five for Toby Norton, ten for Uncle Jas, who was still smiling gnomically at the memory, his only regret that he was sworn to secrecy. Sheik Ibn Fahad, laid to rest.

There was a hundred and thirty-two thousand to Barry Mee: what he and his deadbeat pals lost, right on the button. Made him dead straight. It left Mee more than happy – no losses except for Old's invoice, which he was happy to pay. He knew Old had made a piece from the con but he saw that as Old's business, though Old had expected an argument. He had been conned and because of Old he had got his money back, got even. Very few around who could claim that: to have made a comeback from a con.

Old's fee, of a shade under five thousand, he seemed to see as exceptionally modest. By the time he left Mee at the pay-off, Old even suspected Mee might just pay off his partners, so long as they picked up their share of Old's bill without a gripe. That was between Mee and his conscience, and what a battle that would be.

With all the expenses, wages and Barry Mee, there was a bill of a hundred and sixty-seven thousand pounds. The proceeds of the con plus Old's fee came to thirty-eight. But Ras refused to take any of the fee as he said he didn't earn any until the scam. So he took half of thirty-three which Old insisted on calling seventeen. Leaving Old twenty-one.

It had been a great idea, even Silvester said so. As Shawaz, Ras had fooled Silvester completely: his con, his act. And he had the best time he could remember since he took control of his bar from its dissolute owner. Satya had not approved in principle, but she admired the nerve, the front, and she loved to see Ras so happy. She knew he missed the Army, the humdrum spiced with flashes of the sudden, terrifying and dramatic. That was it. He loved the drama. Well he'd had a dose, as had his uncle Jas, the two of them playing their double act, and perhaps he could settle down a little.

Because there was good reason to settle down if her instincts were right. And she was sure the Predictor kit in her handbag would confirm her instinct in the morning.

Old came back from Ras's flushed with success. He

was twenty-one thousand pounds ahead, all to be given back to Toby to join the two hundred thousand that Ras had returned to Toby not two hours after he had picked it up. All in all he was getting to be a fairly wealthy kind of chap, he thought, with a little too much self-satisfaction.

Sam noticed the door first. It was closed but not properly fastened. They went into the front room. First targets for any burglar – CD player, CDs, TV and video – all intact. But the mantelpiece was swept clean. All the family photos and bits and bobs lay heaped on the floor to the left of the mantelpiece. Also missing was Dennis Warriner's jade figurine. Written in foot-high letters in red spray paint was a message:

WHO'S A
NAUGHTY
BOY THEN?

SIGNET

Published or forthcoming

PITY THE SINNER

Mark Daniel

Neil Munrow, steeplechase jockey, has a problem. His wife Katya is suing for a costly divorce and custody of his beloved daughter – and money is getting tight. At least that's what he thought – until he checked his bank account and found that someone had given him £80,000.

But as soon as he discovers the money, he finds Katya has spent it. Now Neil has a mysterious benefactor seeking recompense – but not of the financial kind. And with his greatest treasure under threat, he must show his hand and state his price … for cheating, for stealing, for murder …

LOOSE AMONG THE LAMBS

Jay Brandon

In the endless heat of a San Antonio summer, three children are abducted and abused. As the city howls for justice, a man steps forward to offer his confession. An innocent man …

District Attorney Mark Blackwell and Prosecutor Becky Schirhart get on the case and begin to peel back the complex web of lies and deceit protecting those who think they are beyond the law. Starting with their own department …

'The pace is effortlessly sustained to produce a gripping story whose outcome is uncertain till the final pages' – *Sunday Telegraph*

IT TAKES TWO

Maeve Haran

Hotshot lawyer Tess Brien and her ad-man husband Stephen know that a good marriage is hard to keep. They should. Enough of their friends' relationships are crumbling around them. But theirs is a happy home, a secure base for their two lively teenagers.

But when Stephen suddenly gives up his job, leaving a stressed and angry Tess to pick up the bills, and another woman seems determined to have Stephen at any cost, distrust and disruption threaten to destroy their idyllic home …

'Maeve Haran has a feel for the substantial concerns of her readers … which is why she has become required reading for modern romantics' – *The Times*

Published or forthcoming

FINAL
ARGUMENT

Clifford Irving

Can a lawyer defend a man he once prosecuted?

Ted Jaffe has always felt guilty about the Zide case, mostly because of his affair with the victim's wife. And now, risking his career, his family's well being and his own safety, Jaffe probes his hazy twelve-year-old memories – and discovers his instinct was right: the man convicted was not a murderer.

But if Jaffe wins the battle for a new hearing, he'll have to put Connie Zide on the stand. And put his own past on public trial …